STARING INTO THE ABYSS

Edited by Patrick Thomas & John L. French

PADWOLF PUBLISHING INC.
WWW.PADWOLF.COM
www.facebook.com/Padwolf

www.theagentsoftheabyss.com

STARING INTO THE ABYSS
edited by Patrick Thomas
copyedited by John L. French
© 2022 Patrick Thomas

cover by Patrick Thomas

*Agents of the Abyss created by Patrick Thomas and
all related characters and settings are © and ™ Patrick Thomas*

ISBN 978-1-890096-98-4
FIrst Printing.

From the writings of Abraham Van Helsing, founder and Lord Protector of the Sway:

Monsters have always been with mankind. In days of old, people had the good sense to kill them on sight as befits enemies of mankind. There has been a shift in the world in recent decades. Governments, foolishly thinking they can control the monsters, have recruited them as assets on the world stage, granting them legitimacy and equal status with humans.

France has the body-stealing Phantom and a simian leader. The British have Invisibles and Hydes. Israel has the mummy of Rames II. The Russians have Rasputin, Baba Yaga, and Night Witches. China has worse. And Americans have everything they can get their hands on.

Most disturbing of all, the worst monster of all has his own country. No longer content to be a lowly count, Dracula has crowned himself King of Transylvania and defends his borders not only with his unholy powers but with technology plundered from the second Martian invasion, granting him a place on the world stage as one of the global superpowers.

It is madness. Humanity either does not see the danger or does not care. Certainly, in the short term, some lives are saved but in the end, will those lives be worth it if humanity is supplanted and made subservient or extinct by the monsters? The Abyss be damned. Working from the shadows, we Sway will destroy the monsters beneath the heels of true humans.

*For those who worked to make
Agents of the Abyss a reality-*

The Authors of the Abyss

*John L. French, Christy Nicholas, Robert E Waters,
David Lee Summers, Lee O'Connell, Aleathia Drehmer,
Russ Colchamiro, Thomas Karwacki, G.H. Monroe,
Melora Johnson, Elyssa Mikaela, Dave Muffley,
Anna Hoyler, Max Birkett, and Diane Raetz.*

Contents

Excerpt from Hidden Geography, the Sway training manual:

Monsters seek to supplant humanity. It is the Sway's purpose and duty to stop this from happening by any means at our disposal.

There are places upon earth where monsters congregate. Some like Transylvania are by design, others by happenstance.

One appears to be both. The French named it La Bête Isle. It is also known as the Isle of Beasts. Monsters from the past call it home and new monsters seek to join them.

Fortunately, it is a savage place and the beasts assure each other's extermination. It is our recommendation to avoid the Isle as the few humans who stumble across it do not survive long enough to leave.

Once Faced and Settled

Mattea Orr

Amelia had come here to suffer, but it wasn't really working. She stared out the bank of windows to her right and tried her best to ignore the beautiful day outside.

"This time you've gone too far. I learned long ago that you've no respect for your own safety, but can't you think of those who care about you? How you make us feel? What you must put your poor mother through. Why, it doesn't bear thinking of." Sister Agnes's voice quivered, rising.

What Amelia wanted to say was that Mother had always encouraged the dreams of her daughters—whether it was chasing tree toads, building their own roller coaster, or learning to fly. She had insisted they have the education to do whatever they wanted. But Amelia didn't say any of those things. Instead, Amelia bowed her head and let her former boss deliver the scolding she'd come here hoping to receive. She sipped the harsh words as though they were a hot, rich broth from a bowl. These words sustained and fortified her against the empty praise and adulation of the cheering crowds, against the ticker tape sticking to her sweaty neck like spiderwebs.

Sister Agnes's jawline vibrated the way Grandmother Otis's had when she grew agitated, and now it shook wildly as the older woman worked up steam. "You can't possibly plan to continue hopping around the country, hawking this and that. Books, luggage, clothing. Honestly, what can your Mr. Putnam have in mind by putting you as the new face of a *cigarette* company?"

The summer sun had not yet built to a boil. The wood-paneled office of the mother superior, who had kindly allowed Sister Agnes to receive Amelia there, acted a bit like an oven with its polished walls reflecting and amplifying the sunlight. Amelia wiped a bead of sweat from her temple. The criticism spread over her like a healing balm. She lowered her shoulders and breathed deeply for the first time in weeks, even the nearly ever-present pressure in her sinuses faded a little. Sister Agnes's words were the whetstone that Amelia would use to sharpen her thoughts to a fine edge to cut through the false accolades and see her way forward.

"Amelia! What have you got to say for yourself?" said the former nurse turned nun.

As the woman pressed closer, the bitter notes of her morning coffee floated by on her breath.

For the first time in twenty minutes, Amelia spoke. "I have no defense. You are utterly correct, Sister."

The older woman's mouth opened and then closed again. She blinked. "Of course I am. Now, do you plan to give up this harried schedule and these terrifying stunts so you can get back to teaching?"

Amelia tucked one of her short, light curls behind her ear. "Absolutely not."

Sister Agnes' cheeks tightened, but her eyes softened as she stared at the younger woman's smile. "You used to get that same look on your face whenever Matron told you we had an incurable patient. I can see I've made no impression on you whatsoever. Did you even hear a word I said, or was your head in the clouds this whole time?"

"On the contrary, Agnes, you were an enormous help. Exactly what I needed to hear," Amelia said, standing.

The nun took Amelia's hands and pressed her thumbs gently onto the younger woman's knuckles. "What if the next time you take flight and make a run for the heavens, you don't come back to us?"

Amelia returned the nun's light squeeze. "I answered that question the first time I flew. We were no more than two hundred feet off the ground, and I just knew I needed to fly myself one day. You haven't seen a tree until you've seen its shadow from the sky. Perhaps it's how God sees the Earth, sees us. I know that I'm never closer to both God and man than when I'm thousands of feet in the air."

The older woman just shook her head. Amelia placed her purse over her shoulder and leaned in to embrace her old boss and friend before saying goodbye. Sister Agnes's cheek yielded like pudding under her lips. Somewhere close by a telephone rang. "I'm sorry, but I have to go. George booked me to speak at the local women's association this afternoon."

"Will you at least promise to be careful?" Sister Agnes asked as they walked to the door of the convent, their footsteps echoing in the empty hallway.

Amelia sighed, not wanting to hurt her friend. "Listen, if I can find a way to do more than keep the flight log and be careful at the same time, I will."

Amelia had planned the chastisement at Agnes's hands because she knew a different kind of agony would find her later that day. After ninety minutes of jabbering about the nature of women and adventure, she was worn as thin as the elbows of a favorite sweater.

"And finally, I want to leave you with this. Women must try to do things as men have tried. When they fail, their failure must be but a challenge to other women to try even harder. Thank you," Amelia said.

The rapid applause tumbled over her thanks as she waved at the crowd and headed backstage, shaking hands and offering smiles as she went. If it got the word out about the love of flying, she'd speak from the top of a milk crate next to a cow pasture. Luckily, the venues George had scheduled for her reached many more people. He had seen to that. This trip might have been his idea, but she was a willing participant. Every bit of press she garnered would put the idea of women and flight in people's minds, and it would make Amelia enough money to get back up into the air—perhaps even in a new plane.

A twisted knot of pain pulsed above and below each eye. She longed for some aspirin and a nap, but obligations chewed at her heels. She and George had dinner plans with the Mayor and his wife, and then they were due at the train station this evening in order to reach Pittsburgh by the morning.

At the exit door of the theater, she turned the handle and took a moment to breathe the heavy summer air outside. Before she'd taken ten steps, someone called her name.

"Miss Earhart. Miss Earhart!"

Amelia sighed. She'd arrived early today so she could sign autographs, shake hands, and take some photos because long engagements always left her exhausted. Her headaches had been particularly bad lately. Slipping out of the theater unnoticed had been too much to hope for. Amelia plastered on a smile and turned, her skirt brushing against the stockings covering her calves.

A short woman with black hair cut in a severe bob stood beside the stage door. She must have been waiting right outside the building, and Amelia walked past without seeing her. A fact made all the stranger since the woman's bright red suit sparked against the white brick wall behind.

"I'm sorry, you've caught me short on time," Amelia said.

The woman approached Amelia and stuck out her hand. "I'm Agent Beyer. I promise not to take up much of your time. If you're not interested in what I have to say, I'll be on my way."

The agent's grip felt strong and warm. On her deep brown wrist, she wore a heavy wristwatch with an oversized dial unlike any Amelia had ever seen.

"I hope you enjoyed the lecture, but if you've any business you wish to discuss I should direct you to my manager, George Putnam." Amelia released the woman's hand.

Somewhere nearby a car horn chirped merrily.

Agent Beyer smiled. "I actually missed the talk. I couldn't stomach all the kudos and glory for someone who only took to the air like a passenger on a bus."

Amelia had been about to turn away, but this woman's words skewered her attention and jerked her head back around. "Pardon me, what did you say?"

"I think you said it best yourself. You were baggage up there. A sack of potatoes." Agent Beyer turned down her lips. "If it were me, I'd be sick over it. I don't even like eating a meal I haven't earned, let alone allowing people to throw me a parade just for doing something while wearing a skirt."

Her headache forgotten, Amelia shook her head as if to clear the cobwebs. She'd gone to see Sister Agnes for this very reason—to hear the truth. Now that the truth stood in front of her, Amelia felt divided. Part of her wanted to ask for more so she could take it out to look at it when the going got tough. A good luck charm. The other part wanted to slap the woman's loose smile off her face.

"Honestly, Agent Beyer, I couldn't have flown the flight by myself, I'm not trained for it yet. If you'd bought a ticket for the lecture, you'd have heard me explain as much. Now, if you'll—"

"Care to do something about it?"

"About what?"

Amelia realized she'd only just noticed that while Agent Beyer stood no taller than her shoulder her demeanor loomed very large.

"Like I said, I have an offer for you, and it includes plenty of flight time with you in the pilot's seat. We both know you're better at navigating than those flyboys will ever admit. Agree to a job with us, and you'll be able to earn all this praise you've been getting. Maybe someday you'll fly across the Atlantic alone, or around the world." Agent Beyer glued her small, dark eyes to Amelia's face and didn't look away.

"Who's us? Who do you work for? The FBI? The Army? The government?" Amelia asked, knowing even as the words left her mouth that each name grew less likely than the last. Those organizations didn't hire women, and certainly not black women.

Agent Beyer laughed, a surprisingly delicate sound. "On the

contrary Miss Earhart, those nice fellas work for me."

Amelia found no sense of unease or deception in Agent Beyer's calm gaze and frank manner. She stared at the woman openly. Was she crazy? Could she be a danger?

"You'll have to excuse me if that sounds preposterous," Amelia said.

"Trust me, I know exactly how it sounds. It's worse when I'm talking to a man, or a woman without a level head on her shoulders, but you're an adventurer, naturally curious. If you walk away now, you'll always wonder. Now, about that job." Agent Beyer glanced at that oversized watch. "Are you familiar with the Bermuda Triangle?"

A rush of heat flickered in Amelia's high cheeks. "I believe you may be playing me for a fool, Agent Beyer. Good day." She turned to walk to the street where her driver, Harry, waited to take her back to the hotel.

The shorter woman managed to keep up with Amelia's longer strides. "Like lots of things in this world that exist, the Bermuda Triangle doesn't need you to believe in it. Most people do the best they can to forget about them until they're forced to do otherwise."

The heat of the day grew oppressive as they walked, and Amelia squinted against the glare of the sun. Part of her reasoned that the quickest way to get rid of this strange woman would be to agree with her demands, arrange to meet her at a later date to discuss the details, and then simply not show up.

Just tell her what she wants to hear; then do whatever the hell you want. She decided as they approached the black car waiting for her on a side street.

The sun had shifted over the course of the afternoon, and the car sat baking in the full sun. The driver's seat stood empty. Amelia frowned, then spied the tall man in the shade of a neighboring building. It would have been impossible for Harry to wait inside the car. Heat wavered off the scorching metal. She glared at the vehicle, her dress already sticking to her back and imagined the stifling interior.

"Glad I brought the convertible. What it lacks in shade it makes up for with a delicious breeze," Agent Beyer said as she gestured toward a gorgeous automobile parked behind the black oven-on-wheels waiting for Amelia.

The lines of Agent Beyer's car stunned Amelia. The metal had the look of waves over the tires. As with Beyer's watch, she'd never seen anything like it. It must be the latest technology. She cut her eyes toward the woman who stood watching her.

"At least let me give you a ride back to your hotel. If I haven't convinced you by then, I won't bother you anymore. Your driver can follow us," she added when Amelia glanced over to where Harry approached.

The truth was, she wanted to ride in that exquisite machine. Amelia smiled and nodded. "I'm staying at the Algonquin."

"There are plenty of pilots around, Agent Beyer. Why do your bosses want me for this job?" Amelia ran a hand over her short-cropped curls, lifting them off her neck so they could dry.

"Not for the same reason that you're getting most of your gigs these days. You're the pretty face the country's slapped on 'women in flight,' but I've seen your resume. You have almost 600 in-flight hours, all without a serious accident. Which would be impressive for a pilot of any stripe, but what we really need for this job are two particular things. The first is an outsized sense of adventure, something I can see you have in spades." Agent Beyer pulled her car into a smooth turn.

Amelia grinned fiercely. "You have me there. Adventure is worthwhile in itself, but it doesn't often do to be too foolhardy. Though a little more foolhardiness would do *some* people good." She surprised herself by laughing, putting a long-fingered hand up to cover her lips for a moment. "What's the second requirement?"

Now it was Agent Beyer's turn to laugh. "Honestly, there's more than two. Tenacious. Restless. Calm in the face of danger. But, mainly, after being forced into the passenger seat, I know you're hungry to prove yourself."

A blade of determination caught at Amelia's tired shoulders and straightened them. "I am, certainly. That's why I'm on this tour, to raise funds for a solo trip across the Atlantic. But I have commitments, I can't abandon them."

Agent Beyer shook her head, the stiff wind pushing wisps of hair across her full cheeks. "I'm not asking you to. This is a quick job. Get in, get what you came for, get out. Two days at the most. We can sneak it in between engagements."

"Still—"

Something in her tone must have suggested a weakening resolve as Agent Beyer pressed on.

"Name the plane you want for the job, and I'll have it waiting at the airfield for you. No matter the outcome of this mission, you keep the plane. If you succeed, though? I'll make sure you have what you need for a record-setting trip across the pond. What do you say?"

"Any plane?" Amelia asked, rubbing her hand over the smooth chrome of the car's dash.

"Miss Earhart, make my bosses happy, and a fancy new ride will be just the tip of the iceberg."

A shift in the morning breeze lightened the smell of salt and dead fish that lingered over the airfield. Thin grass poked through the sandy soil in spots, and the long black car that deposited Amelia near the cluster of low buildings left barely any mark behind as it pulled away. She hefted a light knapsack holding a change of clothes, a toothbrush and comb, two handkerchiefs, and a tube of cold cream. Draped over her other arm were her leather jacket and pilot's cap. Agent Beyer had explained that her agency would include any other equipment and provisions for the mission.

A few workers walked between a side building and a couple of planes, but no one else presented themselves for her arrival, so Amelia headed to the door of the main building.

Before entering, she spied a piece of a cherry red airplane wing sticking out from behind the structure and her breath caught in her throat. Amelia detoured around the corner where the cinder block surface caught at the cotton twill of the riding pants she used for flying.

The morning sun glinted off the single wing crossing over the top of the fuselage and the sharply curved hoods over the landing gear. Over twenty-eight feet long, it could hold up to six passengers—more than enough room in case she wanted company when she crossed the Atlantic. Amelia stared at the immense span of the wings, nearly twice the length of the aircraft, and smiled. She liked how the airplane seemed to hover low to the ground. If she stood on her tiptoes, Amelia could probably reach the peak.

It had to be her plane, the Lockheed Vega 5B. Rumors of this model had circulated through the flying community for months, ever since Lockheed released the Vega 1 last year and it broke every important speed record. This one was supposed to be even faster, topping out at speeds of 165 miles per hour. With it, she could hope to break every record in the books. She wanted to get close and inspect every inch of the eight-foot-high plane, to open the door and climb inside the cockpit to learn the plane's language—the one it spoke just for her. But first, she had to earn it. Amelia simply nodded once at the beautiful machine before retracing her steps to the front of the building.

Inside, she found Agent Beyer seated at a desk inside a small office with a concrete floor and walls plastered with maps. There was also a table and chairs along with a filing cabinet.

Agent Beyer looked up and grinned. "You're early. I like that." With a single finger, she beckoned for the younger woman to join her. "Pull up a chair, and I'll show you where you're headed."

Once Amelia did so, the older woman pointed to a map she had anchored to the desk with a book, a paperweight, and two rocks. Amelia noticed an OTA in Art Deco lettering near the right-hand bottom corner. She had never seen the logo before.

"What's that?" she asked, tapping a finger on the letters.

Agent Beyer's eyes flickered to Amelia's face, considering. "That is your moment of choice. It's not when you agreed to take this job, or when you climb aboard that fancy new plane out back, or even when you take off. This right here is the moment when you're going to have to choose to be in on this secret, or out. There's no halfway about it. Because after this you'll know too much." The woman's tone, so light and casual, had turned flat and serious.

Tendrils of doubt and excitement wavered in Amelia's gut.

"If you're in, you'll have to sign this." Agent Beyer pulled a paper and pen from a briefcase on the floor at her feet and handed them to

Amelia. "Read it over, but we kept it to a single page. You're agreeing to keep your mouth shut but so are we. Get lost out there, and you're on your own. We won't come looking for you, won't make up some fancy story, and won't notify your next of kin."

Amelia read the brief legal document, glanced at the blank back, and stared into Agent Beyer's eyes, she didn't see their serious brown color, but instead, pictured the gleaming red bird waiting outside. Nothing else mattered. "What's your first name?" she said.

"Dorothy," Agent Beyer replied, looking startled.

Amelia signed the paper in her careful, clear script and handed it back.

Agent Beyer replaced everything in the briefcase and pointed at the letters on the map. "The Office of the Aberrant, OTA, is a secret division of the United States government tasked with the oversight and regulation of all those bits and pieces in the world which don't require your belief but which exist nonetheless." Amelia's skepticism must have shown on her face because Agent Beyer winked at her. "I won't run down the list of aberrant items and people we've collected now, not when we are getting along so well. If all goes as planned over the next forty-eight hours, my bosses might have other jobs for you, and you'll get to peek at the list. For now, best stay on task."

Amelia nodded, deciding that since she'd committed to doing this, she might as well learn only what she needed to get by in case she wanted, or had, to forget it later. "Fair enough. I'm ready to fly if this other agent you talked about is ready to leave, but the maps and flight plans you gave me don't match up with any known islands in the Bermuda Triangle, as you called it."

Agent Beyer glanced over her shoulder at a heavy metal door that was firmly closed. "Agent Sadler will be with us shortly. Now, just follow the maps I gave you, and you'll have no problems. I promise you, there is an island. Your equipment, compasses, and whatnot might start acting funny as you draw close, so I don't suggest you rely on them. Use your own senses instead."

"Dead reckoning?" Amelia's stomach fluttered. She wasn't proficient in that method of navigation. "Perhaps—" she began, but Agent Beyer went on.

"Land on the southern tip of the island in this open field." Agent Beyer pulled another map on top of the first. This one was a close up of an island with jagged edges and staggering elevations. She traced her finger along a snaking, blue line. "From there, follow the largest trail inland due north. We don't have more specific directions as the last successful mission to the isle was some years ago."

Amelia studied the route for a minute before nodding. "Seems simple enough."

Agent Beyer tipped her head, glancing up at the taller woman before continuing. "You and Agent Sadler will make your way through the jungle to a bastion of civilization." She pointed to a narrow valley about a third of the way toward the center of the island. "Here."

"Civilization? Who lives there?" Amelia said.

"People from all over the globe. They travel to the isle for many reasons. Most want to get far away from where they were. It's for the desperate. For example, Doctor Fabrice Apollinaire.

"During the war, our government and its allies uncovered some, well, *unusual* technologies. It was decided that the world would be better off without these discoveries, and as part of The Treaty of Versailles, all the diplomats agreed they should be destroyed. If they fall into the wrong hands, the cost in human life would be too high.

"Apollinaire, a brilliant scientist, worked for my counterpart in the French government, the Directorate of Altérité Security, and he disagreed with their plan. However, before the treaty was signed, indeed, before the war was even over, Apollinaire died. Or so we thought." Agent Beyer leaned back in her chair and crossed her arms.

Amelia's head spun. She'd been a nurse in Toronto during The Great War and had contracted the flu herself. Chronic sinusitis had plagued her ever since. At the very mention of that memory, a sour taste bloomed on the back of her tongue. She swallowed hard.

"We've recently discovered that Apollinaire faked his death. Prior to this, he took notes and photographs on as much of the technology as possible. He disappeared with illicit papers. We believe he settled on the isle and has been conducting research on this technology ever since. With almost ten years to work on deciphering this technology for his own use, there's no telling what he's managed to recreate."

Trying to shake off her own ghosts, Amelia leaned forward, elbow on the desk. "So what do we do?"

"Bring him back. Him and all his research. What you can't bring back, completely destroy before you leave. The equipment and all his documentation. My bosses want to spend the next ten years questioning Apollinaire," Agent Beyer said as she folded up the second map and handed it to Amelia.

"What if he won't come?" she said.

"Not really your job, Miss Earhart. Agent Sadler is one of our best field agents and has been fully briefed for this mission. She'll handle Dr. Apollinaire. Just follow her lead. Your job is to fly everyone safely there and back again."

A thin young man dressed in coveralls hoisted a crate through the open door of the Vega. Amelia stuck her head out the cockpit into the passenger area like a nervous but proud parent.

When he noticed her, he gestured with the crate. "Where would you like the food, Miss?"

She pointed under the rear seats. "Please secure it there next to the water." They'd been loading the plane for the better part of thirty minutes and were almost finished. Amelia itched to get started. The sun had fully risen about fifteen minutes ago. They needed to make the most of the daylight.

While he contorted himself at the rear of the fuselage, she peered out the nearest window, scouring the field for any sign of Agent Sadler. With their coveralls and grease-stained handkerchiefs, none of the figures in the scrubby grass around the plane seemed likely. She resumed her final examination of the cockpit when a voice called to her from the airplane door.

"Miss?"

She turned around. "Yes?"

The young woman poking her head in the door had her blonde hair tucked under a worker's cap. "The boys want to know if you're ready for Agent Sadler to board."

Amelia's frown lowered the corners of her eyes. Why didn't Sadler just come aboard by herself? "Of course, tell her to come right in."

The young woman nodded and popped out of sight. Amelia approached the opening to greet Sadler, only to encounter two men carrying a body on a stretcher. Her heart dropped, and she bit her lip at the sight of the agent supposed to be her partner.

"Is Agent Sadler alright?" she asked.

A third man hopped into the plane to grasp the front handles of the stretcher. "Bit too much to drink last night," he said, winking. The ropey muscles of his forearms twisted and bulged as he helped the two men outside maneuver the unmoving form of the agent into the passenger area.

"And this morning as well from the smell of it," she said as the caustic fumes of several forms of alcohol wafted off Sadler's prone form, filling the small cabin. "None of those crates has any liquor in it, do they?"

The young woman from before spoke from the door. "No, Miss. I oversaw the packing myself."

Amelia nodded. "Thank you. Perhaps if you tried laying her across two seats?" she said to the three men trying to load Agent Sadler into one of the leather seats.

The edge of Amelia's lip curled at the memory of the stink of the nursing ward. *I hope she doesn't start vomiting mid-flight.*

The men complied, buckling the unconscious woman to the seats. Because the Vega's seats lacked seat belts, they had scared up several men's trouser belts from the dormitory. Sadler's black hair contrasted sharply with her bright red lips and pale cheeks. The woman's neck looked vulnerable with her head leaning steeply to the side.

Amelia finished the preflight procedures, doing her best to ignore Sadler's broad snores, occasionally muttering under her breath.

When she completed the preflight checklist, Amelia snagged the arm of the young blonde woman again. She took another long, incredulous look at her drunken partner. "Where's Agent Beyer?"

"Gone back to town. Is there anything you need?"

Amelia shook her head. "No. Thank you. I'll see her when we get back."

Empty-handed, if Agent Sadler is any indication.

Amelia felt as though ownership of the Vega and the funds to attempt her own transatlantic flight were being held out of reach by a woman who didn't know a glass from a bottle.

With the farewells and shouts of good luck still ringing in her ears, Amelia tugged on her tight leather pilot's cap, signaled to those lining the runway, and started the Vega's engine.

Shut into the shallow box that was the cockpit, Amelia's world narrowed to V-shaped windows, a bank of glass-fronted dials, and the pedals under her feet. After only a few minutes into the flight, the low buzz from the engines that vibrated through her body faded, no more noticeable than her own heartbeat. The stick in her hands moved like the flank of a large animal breathing, her plane nestled against the beast's broad side.

She caught herself smiling inside this tight circle of concentration, the never-ending speaking engagements and the hollow adulation of unearned achievements. Even the unconscious agent in the cabin behind her slipped away from immediate concern. She breathed evenly when the plane hit a rough air pocket and lost some altitude. The familiar lightness lifted the backs of her thighs. Amelia adjusted for the lost altitude and smiled. This was what she lived for.

They'd been airborne for several hours, Amelia's eyes rarely leaving the horizon except to get a read on their current position. She used the controls on the dash to double check her rusty dead reckoning skills. So far, both methods of navigation indicated they remained on course but worry snipped at her thoughts. Agent Beyer's warning that navigational controls would become less accurate as they approached the island never strayed far from her concerns.

Even given all that—the calm weather and uneventful journey— when the equipment failed, it happened suddenly. The dials in front of her shivered, several needles sagging. To Amelia, it felt like the cold ocean depths opening beneath her when she swam too far from shore.

Amelia spoke for the first time since they had taken off. "Damn."

Now that she'd snapped the outer thread of the island's web, she was stuck. If she didn't successfully finish their course to the island, she would have no fixed object to navigate from on the return trip. Amelia glanced out the window again, scribbling on a piece of paper at her side.

At that moment, the door of the cockpit opened, bringing a puff of fresh air that was quickly squashed by the scented tendrils of whiskey Agent Sadler seemed to wear as easily as her khaki suit. Amelia looked up, startled.

"Goodness, I've awoken tied up before but never by a couple of gentlemen's belts. Please tell me they were at least handsome," Sadler said, speaking loud enough to be easily heard despite the noisy cockpit. Her red lips quirked into a half-smile. She held a flask in the other hand, a dark brown bangle inlaid with silver medallions encircled the same wrist. "Are we almost there?"

Amelia kept her focus on the job. "How nice of you to finally join the mission."

Sadler ignored the jab and leaned farther into the cockpit, blocking Amelia's view to the south. "What's all this?" She reached out a finger and tapped one of the misbehaving dials. "Are we *that* close then?" Sadler pushed her face to the nearest window, bumping Amelia's shoulder.

"Do you mind! I'm trying to fly and not crash here!" she snapped.

"Sorry," the dark-haired woman said pulling back, but not leaving the cramped space. "Agent Ursula Sadler."

The woman's hand snaked into Amelia's peripheral vision, offering to shake.

"I'm a little busy." Amelia raised higher, trying to get a better look at the horizon that had disappeared below the line of the windshield. She eased the control stick forward.

Agent Sadler bumped heavily against her seat, and something splashed down the back of Amelia's collar.

"Whoops! Sorry about that . . ." Sadler stopped. "What did you say your name was again?"

"I didn't. It's Amelia Earhart. Now, will you please return to your seat? We're close enough to the island that my controls have failed, and it's taking all I have to keep us on course."

"Aren't you clever? Sounds dreadfully tricky."

Amelia couldn't detect any sarcasm in the woman's voice. But with her high society New England accent, she reminded Amelia of so many other women who'd judged her when they learned what she did for a living. It raised her hackles. She was about to offer a sharp retort when Sadler spoke again.

"Why didn't you say so before? I'll just go back and have a rummage in the crates. I'm a might peckish."

The woman left, forgetting to close the cockpit door. Amelia's hands were glued to the stick. She didn't dare turn to shut it. However, any hint of Sadler's presence soon faded under the rumble of the engines. Their hum had grown to a straining whine. Amelia scowled.

That doesn't sound right.

"Look, oranges!" Sadler said, popping her head back through the door, a large fruit in each hand. "Shall I peel you one?"

"No thank you," Amelia said, jaw clenched.

"Suit yourself." Sadler left again.

The plane shuddered, and for a terrible moment the usual resistance on the stick fell away. When she pushed forward, the beast of the sky didn't push back.

Panic gripped her throat like a hot hand, and she nearly stood up, desperate to find the sun above the horizon again.

It was gone.

She searched the empty blue sky for the longest moment of her life. Amelia wandered in her heart and bones, tried to orient her mind, strained to feel due north. But it escaped her. She banged on the shiny new console full of useless numbers in front of her.

Slowly, she turned the plane from side-to-side in ever-widening degrees.

Nothing.

She banked the aircraft again, turning more sharply. *There!* Somehow the sun had gotten nearly behind her. Had Sadler distracted her that badly?

Amelia swallowed hard.

Sadler's voice drifted in from the cabin, muffled by distance and the pounding of blood in Amelia's ears. She ignored the troublesome agent, glancing instead at her watch only to see that the timepiece looked frozen.

"La Bête Isle!" Sadler shouted very close to her ear.

Amelia jumped in her seat. "*What?*"

"The Island of the Beasts," Sadler grabbed her shoulder and pointed out the window to Amelia's left. "We're right over it!"

"That's not possible." Amelia shook her head.

"I saw it out the window." Sadler pointed down, her bangle clacking off Amelia's seat.

"I'm telling you, it's just below us."

If she banked the plane again, they would lose their heading. Precarious as it already was, Amelia couldn't afford to be wrong.

"You're drunk, Agent Sadler. I'm the pilot here, and I know what I'm doing. Now, take your seat and close the door behind you." Amelia straightened her shoulders.

Sadler sucked in air through her teeth and backed away from Amelia, taking the sharp reek of alcohol with her. A moment later, Amelia heard a click, and the woman reappeared beside her.

Pushed to her breaking point, Amelia yelled, "I said, take your *seat!*"

Sadler held the tip of something small and metal against Amelia's cheek. "Bring the plane around!"

She flicked her gaze to the side, staring with horror at the barrel of Sadler's pistol. "You'll kill us both if you fire that."

"I'm not drunk, sweetheart, at least no more than usual. But we are *over* the island. I assure you. Didn't Agent Beyer warn you about this place? Your instruments, your sense of direction, time itself—they all act differently here. I know what I'm saying. Now, bring us *around*," she said, the cold iron in her voice unmistakable.

"If you're wrong, I won't be able to get us back on course." Amelia turned her head to lock eyes with Sadler. "I'm not wrong." The agent used her pistol to point at the control stick.

Amelia pushed it forward on an angle, and Sadler used her free hand to grip the back of the pilot's seat as the plane banked sharply.

The dark outline of a rocky coast soon came into view. Amelia stared in wonder. How had she missed an entire island? The V-shaped windows of the cockpit had blocked the island from view when the plane was directly over the landmass, but that didn't explain how she'd overlooked such a massive chunk of land in a calm sea on a clear day.

"See, it's right—"

"I have it now," Amelia interjected.

A long pause filled the small space.

Agent Sadler's pistol moved out of sight. "I'd better take my seat for the landing. After we're down, I'll poke about in the crate and see if Beyer managed to remember bullets for this gun."

Angry at being fooled, Amelia's knuckles turned white as she clenched the stick. She took a deep breath. Sadler might be ill-mannered and aggravating, but she wasn't wrong. The island filled more of the cockpit window, and Amelia admitted to herself that the agent probably just saved their lives. They could always fight about methods later. Right now, she needed to land this plane.

Circling to where the rough rock of the shore opened up, Amelia searched the edges of the island for the promised clearing, large and smooth enough to act as a landing field. The rocky cliffs and beaches stood out around the dense jungle of the island's center, and after ten minutes of searching, she spied the landing site.

Amelia adjusted the flaps and angled toward the strip, calculating their descent rate. Two large promontories surrounded the entrance to the open area and forced her to approach from a steep angle, lowering the plane over the water to safely clear the obstacles. There must be large rocks underwater at the shoreline as well because the water chopped at the land. White foam frothed on the beach like a mad dog.

Near the island, they flew past an enormous rock jutting up from the sea just like the one Agent Beyer had pointed to on the map. A surge of confidence buoyed Amelia past the welcomed landmark.

They cleared the shadow of the looming cliff, and the sea exploded.

A gaping jaw lined with a double row of pointed teeth, each one longer than her arm, flashed outside her windows. The beast lunging at them unhinged its mouth to an astonishing size, looking ready to swallow the entire plane. Then a rush of water slapped against the fuselage, and she struggled to hold the plane steady. Sheets of seawater rained down on the Vega's roof. Deafened and panicked, Amelia yanked on the controls. The nimble craft rose quickly but not fast enough to escape the thunderous wrench as something scraped the side of the plane.

Seawater turned her windshield into a blurry maze. Acting on instinct, Amelia pulled the plane higher, her arms shaking.

"What was that?" Sadler yelled, bursting into the cockpit holding the side of her head as though she'd bumped it.

"I don't know! But it was big enough to eat us whole. I'll tilt the plane, and you go look out the back windows."

"Our supposed ally, The Phantom, didn't mention sea monsters," Sadler said to herself before lurching away, grabbing heavily onto the doorway as the plane tipped. She stumbled back moments later, a pair of binoculars clutched to her chest. "Eels!"

"*Eels?* Eels just attacked the plane?"

"No. Well, yes. They aren't *regular* eels." Sadler gestured at the sea out the right-hand window. "Don't you know your French? It's an island of *beasts*."

"Thanks," Amelia noted dryly, "I gathered as much. Whatever they are, what are we going to *do* about them?" She kept the plane steady, the shaking of her hands feeding the part of her that loved this thrill. The part that never slept for long.

"Our first pass woke them up. They're frenzied now. I need you to get us closer, no more than 500 yards or so. When I direct you, pass by the swarm in the water, keeping the plane's door facing them. Oh, and I've some whiskey if you need to steady your nerves. The plane is hopping around like an angry horse," Sadler said. Amelia glared at her. "Suit yourself. Fly slow and steady and be ready for my signal."

Sadler quickly reached down and jammed her pistol into the pocket of Amelia's leather jacket where it hung on the back of the seat. "Just in case I don't survive this, you might need a weapon. I'm going to get a bigger gun."

"I thought this wasn't loaded?" Amelia asked, her voice higher than she liked.

"Of course it was loaded." Sadler flicked her head to the side. "Sorry," she added insincerely before exiting the cockpit.

Amelia's indignant sputters faded as she flew in tight circles, preparing herself for whatever crazy idea Sadler had planned. A few loud crashes and an ominous *clank* broke through the whine of the motors. She was on the verge of calling for Sadler to ask if everything was alright, when the agent's shout reached her.

"I'm all set up! Take us around!"

"Roger that!" Amelia yelled, easing the stick to the left. She executed another tight circle, bringing the plane as close to the giant rock as she dared. When they emerged out of its shadow, even though they were farther away this time, the sea erupted in a writhing mass. The thick, dark green bodies of the disgusting creatures grappled with each other, pushing their comrades beneath the water, each fighting to get close enough to snap the plane out of the air.

One of the largest muscled its way to the top of the monstrous living pile and flung itself at them. A wicked cracking filled the air as Sadler fired something clearly larger than her pistol. Several more shots followed quickly.

Amelia ducked her shoulders at the first report, forcing herself to keep her eyes open. They zoomed past the place where the eels attacked, and she lost sight of the vicious beasts The Vega vibrated under her hands and seat as the engines accelerated them up and away.

Sadler clambered back into the cockpit, puffing. "Should be safe to fly in now."

"Safe?"

"Safe from the eels at any rate. Take a peek if you don't believe me." Sadler perched herself just off Amelia's right shoulder.

She flew around again, this time aiming the plane straight so it flew broadside to the school of eels. Her jaw dropped in amazement at the unnatural mass rising from the ocean. A giant cluster of eel bodies writhed below. The sea always moved, shifting and tracing a sometimes-dizzying pattern beneath your boat or plane, Amelia knew, but she'd never seen anything like this. Beige tubes as thick as tree trunks wrestled with each other, their speckled bodies slick with bloody, pink froth.

As they drew nearer, Amelia scrunched her nose and tried not to gag. The sulfurous stink of shredded entrails lay heavy over a smell far too salty to be seawater alone. At her shoulder, Sadler made a clicking sound in the back of her throat.

"What did you do?" Amelia asked, half in wonder, half in disgust.

"A few well-placed shots from my Enfield rifle took down one of the eels. Its brethren took care of the rest. Must have scented blood in the water."

"They're eating each other?" She paused and answered herself. "They're eating each other." She shuddered, grateful the cockpit's high windows soon cut off her view.

"Ready to try the landing again?" Sadler said, slapping the back of Amelia's seat.

Amelia swallowed against the queasy knot in her throat. "Yeah."

The agent left the cabin, presumably to take her seat, while Amelia pushed away her worries over how they'd get off the island when the time came. She needed to concentrate on the landing ahead.

Just as she had for the first attempt, she opened the flaps and pointed the plane directly down the corridor of eels, now distracted by their horrifying food frenzy. As the plane cleared the large rock, she held her breath for fear that another beast would spring into their path and grab them.

Nothing.

From the cabin, Agent Sadler shrieked with delight, cursing at the giant cannibal fish. Amelia shook her head and sighed gently, steering the plane through the cliffs and down onto the cleared strip of land at the edge of the jungle.

Amelia hefted her pack onto her shoulders, tightened the straps, and tried to get used to balancing under its weight. They didn't plan to be gone long and had packed light, but after flying for a few hours her legs always felt strangely heavy on the ground.

"All set, Amelia?" Sadler asked, already strapped into her own pack.

The agent's bag bulged more than Amelia's, and she frowned, wondering what other surprises Sadler had in store. There were lots of things Amelia couldn't control in this situation, so she decided to fix what she could.

"Listen, call me A.E. Nearly everyone does."

Sadler smiled. "Call me Ursula. You'll be the first." Her bracelet's silver inlays shimmered in the high sun as she popped a dripping segment of an orange into her mouth and strode off toward an opening in the trees.

A high-pitched shriek echoed from the jungle, sending a wild boar rocketing out of the undergrowth and across the sandy soil to another cove of trees farther up the beach. With one hand, Amelia pressed the outline of the pistol in her pocket and took off after Sadler.

Amelia's longer strides soon closed the gap between them, and they entered the trees together. No more than a few hundred feet from the jungle's edge, the natural lighting changed. The sun's rays couldn't penetrate the leafy canopy, and only a meager amount managed to filter through. Even once her eyes adjusted, Amelia found herself squinting. The air under the trees seemed thicker somehow, and with limited sight her other senses dialed into a sharper focus.

The warm, rich earth released such a heavy odor of green and growing things that she couldn't smell the lavish pink blossoms of an overhanging bush until she came very near them. Their scent, musky like vanilla, faded quickly. The wet vegetation and rocks made the path slippery, and even in their stout hiking boots, Amelia and Sadler had to watch their footing.

Another shrill call from far off in the distance startled a flock of birds out of the leafy treetops overhead. Their clatter left Amelia's pulse pushing wildly against the base of her throat.

Sadler seemed unaffected—just as she had by the aftereffects of too much alcohol, holding a gun to someone's head, or almost being bitten in two by giant eels. She marched along cheerily, the jacket of her beige pantsuit soaked with a dark triangle of sweat between her shoulder blades.

Amelia glared at the other woman's back. *Perhaps I'm being unfair. Maybe only holding a gun to my head failed to bother her.*

She put on her brightest tone, determined to make Sadler explain. "So. You called this Island of the Beasts. If this place is surrounded by sea serpents, what can we expect to find inland?"

"The whole thing's chock a block with dangerous, deadly, venomous creatures," the agent said over her shoulder.

Despite her resolve, Amelia couldn't stop peering into the thick canopy above, grateful their heavy shade kept the undergrowth controlled. "Like snakes, spiders, or panthers?"

"Those too, I suppose. I was just talking about the people, though."

"People? Surely you're joking."

"Not at all. There were, of course, a small group of natives populating the island when it was first discovered, but over time, the isle's isolation has drawn anyone and everyone looking to escape . . . or to never be found again." This time Sadler did turn, shooting a wicked grin at her companion.

Amelia stepped over a rotting log on the path. "Then how did we get a map of the place?"

"A little misunderstanding between one of my colleagues and our government." She paused. "Several foreign governments as well. The Phantom needed to make himself scarce for a while, and he needed someplace that could support his unusual lifestyle. When he heard rumors that Apollinaire had set up shop here, it seemed like the perfect match."

"Why did he leave?"

Sadler spun around and stopped, shrugging. "The Phantom's not really someone you sit down with for a personal chat. Maybe he ran out of accessible bodies on such a small island."

"Bodies? What do you mean?" Amelia asked.

"When you more or less wear the bodies of others like clothes, you need a very big closet. He no longer has a body of his own but manages to get quite a few useful things accomplished by taking over others."

Amelia shuddered. "That's horrible."

Sadler grinned. "It certainly is for the bodies in question. However, I'm glad to hear you moved right past 'impossible.'"

"There were giant eels. It's hard to go back to the conventional after that."

Sadler nodded. "Anyway, when The Phantom returned, he used his intel of the island to buy himself back into my superior's good graces at the OTA because the DAT wanted a favor from them. Can we get on with this blasted trudge through this Godforsaken jungle now?"

Amelia flicked her eyes past Sadler's shoulder. Looking deeper into the brush, an outline of a dark shadow took shape far to the right of the path behind a cluster of thick tree trunks. An outline she recognized all too well. "Are we the only ones after Apollinaire?"

Sadler huffed. "*More* questions?"

Despite the agent's attempt at a rebuff, Amelia noticed a fast quirk of the woman's heavily made-up lips. "We aren't the first agents sent here, are we?" She pointed past Sadler at the wreck of an airplane in the jungle.

The agent turned her head, and after a few seconds she gasped, "Ambrose!" Sadler took off into the trees.

Amelia ran after her, and they reached the downed craft together. Sadler stopped first, badly out of breath.

Amelia circled the ragged pieces of what remained of the plane's fuselage. After a few steps, she realized this was the same model of aircraft they'd just left on the beach. A Lockheed Vega 5B that shouldn't even be on the market yet—just like hers. Cold threads of panic left her hands and chest quivering. She twisted her head, searching for the identification numbers on the wings. A strange thought entered her head—an imagined déjà vu. Had they actually crashed or been eaten by the enormous eels, and this place was some kind of purgatory?

There! NR-7948.

They were different numbers. Dizzy with relief at no longer being faced with the idea of her own death, Amelia started walking again.

Sadler met her when she finished her circle around the wreck.

"How did the plane get so far past the tree line?" Amelia wondered aloud.

"What do you mean?"

Amelia pointed at the intact canopy above, talking a little too loudly as if to push away her fears. "I would have expected it to take trees or at least some of the larger limbs down. We'd be able to see the sky, and the plants in this area would be growing like mad, trying to reach sunlight." She gestured at the undisturbed jungle floor. "There's no sign of an impact on the ground or to the body of the plane. I've seen crashes before," she cleared her throat against the memories gathered there, "they never look like this."

Sadler scowled, pointing at the gaping hole in the side of the plane. "The bodies would have been carried away by scavengers."

"That's not what I mean. The *wreckage* wouldn't look like, like *this*." She squatted down and pointed at the underside of the fuselage, now facing sideways. "The landing gear and windscreen are intact, the wings are fine, but," Amelia stood and gestured to where only a few pieces of cloth from the tail remained, "weirdly, it looks like the tail assembly took the brunt of the damage."

Sadler's dark eyebrows lowered in confusion. "What?"

"The wrong parts of the plane are broken."

"Why didn't you just . . .?" She shook her head. "This plane didn't crash?"

"I'd bet my pilot's license on it," Amelia said, approaching what remained of the cockpit, where it balanced precariously, looking more like an overturned bowl. The propeller was missing. "I might be able to find the logbook."

Amelia dropped to her knees, sending up the sickly scent of rotting jungle vegetation. The opening to the cockpit rested against the ground, and Amelia had to twist herself awkwardly to reach inside. Unable to see the darkened interior clearly, she groped blindly, envisioning her Vega's cockpit to guide her hands. She pressed against the wreckage so hard that it groaned under her weight, tipping wildly.

Amelia grunted in pain, but pressed on, hunting for a flat, oblong object. Her hand finally clasped what felt like the logbook, however, when she tried to pull her arm out with the book she realized she was now stuck. If she let go, the book would fall into the footwell where it would be impossible to reach. Amelia supported the weight of the whole cockpit now against her chest as she squatted on the ground. The muscles in her legs and shoulders burned. She pushed harder. The only option to avoid crushing her arm was to flip the thing over completely.

Something slammed hard against the wall of the overturned cockpit. The pressure on her arm released, and the cockpit flipped, lumbering back down to the ground with a crash and the tinkle of breaking glass. Amelia turned her back to the piece and leaned into it, chest heaving. She looked up at Sadler. She held out the logbook to the agent. "Thanks."

Sadler shook her head. "You're the pilot. You should read it."

Amelia cracked open the book. Inside, a messy scrawl cataloged descriptions of weather, flight time, and altitude that mirrored their own almost exactly. It was eerily similar. She'd already checked the numbers once, but a sharp thread of worry drew her eyes back to the call letters on the wings of the wreck. She needed to make sure they were still different than her own Vega.

Nothing unusual struck her about the entries she scanned, so instead, she flipped to the front of the book and read aloud the pilot's name. "Roger Gantz? Is that a pilot for the Office of the Aberrant?"

Sadler leaned in to get a closer look at the book. "Yes, he'd recently joined the organization. Gantz flew Ambrose Masters in a few weeks ago, but they never came back. We don't have many pilots to spare, so I suppose that's why they drafted you and me this time."

Amelia climbed to her feet. "What do you mean?"

Sadler snorted. An act that seemed at odds with her perfect hair, makeup, and outfit, but one Amelia was learning fit the agent perfectly. "What's the difference between the two of them and the two of us?"

Amelia paused, then pursed her lips. "We're women." Amelia dropped the logbook into her pack before taking a swig of water from her canteen. The air had grown hotter, more heavily laced with the smell of flowers and sulfur.

"Indeed." Sadler noticed Amelia's frown and laughed. "You didn't think we were the first-stringers, did you? Ambrose and Roger are either dead or prisoners, no sense sending good money after bad when they could have the two of us for the cost of . . ." the agent glanced at the wreck behind her, "the cost of that fancy new plane on the beach. I sure hope you bargained for more than that."

Amelia tilted her chin up. "That's none of your business."

The other woman sighed and left it at that. "Fine. Then let's get a move on, shall we? Once we get what we came for, you can get back to setting records."

That remark hinted Sadler knew more about Amelia than she let on. Still, she trailed the agent, fuming. What right did this hoity-toity, drunken, know-it-all have to accuse Amelia of taking a bad deal?

"Why are *you* here?" she demanded, grabbing Sadler's arm and forcing her to stop.

A dark smile carved Sadler's round face. "You sure you really want to know?" Amelia nodded. "Okay, then, tell me something, A.E. When you're up there at night in your little flying box, do you ever see Mars? Just a little orange speck in the great big sky?"

Amelia shook her head. "It's not really used for navigation."

"That's a shame. Next time you should take a closer look, because Mars sees you. It sees all of us. We managed to fight them off once, barely, and we paid for it dearly."

A flicker of memory licked the underside of Amelia's brain. It left her feeling sick and feverish. She put a hand to her head, as though trying to press the memories back where they seemed to throb just under her temples.

Sadler went on as though she hadn't noticed. "But they left some of their bag of tricks behind. If the Martians managed to kill that many of us with their technology, just imagine the horrors we could visit on ourselves trying to pretend we know how to use it. But Apollinaire thought he knew better. He decided for the rest of humanity. That crackpot thinks we ought to make a deal with the devil, and he's hiding out on this island playing *Faust*."

Amelia's anger drove off whatever spell had fallen over her while Sadler spoke. She shook her head. "Martians? You people really are crazy. Earth germs killed the invaders years ago—they're dead and gone! I can't believe I risked my life for this farce!" She turned toward the path. "I'm going to wait back at the plane. I'll give you twenty-four hours. If you're not back by then, you can find your own way off this island."

The leaves of a bush with serrated edges snagged on Amelia's pack, and she stopped to yank free. Some sap from the plant stuck to her fingers, and the sharp scent of citrus reached her nose.

She clomped down the path, trying to leave behind her anger at having been played for a fool. Amelia had been walking for only a few minutes when rustling from behind made her pause again.

Probably Sadler trying to convince me to come back.

"You might as well go on ahead. I'm just the pilot, remember? I better stick with what I know!" she called into the trees. The noise stopped. When the agent didn't appear, Amelia scanned the path, looking for her. "Sadler?"

Something large slammed into Amelia, sending her sprawling off the path. Stunned, she tried to get her bearings, pushing the fronds of a plant off her face.

A low growl stilled her hands.

Breathing hard, she fumbled in her pocket for her pistol.

Empty.

Amelia rolled to one side, deeper under the bushes. Dirt and leaves clung to her cheek. A giant claw sliced the air and earth where she'd lain moments before. Bits of the forest floor sprayed out from the track the claw carved, flying into her open mouth. The sour taste of rot coated her tongue.

Fear mixed with the soil spread across her face as she crawled through the undergrowth, heading anywhere so long as it was away from what chased her. The jungle growth above her head rustled and shivered as though something monstrous parted them as easily as a child searching for Easter eggs in the grass.

Her left elbow cracked against a tree and left her arm numb. She scooted around the enormous trunk with her good arm and the toes of her boots digging into the earth. Amelia curled into a tight ball behind the tree's meager shelter. Nose to knees, she tried to quiet her jagged breaths, smelling the green scent of crushed leaves on her slacks. The ground shook as whatever chased her lumbered past.

Several feet away, it stopped, snuffling loudly in the brush.

Amelia stifled a whimper.

A pistol shot cracked in the forested air, and the beast roared in pain. Trees and bushes whipped viciously as the beast tried to thrash its way free of the foliage hiding its attacker. Three more shots quickly followed. Amelia's eyes lifted just as the clawed foot of a gigantic lizard plunged several inches into the soft dirt by her face. Terror held her down. Between the creature and the gunfire, she didn't dare move.

A flurry of shots, closer this time, echoed through the trees. Amelia's ears rang like a cathedral bell and even the thunderous crash of the beast hitting the forest floor sounded like the whisper of a distant waterfall.

Finally, it lay still.

Just as suddenly as the attack began, it ended. Her joints were locked in panic, and Amelia had to force her limbs to respond. Slowly, like an old woman, she climbed to her feet and peered through the trees.

"Sadler! I'm over here!" she shouted. The agent might be an insane liar, but she sure was handy with a firearm.

A branch snapped behind her, and Amelia turned, coming face-to-face with a tiger. At least that's what her struggling brain decided it was after flipping back and forth between a man in a tiger mask or a giant cat standing on its hind legs. Its large eyes blinked at her, and the muzzle pulled back in a deep-throated snarl.

Amelia held up her hands, stepping away slowly. The tiger beast didn't follow.

A buzz came from behind her, and then a man spoke. "We've located the intruder, sir. Do you want us to bring her in?"

She whirled around, glad to face a human threat at least, but soon realized her mistake.

It wasn't a man, at least, only as much as the tiger creature had been. He had the overall outline of a human, but his heavily muscled frame bulged in the wrong places under his loose, gray outfit of slacks and a vest. The skin of his bare arms, neck, and bald head was covered in thick, rough scales. Where fingernails should have been, stout claws sprouted instead, clutching a black metal box in one hand. A thick, metal wire poked from the top of the still-buzzing contraption.

The static cut out, and another man's voice came from the box, this time speaking in a slight French accent. "Her, you say? Yes, bring her to me. I have many questions."

Amelia groped at both pockets, again feeling for the weight and outline of her pistol. They were empty. Either she'd transferred the weapon to her pack or had lost it during her flight from the huge beast.

Something hard struck the side of her head, and she dropped to the jungle floor again. Dazed, she felt rough hands tug off her pack and grab her hands. When she tried to pull away, her efforts only bought her a swift jab to her stomach. Amelia coiled around her injury, coughing, trying to drag in a breath.

One of the creatures secured her hands behind her back with what felt like metal cuffs, and they carried her for a minute before dumping her into the open trailer of a vehicle. The familiar scent of grease and rubber was almost soothing. As the hands of her captor receded, she decided it had been the tiger-faced man. No claws had dug at her wrist.

A few feet away, the second man spoke again, his voice now too soft to hear. Amelia peered through the metal grate around her that extended overhead like a tall cage. The man-creatures ignored her. Instead, the lizard-man stroked the head and ears of the tiger-man, who purred happily in response. A flexible, pink tongue erupted from the tiger-man's mouth, licking the arms and cheeks of his companion in long, slow lines.

Amelia watched in horror and fascination until she realized the display that she witnessed was meant to be private, as though between two lovers. The tiger-man didn't seem to be able to speak. When he opened his mouth, only a low purr came out. The lizard-man pulled the other into a rough embrace, and they kissed after a fashion.

She dropped her eyes to the dirt. *What happened to Sadler?*

After a long, bumpy drive down a winding path, the truck descended into a valley where the trees thinned significantly enough for a larger view. Few noises were loud enough to compete with the rumble of the vehicle's motor, but Amelia used her heels and back to lever herself into a sitting position so she could track their path, doing her best to memorize any turns they took.

As they continued, when she wasn't busy trying to make a mental map, she used her time to conjure escape plans, but nothing realistic developed. Even if she could get free of this cage, she still couldn't see what held her hands, let alone escape from it. Her wrists had swollen, and the metal cuffs felt uncomfortably tight now.

At the bottom of the valley, they approached several large, windowless buildings made of what looked like unpainted concrete blocks and metal sheeting, surrounded by several smaller structures. Once inside, her captors had tossed a mildewed tarp over her cage and carried her to the room where she waited.

The bottom grill of the cage dug uncomfortably into Amelia no matter how she positioned herself. She'd been kept in this cage for several hours already with the clock on the wall a mute witness. They'd left her in the center of a large room containing a desk, book-lined shelves, and metal cabinets with locks on the doors. Thirst ate at the back of her throat and tongue. At the far end of the room, something green bubbled in a shallow tank, filling the air with a sour smell. She wondered if the noxious brew would kill her if she drank it.

The large double doors on one wall of the room opened, and the same man-creatures entered. Once the door swung closed behind them, tiger-man turned his companion against the wall and nuzzled his neck. Lizard-man smiled and stroked the other behind the ears.

"Shhh . . . Later," he whispered, pointing at Amelia.

The first creature pulled away reluctantly, and they turned toward her.

This time, she was ready. "Please, let me go. I've done nothing to harm you. I promise to leave the island and never return. I won't breathe a word of what I've seen here."

The creatures shared a glance as they bent down to lift her cage.

"Please!" Her voice rose with genuine panic. "Let me go! I can get you off the island, too. I know where there's an airplane."

At that, the man with the tiger face fumbled her cage, and she tipped painfully against the side. "Planes! You know planes? Yes, I can—"

"Leave him alone," the lizard-man said. "He only tripped. Just make things easy on yourself and tell the doctor what he wants to know."

Amelia tried again to speak to them, but both ignored her. They carried her down a short hallway and into a second room. This one was full of two large steel tanks with flashing lights and pressure gauges at the top of a ladder that climbed each side. The tank on the right hissed out steam that floated toward a ceiling fan near a vent.

Two metal exam tables, along with gleaming surgical instruments, lined one wall. The third wall held a worktable where a man with closely cropped, white hair sat bent over a glowing object shaped like a book. He looked up as they entered, his pinched face expanding back to normal, and the light from the object faded.

"Excellent!" He rose from the desk. "Just set her over here." He gestured to the empty floor between the two tanks. His bushy eyebrows and small nose gave him the look of a terrier.

The creatures set her down, and the man waved them away, saying as they left, "Bring me a number three from storage," he said before turning to Amelia. "I am Dr. Fabrice Apollinaire, and I believe you've come to see me."

Amelia pried her thick, dry tongue from the roof of her mouth. "Why would you think that?"

He shrugged with his dark eyes wide. "Simple. No one else currently residing on the Isle of the Beasts is of any interest. Erik must have blabbed." He scoffed. "And after all I did for him. Who sent you? The DAT? OTA? AOTA?"

She shook her head. "I don't know who that is. Please, just let me go. I won't tell anybody about you. I promise."

The doctor laughed, though not unkindly. "Let's see. Your accent is American, midwestern if I'm not mistaken. You're probably from the Office of the Aberrant. Not that it matters. All those heartless bureaucrats hide behind their fancy initials. I know it may appear to you that I have all the time in the world, living isolated as I do, but you are incorrect. I'm actually on the edge of quite a breakthrough. If you won't provide me information, I'll have to find another use for you. Just as I did for your predecessors."

Amelia's heart thumped heavily in her chest as she remembered the lizard-man's warning that she should answer the doctor's questions. "My predecessors?"

"Why, Agents Masters and Gantz of course. They've been your guides around the island so far."

Unable to stop herself, she recoiled in horror. Amelia stared at the door where the man creatures had gone. Surely, he meant they were the agents who had arrived in the wreck of the Vega. But how could that be possible? They were monsters now—more beast than man.

Apollinaire cackled, obviously delighted. "What's wrong? Didn't you recognize them? Magnificent specimens, aren't they? Moreau was a genius, and I don't use that word lightly. However, his process was unstable and lengthy at best. What I've done with it," he turned and gestured toward the tanks behind him, "will allow us to create a race of unstoppable soldiers, protecting us from attack when the Martians return."

"You turned them into monsters," Amelia said, the words escaping her mouth before she could think better of it. Sadler had known these men. One had been a pilot like Amelia. What would Sadler think of them? Or of Amelia for getting herself captured? At the thought of the unflappable agent, she pressed her lips together.

The doctor continued. "On the contrary, I've improved them. Deciphering the Martian technology has been a long, slow journey, rife with many missteps—made more so by my isolation here." He waved his hand at the laboratory.

He spoke as though Amelia were the first person he'd seen in a long time. Amelia thought that Sadler must still be out there. He must not know about her. Amelia needed to stall Apollinaire until the agent arrived. However, Amelia wasn't an agent at the OTA and knew so little about any of this. He would soon see past such tactics. The only valuable information she held would give up Sadler, and the agent was her only chance at escape.

"Nobody forced you here. You abandoned the world," Amelia said.

He clicked his tongue. "I needed the space to experiment without anyone meddling. I must admit that not all my experiments turned out so well. A true scientist always admits their failures. And I am nothing if not a true scientist. Not like those other bureaucratic fools. Everyone I loved lost their lives to the disease we created to fend off the Martians." He must have noticed her confusion because he added, "The governments all made sure that the Martians, for all their murderous inventions, would be quite susceptible to influenza. Unfortunately, so were we. You and everyone else thinks our germs killed them all, but what about those still on Mars? They never got sick, now did they? What makes you think they aren't working on a vaccine so they can come back and try to conquer us again?" Apollinaire checked the controls at the base of the nearest tank.

The bars of her cage bit into Amelia's hands and knees. She'd risen to a crouch to brace herself but didn't know against what. Now she sagged back. A rush of blood to her face made her feel feverish again, robbing her strength. The same feelings of pain, illness, and déjà vu crept over her as when Beyer and Sadler had mentioned the war. This time, Apollinaire's words roused her fearful, suppressed memories to a sickening pitch. The room around her tumbled away as her ears filled with shouts and screams.

She'd served as a nurse in Canada, taking care of soldiers until she fell ill herself. Even all these years later, she hardly had words to describe what had happened. Instead of airplanes, giant, flat warships crowded the skies, slicing the air with beams of light and fire. Tripods that burned cities, destroyed the land, and killed millions of people.

She, and so many others, woke up screaming from the memories until the best way to survive was to try to forget the horrors. But she could never forget those soldiers under her care, and the illness she suffered as well. The awful bone-wrenching chills and scorching fevers decimating even the young and strong. Fluid in the lungs that drowned and choked, the worst sickness she'd ever seen, killing millions worldwide.

The doctor turned to her, about to speak, then stopped when he noticed her distress. "Did you also lose someone to the battles? Or to Earth's great killing machine, influenza?"

She nodded, unable to speak.

He shook his head sadly. "I lost everyone I cared about, my family—" his voice cracked, and he blinked rapidly. "They're gone. Stolen from me by the powers that be, and what they saw fit to unleash upon the world. We may have driven off our alien foes, but at what cost?"

Amelia wiped her cheeks, surprised to find tears mingled with the beads of sweat.

Apollinaire gestured at the equipment around them. "We should have the courage to seize the opportunity purchased with their sacrifice! If we don't unlock the Martian's technology, where does that leave us? We cannot hope to compete with them a second time." His voice grew quiet, hard, and cold as ice. "We have to make sure we're prepared so that it never happens again."

Her voice shook as she finally composed herself enough to speak. "Perhaps if you showed the government what you've accomplished, they'll change their minds. I could act as your messenger. Send me back with a letter."

"That's not a terrible idea." Apollinaire approached her cage, tipping his head back and forth as though examining her face and body. "But not a letter. No, a letter can be faked. Tell me, ma'am, do you have a favorite animal?"

Amelia's heart clenched, and a chilling numbness swept over her legs. Before she could answer, or beg for her humanity, the creatures that had been Ambrose Masters and Paul Gantz returned, carrying a large metal canister between them.

Apollinaire turned. "Just in time! Hook it up to tank one." While the two half-men struggled under their load, he turned back to the captive pilot, saying conversationally, "No need for fear. I'm making improvements all the time. The process is much less painful now. Also, I'll be sure to leave your speaking organs intact so that you can answer my questions once you've been altered."

A hose snaked out of the bottom of each tank, and Gantz used his more nimble, fully human hands to attach it to a nozzle on the canister. Masters disengaged the latch on the side of the larger contraption, and the front opened like a split bun. Inside, a vaguely human shape was outlined in shining steel like a giant cookie cutter, bonds visible at the neck and ankles. Metal sleeves like elongated evening gloves covered the area from hands to elbows.

Her voice stuck in her throat, and she couldn't catch her breath. He meant to transform her into some hideous hybrid creature—to steal her choice and freedom and to remove whatever made her whole. Masters and Gantz drew her gaze like a dreadful magnet, their human actions made all the more terrifying by their beastly appearance.

Like ripping off a hangnail, she dragged her eyes from them, panic threatening to stop her mind. She needed to distract herself, to find a way out of her distress if she hoped to escape. Her brain latched onto the activity in the room. The doctor had pulled out several more glowing, book-like objects—identical to the one he'd been reading when she arrived. He studied their surfaces, reached down, removed a glowing rectangle the size of a cigarette lighter, and held it up to the light.

He noticed her watching and brought it closer, hand extended. "See? This is just one of the many Martian innovations we could use to our advantage. It took me two solid years of investigation to understand its workings—it is that clever. These tablets use an organic method to encode a staggering amount of information in a minuscule space. Nothing short of the most ingenious method of data storage ever imagined. Though I've had a recent breakthrough. I believe we have unknown wonders on the horizon, but I won't know for some time yet, possibly several years."

When she didn't speak, Apollinaire shrugged and returned the rectangle to one of the flat tomes on his desk. He pulled out another, examining it under the light as well. "Ah! Here it is. The American bald eagle, fitting wouldn't you say?"

Dread reached into her bones, stiffening her thoughts. Amelia crouched in preparation to bolt, to defend herself, to do *something*. But she saw through her own deception. She looked more like a scared rabbit, crumpled into a ball, trying to hide, just as she had when she'd been attacked in the forest.

On the doctor's instruction, Gantz unlocked the side of her cage, and they dragged her out. She kept her legs under her, the muscles so tight they threatened to knot.

Just before they reached the tank, she burst up with a thrust of speed from her long, powerful legs. She ripped her arms down and away from their grasp at the same time.

Amelia thought she was free. For one glorious moment her heart burst, and she leapt away, only to have Masters' unnaturally long arms grab her around the neck and bring her crashing to the ground. On the way down, she hit her temple against the edge of the tank. She lay on the concrete floor, confused by the overwhelming scent of blood and mildew. Once more, she was lifted like a sack of potatoes, into the cylinder, into the tank. The two former agents locked a belt around her waist and started securing the rest of her in place.

"There's no need to resist. Think of this as your next great adventure," Apollinaire said. "Leave her left arm free. I'll need to inject her," he added to Masters.

Cold steel clicked into place around her neck, right forearm, and ankles. The doctor approached with a large hypodermic needle. She couldn't watch and clamped her eyes shut. A light burning sensation began at the inside crook of her elbow, spreading up her arm and across her neck and chest.

Tears flooded under her lids, and she shrieked in frustration, the sound echoing strangely in the spare room. Did she sound avian? Was she already turning into an eagle? When she opened her eyes, they were wild with panic. Her bones creaked, and pain arced through her limbs as she yanked at her bonds, determined to be free of die trying. The bonds cut into her wrist and neck. She strained so hard that when an actual explosion ripped through the room, Amelia believed she had burst her bindings and torn free.

But in front of her, the three men dove for the floor as fire, smoke, and debris shot across the room. She tried moving but cried out again when she remained captive.

Another figure catapulted through the smoke, and she screamed at them, "Help! Get me out of here!" Ears still ringing, her voice sounded muffled. She didn't know if she'd been heard. Amelia tried using her free arm to reach around and release herself, but the limb lagged, half asleep from whatever now coursed through her. She couldn't bend down to look with the strap of metal across her neck holding her head in place.

When Sadler strolled out of the smoke, the sight of her put the taste of courage in Amelia's mouth. She rolled it across her tongue like a ball of hard candy, its sweetness spreading. With renewed vigor, Amelia ripped at the clasp of the fetter across her throat.

Sadler cast about in the smoke, looking for something. She dove at the nearest figure rising from the floor, wrapped an arm like steel around its throat, and dragged it fully to its feet.

She put a pistol to its head. "Apollinaire!" she shouted. "Get over here, or I shoot your thug."

The beast that had been Masters didn't struggle in Sadler's grasp but stood still.

With a cry of triumph, Amelia finally pulled open the clasp on the band of steel across her neck. She twisted toward her other arm, and now that she could see, made quick work of the second clasp. She tried to keep an eye on what was happening in the room, but thick smoke and dust lingered in the air. The last time she'd seen him, Apollinaire had disappeared behind his desk. Instead of clearing, the haze appeared to grow.

"Behind the desk!" she yelled, working on the thick leather belt. Sadler whirled with her captive to face the other direction. In a few seconds, Amelia freed herself at the waist and bent to attend to the manacles at her ankles, the numbness in her arm had dissipated.

A sound like an electric saw shredded the air. Amelia glanced up, one ankle still chained, in time to see a bright blue light blaze from behind the desk, burning a path straight at Sadler.

"Watch out!" Amelia shouted at Sadler.

She released her hold on Masters and spun away, diving for the floor. Masters wasn't so lucky. The light hit him square in the chest, burst out his back, and slammed into the far wall where it punched a hole through to the outside.

From behind one of the metal examining tables, the agent took aim and pointed into the quickly growing smoke. A burning trail sparked where the blast had left a straight line. Amelia smelled the sharp, hot scent of melting wires and woodsmoke.

Small fires burst to life, filling the room with a strange light.

Sadler aimed two shots in Apollinaire's direction, but before she could get closer or fire another volley, a dark shape hurtled across the room. Amelia watched in horror as Gantz crashed into the desk and lifted the entire piece, tossing it as though it had been a pillow. He wrapped his arms around Apollinaire who fumbled with the weapon at his feet. Either it was jammed or needed charging.

Amelia used the distraction to bend, and now familiar with the clasps, released herself in seconds. She leapt down from the cylinder platform, landing unsteadily.

But Sadler was there, appearing out of the flames and the dark to grab her arm.

"Where have you been?" Amelia said, her voice shaking with nerves.

"Following you. Not all of us got a cushy ride through the jungle. Next time I deserve the scenic tour, and you hoof it through a bug-infested playground filled with dinosaurs and headhunters."

"I'd take them over Martian technology any day," Amelia said.

The agent grinned. "Do you believe me now?"

She nodded but pointed at the others in the room. "You can't shoot them. We need them." She spied the form of Masters, still writhing on the floor despite his grave wound. She dropped to her knees next to him.

"What are you doing?" Sadler said. "Leave that thing be."

Amelia ignored her. "Is there anything I can do? Is there a first aid kit?" she asked Masters. He shook his head.

Across the room, Gantz screamed like the wildcat Apollinaire had turned him into, slamming the doctor's body into the concrete wall as though it were the limp body of a mouse.

"Stop, him…" Masters said, struggling to breathe.

Amelia tried to find something to press on the wound in his chest, but the injury was so massive, there was little she could do. She hadn't been a field nurse, only worked in the hospital, and had never seen a wound like this.

Sadler pointed her pistol at the two men, getting close enough to aim directly at Gantz. "Stop! I want him alive!"

Gantz paused, his hand around Apollinaire's throat, the weapon of such destruction now abandoned on the floor. His chest rippled with his breaths, and his thick whiskers quivered. Gantz's eyes narrowed to slits.

"Don't shoot him!" Amelia yelled to Sadler. "That's Gantz! This is Masters!"

Sadler didn't turn but visibly stiffened. She spoke again, her voice hard and terrible. "I don't know what he did to you, but if you are Gantz, and you're still in there, then listen to me now. I *need* him. I'm supposed to take him back to the OTA. We have to figure out what he's done so that more people don't get hurt."

Gantz's eyes flickered, and then he noticed Amelia on the floor next to Masters. The man Amelia guessed had meant much more to him than just a fellow agent. His face softened for a moment, looking almost human under its striped fur. He flung Apollinaire into a crumpled heap at his feet and turned to face Sadler. Gantz shook his head. With his still human hand, he pointed at the tank where Amelia had been held captive.

"What?" Sadler asked.

He pointed again.

Masters spoke up, his voice a whisper from the floor next to Amelia. "He wants to turn him."

"He wants to turn Apollinaire into a beast," she called out with dawning horror. She might have been seconds away from the same fate but found herself unable to wish it on anyone else.

Sadler looked at Masters and then back at Gantz. She had a clear shot at the tiger-man, and the muscles of her forearm rippled under their layer of sweat and grime, tensing her fingers on the trigger. The air still crackled with fire. If she waited too long, they might lose Apollinaire and his research.

Gantz didn't wait for her to decide. Instead, he bent and picked up the unconscious doctor, tossing him over one shoulder and heading for the tank.

"Gantz! Our bosses are going to be quite put out if I don't bring him back. I don't want to have to shoot you!"

The former agent turned his head and bared his teeth, snarling.

Sadler holstered her gun and walked with Gantz. "Okay fine. This is how we'll do it. I help you get him in there, and you give me all his research. Every last bit. Deal?" When he didn't answer, she stepped in front of him. "Hey, do we have a deal?"

"I don't think he can talk," Amelia said, her hands still on Masters' shoulders.

"Just nod then," Sadler said.

When Gantz did so, she stepped aside and climbed onto the ladder next to the platform. From there, she helped Gantz buckle Apollinaire into place. Amelia and Masters watched silently, as Gantz injected the dazed Apollinaire with a vial identical to the one the doctor had administered to Amelia. Once they shut the tank door, Gantz moved the dials on the controls at the bottom of the tank and pushed several buttons.

A coil of smoke erupted from the top of the tank and a muffled scream pierced the air.

Doctor Apollinaire was awake.

Whether he understood what was happening, Amelia couldn't be sure. As his voice rose higher, it changed in tone, becoming a piercing shriek. She wanted to cover her ears. She wanted to leave this horrible place. She wanted to forget that any of this ever happened.

After what felt like an hour, but must have been no more than a few minutes, Apollinaire's screams died away.

Gantz pulled open the tank. Inside, the man's once sparse white hair now clustered thickly, covering his head completely. A wicked-looking beak slumped toward his chest, and dark brown feathers sprouted from his collar and cuffs, turning into longer plumes where his fingers had been. Gantz released Apollinaire, and he slumped to the ground, shivering slightly.

"He will sleep now," Masters said weakly from the floor. "Gantz, give them everything."

The tiger man approached the doctor's desk and righted it. He dug through the drawers and handed several identical looking volumes to Sadler and Amelia. The women packed them away in Sadler's bag.

"What are these?" she asked.

"I'm not sure, but I saw him using them. They're some kind of advanced information storage system," Amelia said.

Sadler nodded, accepting yet another from Gantz. "How many more are there?" Her bag had filled quickly.

Gantz pointed at a low shelf containing several boxes. Beside it lay Amelia's pack. Together, they grabbed the few remaining book-like objects and squeezed them into the bags.

"We could take the same vehicle they used to bring me. Gantz, can you drive it?" Amelia said.

The former agent slammed his eyes closed and whipped his head back and forth. His green eyes snapped open wide and glowed in the flickering firelight. Gantz pointed at the floor where Masters still lay and went to crouch beside him. "We can take him too. There's room on our plane. Maybe there's something in this research that can help you?" Sadler offered with a heavy voice.

Gantz shook his head again and wrapped his arms around Masters.

The injured man whispered something into the other's ear, and he stood again, motioning for them to follow. Coughing, the three of them stumbled through the slowly thickening smoke to a door in the far wall. He unlocked it and handed them the keys. Expecting to find themselves outside or in a garage of some kind, Amelia was dumbfounded to see a cozy, bright room.

They stepped inside a space with soft furniture, sturdy books, toys, and a little bed. Just the right size for a small child. A babble broke through Amelia's amazement. There, in the corner of the room, sat a young toddler in a pen surrounded by several balls and books.

"Who's this?" Sadler asked. She turned toward Amelia. "Did Apollinaire mention a kid?"

"I think . . ." She turned to look for Gantz, but he'd left. She squinted into the growing smoke and flames. Masters had disappeared too. A shiver ran down her spine. Apollinaire hadn't mentioned a child, but he had mentioned a storage system. He couldn't have meant this, could he? Such a thing simply wasn't possible. But then, before today, she'd never seen a human transformed into a beast. She needed time to think.

"A child he stole from someone who lives on the island for an experiment," she said, entering the room.

Sadler grabbed her arm as she passed "We don't have time to go around the island to find the parents."

"Well, we can't leave a toddler here. I'll figure something out," Amelia said, striding across the small room to the pen. When she got close, the child reached its chubby arms up, the sleeves of its loose shirt falling back to reveal delightful rolls of soft skin.

The tall woman bent low, scooped up the child, and returned to where Sadler stood holding both their packs.

The agent held out two wet handkerchiefs. "Tie one over your mouth, then hold the other over the child's mouth until we're out of the smoke." Amelia took the cloths, and Sadler held the toddler while Amelia fixed the cool square of fabric in place.

"The fire's getting thick. We're going to have to run. Are you ready?" Sadler asked, handing the child back.

Amelia tightened her grip on the toddler in her arms, who rested its dark curls against her chest. "Let's get out of here."

Together, they sprinted through the burning building, Amelia trusting Sadler to lead them clear of the flames. The smoke burned yellow and green, the toxic fumes making their eyes water. Amelia sputtered and coughed despite the wet cloth. Luckily, it wasn't long before they burst outside, the air so thick with smoke even outside she could barely see. Night had fallen, and the light looked no different here. If anything, it was darker outside than in.

Sadler tapped her arm and pointed through the haze to where a small truck waited. Once there, Amelia settled the child on Sadler's lap where it began playing with the agent's bangle.

She stripped it off her wrist and handed it over. "Should we have tried to bring Apollinaire back with us?"

Amelia shook her head. "I don't think they would've let us."

They turned to look behind at the compound. Engulfed in flames, it cast flickering shadows onto the surrounding jungle. Amelia thought she saw several forms crawling, leaping, or flying into the trees. But her mind was filled with beasts and she might have been mistaken.

Amelia sat facing the same wide bank of windows she'd gazed at less than a week ago, but she didn't really see them this time either. When her eyes focused on the finer details of distant hills, seeing each leaf on each tree, things that should have been invisible, Amelia's mind floated away. It wandered in a mysterious jungle, coursed past smoke and flame, and rose over a dark ocean. In quiet moments, in dreams, her heart whispered that she was there still. She felt afraid it was right. That it would always be so.

The door opened, and Sister Agnes entered on the heels of the mother superior, breaking the dark chain of Amelia's thoughts. The older women smiled at her as they sat, Agnes beside her and the mother superior behind the desk.

"Thank you for agreeing to meet with us again," the mother superior drew a sheaf of papers from the top drawer.

"On the contrary, it's I who would like to thank you," Amelia said.

"We wanted to reassure you that 'your daughter,'" the mother superior glanced down at the records, "Mary Grace Ceres, has been placed in a loving home with an upstanding couple who are fine Christians. Her needs will be more than met."

Agnes reached over and squeezed Amelia's hand.

The mother superior smiled. "If you'll just sign here, you can be on your way."

Amelia leaned in and carefully wrote her name on the line. She still didn't know if she'd made a terrible mistake lying to the OTA and hiding her suspicions about the child. But, as Apollinaire had implied, they wouldn't know the complete effects of his experiments on the child for some time, possibly several years. Amelia wasn't willing to risk the child's chances at a normal life on the guesses of a mad man. Also, they didn't know if Apollinaire had survived the fire, and the last thing Amelia wanted was for him to be able to get his hands on Mary. No, this was for the best. She would know how to reach the child. That would have to be good enough.

After a few more minutes of final details, the weight of which felt both unbearably heavy and foreign at the same time, like a memory of another life, she stood to leave.

"Oh," the mother superior said, stopping her. "I almost forgot." She withdrew an envelope from her desk and shook out its contents. "It's our policy that no personal property transfers with the child. Here is your bracelet."

Amelia didn't hesitate, only holding out her hand and slipping on the dark brown bangle inlaid with silver emblems. "Thank you," she said.

As before, Sister Agnes walked her to the gates of the abbey and orphanage. The sound of children's voices laughing and shouting outside in the yard drifted in through the open windows. They didn't speak until Amelia stopped at the gate.

"And the records of Mary's adoption?" she asked Agnes, staring into the nun's face framed in white and dappled with sunshine.

"We find homes for so many of the Lord's children. Things are often lost," Sister Agnes said. "I will see that hers meet that fate." She closed the gates and walked away.

From the writings of Abraham Van Helsing, founder and Lord Protector of the Sway:

Periodically the human race produces minds of such intelligence that to regard them as mere geniuses would be insulting. Leonardo da Vinci, Victor Frankenstein, Dr. Moreau, and Nikola Tesla spring to mind.

There is one intellect that makes the others pale in comparison yet the man wasted his genius on solving mysteries, although to his credit he did use it on numerous occasions to defeat monsters.

At least the detective had the common sense to train one other to think as he did.

The Devil's Work
A Baker Street Abyss tale

John L. French

"**A**re you sure this is proper?" asked the short, ferret-featured man who stood in the doorway behind Sherlock Holmes. "After all, a scene such as this is no place for a member of the fair sex, despite Miss Jane being Doctor Watson's daughter and your goddaughter."

"I shall remind you again, Lestrade," Holmes said, trying but not quite succeeding in keeping his exasperation at Lestrade's prejudices out of his voice, "that my associate is also *Doctor Watson*, a physician and surgeon as qualified as her father, possibly more so as she has had the opportunity to study under him, Doctor Elizabeth Anderson, Doctor Elizabeth Blackwell, and, of course, myself. Jane Watson has been attending autopsies since her twelfth birthday. In fact, it was my present to her. Now then, be silent and let her work."

Concentrating on her work, Jane Marston Watson was unaware of being the subject of conversation between her "uncles" Gregory and Sherlock. Instead, she stood in the center of the room trying to avoid stepping in yet another puddle of blood. Moving carefully so as not to cause any additional spatter, she pulled her now ruined shoe free and looked for a safe place to step. There were not that many. Where there was no blood there were mangled bodies and the limbs torn from them.

Not many people could stand calmly in the middle of what the broadsheets would later call "the room of death." She was one of the few. Later, when the case was closed and she was alone in her Praed Street rooms, then would come the nightmares. But for now, she was a professional with a job to do.

Another careful step, this time avoiding fluids and body parts at the cost of almost losing her balance.

"Careful there," came her companion's unnecessary advice from the doorway. And then, "Are you all right?"

Am I all right? the woman thought. *I am surrounded by bodies that have been torn apart, my new shoes are past saving, my shoulder is throbbing, and my legs are aching from trying not to fall on my posterior.*

Her reply, however, was, "I'm fine, Mr. Holmes. As fine as anyone could be in such a situation."

"Good show, Watson. I knew you were of the right stuff. Your father would be proud. Now then, what can you tell me?"

"That you don't already know?" Having known Sherlock Holmes all her life and having been professionally associated with him for a little more than two years, Jane Watson knew that the detective had seen as much – and possibly more – from his post in the doorway as she had from her closer examination of the room. Still, had Holmes not had need of her medical expertise, it would have been she watching from the doorway as Holmes ruined his shoes.

"She can tell you, Mr. Holmes, that they're dead and most likely to stay that way. And what *I'm* telling you is that neither you nor she is needed. We've made an arrest and the killer is safely behind bars."

Turning away from Jane, Holmes faced the Scotland Yard inspector.

"Lestrade," Holmes said with much-practiced patience, "while it is true that you have made an arrest, there are those who doubt that the killer is behind bars."

"And who might they be, besides yourself and Miss Ja... Doctor Watson over there?"

"Not having all the facts, I have not yet formed an opinion, but it may be that Watson could enlighten both of us. To answer your question, my client certainly has his doubts."

"And who might this client of yours be?"

In answer, Holmes handed the detective an envelope. Removing the single sheet of paper, Lestrade read the instructions to fully cooperate with its bearer. It was signed "D, MI-7."

"Mr. Holmes, I have heard of MI-5 and MI-6, but never MI-7."

"Pray that you don't, Lestrade. It is part of their duties not to be heard of. But if you doubt the *bona fides*, pray look at the endorsements at the bottom."

At the bottom of the single sheet were the initials "M," "C," and finally a regal "George V." Lestrade might have discounted the first two but could not ignore the third.

"You mean?"

"Not another word, Lestrade. It would not be . . . prudent nor proper."

From his post in the room, Jane heard the now sufficiently humbled Scotland Yard man say, "Then by all means, Mr. Holmes, Dr. Watson, please proceed."

"Yes, Watson, please proceed. What are your findings?'

"Thank you, Mr. Holmes. There are four torsos, one female, the rest male. All exhibit signs of a broken neck and all have had at least one limb violently removed. The number of detached limbs agrees with those missing from the victims. There are no extras. That suggests that the killer did not carry away with it any bodies or pieces thereof. But that will have to be verified by the coroner at the morgue."

"You said 'killer' did you not, Doctor, suggesting only one."

"That is correct, Inspector."

"And for one killer to do all this alone, he, or as you said, it would no doubt have to be very strong, quick, and probably agile to kill in such a manner that no one escaped."

"Please listen, Lestrade. Watson did not say that no one escaped."

"But she did refer to the killer as 'it.' That suggests that the one I arrested is the killer."

"You did not let me finish, Inspector. From the damage done to the bodies – the marks on their necks, the apparent angles at which the limbs were torn – your killer is at least six feet tall. As for my use of the word 'it' . . ."

Jane held up a limb. From the shape and size, it had once been attached to the lone dead woman. "Under her nails is something that might be skin, but if it is, it is skin from no race or species that I have encountered. And on her palm there is something that, but for its color and consistency, might be blood."

"Are you sure, Doctor?"

"I'm not certain. The 'skin' appears to be a flexible kind of Parkesine and the fluid is perhaps artificial protoplasm. Laboratory testing will prove or disprove my supposition."

"You mean to say, Doctor, that that Swiss fellow has brought his monster to England."

"That "Swiss fellow,' as you refer to him, Lestrade, was reported dead over one hundred years ago," Holmes said. "And again thirty-nine years ago, then twenty-two. And his first creation is very much alive and unlikely to be our culprit. Or to voluntarily have anything to do with his so-called creator. In any case, he is the one who uses burked body parts, not his creation. What Watson is suggesting is that your killer is an automaton of some sorts."

The detective surveyed the carnage. "What do you think, Watson? One of Victor Frankenstein's disciples."

"Possibly, Mr. Holmes. What about Brainerd and his steam man? Or Coppelius's automaton?"

"The former are in the American West. And despite the intentions of Coppelius, his Olympia is on the side of the angels, working sometimes with the Directorate of Altérité Security in Paris."

"Too much blood was left behind for it to be the Transylvanian king or one of his ilk. That leaves us with Charles Rossum or his father Edward. Or Frankenstein himself."

"The Rossums are more likely, Watson. Victor Frankenstein has not been seen since his last reputed death." Here Holmes smiled. "But just because someone has been reported dead does not mean that he is, as my own history proves."

"Who, Mr. Holmes, are these Rossums?"

"Disgraces to the scientific community, Lestrade," Holmes answered. "The father used what he called 'artificial protoplasm' to form monsters and mutates. The son worked on developing fully artificial humans. It may be that the two are now working together to create obscene amalgams of flesh and machine. I think we'll find that the 'protoplasm' from our killer is part organic and part machine oil."

"That has yet to be confirmed, Mr. Holmes," said Watson, "but no doubt you're correct. Inspector, if I may, I'd like to accompany these bodies to the morgue where I hope to collect more samples. After that, to St. Bart's to have the necessary tests performed."

"Of course, Doctor. And you, Mr. Holmes?"

"I will accompany you, Lestrade, to free my client from his cell."

It was not the first time that the prisoner in the last cell but one had been behind bars. *At least,* he reflected, *British gaols are cleaner than the French ones.* Owing to his nature the prisoner had been given a cell of his own, but a transfer to the cages of Regent's Park seemed likely.

Damn that Dupin, he thought, *and damn the day he told that American writer what had occurred in the Rue Morgue. Ever since then creatures such as I are the first blamed whenever similar crimes occur. I suppose I should be grateful that London constables do not go armed; otherwise, I might have been shot down in the street.*

With nothing to do, the prisoner sat back, awaiting either deliverance or transfer, and observed his fellow inmates.

Watching and listening, he learned how best to forge a beggar's license and which duffer could be trusted to give a good price on stolen goods. The "virtues" of the local dollymops were discussed as were the services they performed and how much each charged.

On hearing two guards discussing his possible transportation to the Zoological Gardens in Regent's Park, the prisoner turned his attention to planning his escape. He was debating the merits of breaking free en route versus waiting until he had been caged among his lesser cousins when . . .

"This way, Mr. Holmes."

The prisoner looked up as Sherlock Holmes entered the cell block.

Holmes was of average height for a human, but there was something about his manner and bearing that made him seem the tallest man in the room. He was accompanied by Inspector Lestrade.

"If I may ask, Mr. Holmes, of what interest is this ape to His Majesty's government?"

"Lestrade, Monsieur Balaoo here is no mere ape. He is of the species *Pan sapiens,* and is as intelligent as you or I. Well, as you at any rate. He is the head of the French Directorate of Altérité Security."

"I have never heard of them."

"Nor should you have. And the less said about this affair the better. Investigate the murders if you feel you must, but do not hope for any success. So if you would release Monsieur Balaoo I will escort him to my client."

"I do not believe that will be necessary, Mr. Holmes."

The voice had come from the doorway. It belonged to Sir Denis Nayland Smith, the man who earlier that day had signed a paper for Holmes with the letter N.

Reaching out his hand to greet the newcomer, Holmes said, "Sir Denis, good to see you again. I take it that your new duties mean that the Chinese doctor is still at bay?"

"Thanks to your help, he is, Mr. Holmes, but he has a way of coming back. It's that damned immortality elixir of his. I think he has pools of it to bathe in. As for Balaoo here, I had no doubt you would secure his release. Now then, Inspector, if you would release Mr. Balaoo, we have vital work to do."

"Moreau active again?"

"His daughter, Mr. Holmes."

"I did not know he had one."

"Neither did we until a week ago."

Reluctantly the inspector ordered Mr. Balaoo's cell door unlocked. Turning to Holmes, the man-ape shook his hand in thanks.

"*Merci, Monsieur Holmes.*"

"*Vous êtes les bienvenus, Monsieur, et bonne chance.*"

After they left, Holmes turned to Lestrade. "You really must stop reading Poe."

"You may be right, Mr. Holmes."

"Now if you'll excuse me . . ." Breaking his sentence, the consulting detective looked into the furthest cell. In it was a young woman dressed as a maid. She was not moving, just staring blankly ahead.

"The prisoner in the far cell. Why is she here?"

"The usual, Mr. Holmes. We believe she slaughtered a family of three, a mother and two children. She's in shock over the horrors of the crime she's committed. We'll know more once she comes around."

"So, another domestic tragedy?"

"Yes, Mr. Holmes."

"Any survivors?"

"The husband, he came in at the end and managed to subdue her. Why?"

"The bloodstains on the maid's clothing are all wrong. They are smeared, not spattered. If I were you, I'd send her under guard to the London School of Medicine for Women for a thorough examination. Then I'd question the husband a bit more thoroughly. With your permission, Lestrade, I would like to return to our crime scene."

Holmes had done more than watch Jane examine the bodies. While the doctor was about her work, Holmes had been examining the room from the doorway. There had been nothing special about the scene of the murders. It was a typical ground floor room in a typical London rooming house.

Except that it was in the rear of the building. No easy access from the street. That, to Holmes's mind, marked the killings as a deliberate act, not one of random violence. The creature had targeted those four people.

Not quite, Sherlock, corrected the voice of logic that was always in his mind, *the monster may have targeted* whoever *was in the room*. And so, the first step, determine whose room it was and who the visitors might have been.

"It was Mr. Pinkney what lived there, Inspector," the landlady told Holmes when he asked. Having seen Holmes earlier she believed that he was with the Yard. He did nothing to disabuse her of this belief.

"What kind of a tenant was he, Mrs. Willoughby?"

A rude noise was her first answer to Holmes's question. Then, "The worst kind, sir. Up at all hours, disturbing the others with his singing, if you could call what he was doing singing. I didn't but he did. Three times I give him notice, but each time he promised to keep regular hours, and of course, he made it right in other ways."

Mrs. Willoughby held out her hand suggestively. Taking several shillings from his pocket, Holmes placed one in her outstretched palm. The rest he held loosely as he asked, "What kind of singing was it, Mrs. Willoughby?'

The landlady's snort was followed by, "I've heard rogering cats make better music."

"Was Mr. Pinkney one for female companionship?"

"What man who is healthy isn't, eh, Inspector?"

"And did he . . ." Holmes looked suggestively towards Pinkney's room.

"I do not run that kind of a house, Inspector," the landlady protested. "Of course, I suppose he might have sneaked one back there. Maybe that was what caused the noise." Then she made the connection. "Are you telling me that one of those that was carried out was a woman?"

"I am afraid so, madam. Now, if I may, I'd like to look around the house. I promise not to bother any of your other lodgers."

Holmes held out another shilling. Mrs. Willoughby accepted it eagerly. "What with all that's been going on today, I don't suppose you can bother them any more than they have been. Look around as much as you like."

Going down the hall, Holmes again took up his position in the doorway, searching the room with his eyes. The bodies and the parts thereof had been removed but otherwise, the scene was intact – blood drying but still wet and tacky, furniture smashed, pictures knocked from the walls, pages from books scattered about.

Books? Again his eyes searched the room. They found no bookcases or shelves, nothing that indicated that *books* had been kept there. Maybe *a* book. Holmes needed a closer look. Thinking, *At least my shoes are not as new as Jane's,* he entered the room.

There were fewer pages than Holmes had hoped. All of the same type of paper, all with the same typeface, and all with words written in a singular corrupt Latin. He had seen its kind only once before, the Golden Dawn case. That case had not gone at all well.

Carefully, Holmes searched the room, moving upended furniture to see what was beneath, doing Jane one better and ruining his suit as well as his shoes. He did not locate the rest of the book, nor did he find any of the instruments that would have been used in the types of ceremonies for which the Golden Dawn had been notorious. Then he studied the pictures that had fallen from the wall.

There were three of them, all of places not found anywhere on Earth. Barren landscapes where black suns cast dark shadows over barely visible creatures, creatures that could not have possibly existed anywhere other than in nightmares.

Reaching into his pocket, he took out the torn pages he had placed there. A title headed one fragment. The detective translated, "The Opening of the Way."

Dark shadows indeed, and deep waters. Creatures quick, strong, and deadly. Matters deemed occult. How do they mix, he wondered. He did not know, yet. But he did know that this was not a case for his leaded cane and John Watson's old Webley revolver. He considered calling on Sir Denis for assistance, this was the sort of thing for which MI-7 was established. Then he thought better of it. Sir Denis might see the torn scraps Holmes held not as the great danger they might be, but as a weapon of great power, one that might destroy them all, and be tempted.

It is folly to act before one has all the facts, said his voice of logic. Find the killer, then decide what to do.

Holmes agreed and, with that goal in mind, searched the room, the hall, and the path to the street, looking for that which would lead him to the killer.

Jane was waiting when Holmes got back to Baker Street.

"Well, Jane?" the detective asked by way of greeting. In private they were family, it was only in front of others that the two used more formal address.

"It was as we suspected, Uncle Sherlock. Whatever killed those people was not human, nor was it natural. The 'skin' and 'blood' were both artificial, and both consistent with what is known of the Rossums' work. Did you find anything when you returned to the boarding house?"

"How did you know I had returned to the boarding house?"

"Where else would you have gone?" She pointed to the crimson stains on his clothes. "And come back looking like that."

"True," Holmes nodded, then told Jane what he had found.

"Surely you don't suspect the occult. In this modern age?"

"The occult, Jane? No, but it could be something indistinguishable from it. Advanced science that seems like magic. Our current age has brought us many wonders, but I am afraid that no machine made by man will eliminate greed, or lust, or the desire for power over one's fellow man. New inventions only mean new sins, or at least new ways to commit the old ones."

Holmes shuddered at his inadvertent use of the phrase "old ones." Jane missed this as Holmes said, "Do we still have those pistols we obtained from the Chinese Doctor down in Limehouse?"

"They are in the safe."

"Fetch them if you will. I have no desire to go against a creature capable of doing what we witnessed armed with only lead and steel. And if you will hand me the Bradshaw, I will see what time the next train to Bancroft leaves."

Holmes paused for Jane to ask the obvious question. Instead, after waiting a minute or so, she said, "You returned to the house. During your investigation, you observed soil, clay, chalk, and the like, which you noted was not indigenous to that part of London. You knew, or you researched, where such a mixture as you found might be located."

She gave Holmes a look as if to ask, "How was that?"

In reply, Holmes said, "Not bad, Jane. You are definitely more astute than was your father. Now add some research into recent shipments of Parkesine and that gives us Bancroft." Holmes consulted his timetable. "There's not much time. Pack just what you need, and do not forget the weapons, and let us be off. But first . . ."

Holmes scribbled on a telegraph form then rang for Miss Hudson's boy. "Send this off," he ordered.

The trip to Bancroft was uneventful, Jane catching up on her medical journals while Holmes enjoyed a pipe and conversation in the smoking car. On arrival, the pair went to the local inn.

"No, no strangers here in town," the landlord replied when Holmes asked, "specially none of the size you mentioned. Still, there's plenty of strangeness to be had outside the town. Less animals around and there's been them what's reported noises coming from the old Selby place."

"What sort of noises? Cries, screams, moans?"

"Nothing like that, Mr. Holmes. Those that heard it say it sounded something like music, but not the good kind, more like they play in the opera houses, only worse."

"Has anyone investigated?"

The man laughed. "Mr. Holmes, this ain't your London. We're simple folk out here, Bancroft has but one constable whose job it is to keep the peace. And until someone breaks that peace or the animals start complaining, there's no one who's going to bother investigating."

"Thank you, landlord." Holmes threw enough coin on the bar to pay for their ales and a little more. "Now if you could direct us to the Selby place . . ."

"It's east of here, toward the coast, but it gets dark early this time of year. If you care to wait until morning, I have two good rooms at a reasonable price. Or will you be needing only the one?" The landlord's leer was unmistakable.

"Two, if you please," Holmes replied in disgust.

The pair were shown to their rooms. Holmes entered Jane's just as the doctor was taking out her kit. The detective went straight to the window and looked out.

"Good, yours has an easier climb down. No one's about. Let's go, Jane. We're sleeping rough tonight."

"I assume you have a reason for giving up warm beds in favor of a night in the woods?"

"When don't I have a reason? Didn't it strike you as odd that with game disappearing and something like music coming from an old house that no one in Bancroft was the least bit curious? Surely someone went out there to investigate and told of his findings over a few pints. And if he went out and didn't return . . ."

Holmes left that thought hanging. "Let's go now, while we can."

Throwing their bags out he clambered out the window, leaving Jane to follow as best she could.

When they were in the woods a good bit away from the inn but still within view of it, Holmes continued as if they were still under roof.

"The murderous creature, how did it get to London? There are no roads out. Most likely it traveled escorted by train. Surely someone noticed a large, almost human-looking creature and the landlord of Bancroft's inn would have heard of it, if only second hand."

"If there is something to hide, why tell us about the Selby place at all?"

"We were told just enough to keep us from leaving. Then given rooms so that word could be sent to Selby House, if indeed there is such a place. Let us wait and watch from here. It won't be the first night we have spent outside. If I am wrong, you will have a pin with which to puncture my ego when it gets too inflated. If I am right, I may have saved both our lives."

A few hours later, with Holmes on watch and Jane asleep, the doctor was awakened from her doze with a shake and a whispered, "Come, the game is afoot."

There was just enough moonlight for Jane to make out a bulky shape approaching the inn. It did not enter through the front door or the back. Instead, it went directly to the side and began climbing up to her room.

Through the quiet night came the sound of the breaking and smashing of the room's appointments. "It will go into my room next. After that, well, I fear for the landlord."

"Holmes, what of the other guests?"

"There are none. I checked before embarking on this course of action."

"And the landlord?"

"If we save him, we might lose all," the detective said coldly. "It was he who set the trap in motion. He must face the consequences."

More smashing, more breaking, then the sound of a loud cry that could have come from no human throat. By the light of the moon, Jane observed the landlord run from his pub and into the night.

"He got away," she said, needlessly.

"Yes, he did." Was there a trace of disappointment in Holmes's voice? Jane couldn't say.

"Now our real work begins. Leave the bags; they will only slow us down. But bring the weapons. I am certain that we will have need of them before the morning comes."

Its work done, the creature lumbered away from the inn, moving slowly enough that Holmes and Jane could keep pace. When the doctor pointed out how easy the creature was to follow, Holmes remarked, "Which may be the point. It is entirely possible that we are walking into a trap. Keep your pistol at the ready and do not hesitate to shoot whatever comes at us – man, beast, or creature."

The two encountered no one and nothing else. Finally, the creature led them to a hunting lodge which had seen better times.

"The Selby place," Watson whispered.

"Or something like it," Holmes replied. "Can you hit the creature from here?'

"I can but try."

"An attempt is all I need. Take mine as well." Holmes handed Jane his pistol. "Destroy that one, then open fire on whatever comes out of the lodge. Then . . ."

"Uncle Sherlock, I may not have been in Afghanistan but you and my father trained me well. I know how to create a diversion." Jane handed the detective's pistol back to him. "And you may need this once you get inside. You're clever but not indestructible."

"And you, my dear, are always right when you need to be. Good luck and take care."

"You too."

As Holmes disappeared into the woods, Jane drew her pistol from its carry bag. It was a bulky piece, larger than her father's reliable Webley. It had an oversized cylinder that held eight missile-like cartridges. Taking careful aim, she fired and sent one toward the creature just as it reached the door of the lodge.

She had seen the effects of the ammunition before, when the Chinese Doctor used it against his own men to effect his escape. The results this time were even more remarkable.

The missile struck the creature in the lower abdomen, the resultant explosion blowing off its legs. The concussion from the blast shattered several of the front windows.

That should draw their attention, Jane thought as she readied her pistol and waited.

As Holmes had surmised, the rear of the lodge was guarded by another of the creations. As he had hoped, the explosion in the front drew it away from the back door. The detective slipped in unseen.

Another explosion. *That's two*, Holmes thought. Then another. *Three. Leave now, dear Jane, your job is done.* He continued through the kitchen and pantry and into the main part of the building.

However many rooms the lodge had had, they had been combined into one large area in the center of which was what seemed to be a stone altar, in front of which a figure in a voluminous hooded black and purple robe was reading from a battered tome and chanting in an unknown language. Behind the robed figure were two rows of creatures, five in a row, each closely resembling the others.

Now that he had time to more closely examine them, Holmes saw that his initial supposition had been correct. They were as much machine as man, with bestial limbs and features augmented by mechanical parts.

As the chant continued, a glowing sphere appeared in front of the altar. This quickly grew to the size of a man. A portal opened revealing a land of bleak colors and twisted shapes, none of which existed in the world Holmes knew.

Too late, was Holmes's first thought. His next was, *Never too late, not while I draw breath.* He knew what must be done, knew the cost of doing so. His only regret was not being able to leave Jane a farewell note.

One shot, then he would fire the rest of his ammunition into the portal in hopes of closing it.

If it is necessary.

Raising his pistol, Holmes took aim at the figure at the altar. "I would very much hate to kill you, Doctor Rossum," he said, "at least not before you close that hellish gate."

Holmes prided himself on seldom being surprised. But even he would admit to being taken aback when a feminine voice answered him.

"I would very much hate it as well, Mr. Holmes," replied the woman as she lowered her hood. "For if you kill me the portal may never close and the hell that would emerge would be on your head. If I may explain?"

"Do so quickly," the detective replied, mindful that half the creatures had turned his way.

"Your guess is partly correct, Mr. Holmes. I am Helena Rossum. Charles Rossum was my husband. Not long ago, he and his father were dragged into the world you see before us. They opened the way seeking a means of making their creations more powerful, longer lived, something more than mindless robots. Something other than the pale imitations of humanity they are."

Holmes's eyes shifted from the woman to the creatures then to the gate. Through it, he noted movement in the background, saw twisted beasts with too many limbs. "And you seek to continue his work?"

"Hardly. I seek vengeance on that which cost me my husband. I plan on sending these creatures though to wreak what damage they can before being destroyed. Once they are inside, only then will I close the portal."

The detective studied the rows of creatures, lined up and ready to march to their destruction. Were they indeed soulless beings designed to do the bidding of he, or she, who controlled them? Or was there already a spark of awareness in each of them, a spark that could be fanned into a flame of understanding and a kind of humanity? This Holmes did not know. He did know what they had been used to do. And this decided him.

He put up his pistol but did not put it away. "You may proceed, Mrs. Rossum."

Her reply of "How kind of you, Mr. Holmes" was heavily sarcastic. She then gave the order that sent the creations into a world unknown. Once they were inside, she read the words and intoned the chant that closed the portal.

"Satisfied, Mr. Holmes?"

"Not quite, Mrs. Rossum. There are four deaths in London for which you are responsible and for which you must pay the price."

"I told the creature to retrieve the book. It contained the instructions on how to open the portal." She paused, then in a more somber voice said, "I did not tell it to kill."

"You set it to its task and so must pay nevertheless. The law will determine the cost."

"I think not, Mr. Holmes." Rossum gave a whistle, and ten more of her creations came into the main room. These were followed by another ten.

"I was not foolish enough to send all the creatures away. I trust that you . . ." There was another explosion from outside. "And your companion will leave me to my work."

"I cannot."

She shook her head then gave the signal that caused her twenty minions to advance toward Holmes.

The book first, then Rossum, he thought, though he doubted the woman's death would suffice to prevent his own. Then three of the advancing creatures moved so as to protect their mistress.

At least the book. Holmes readied himself to fire all his missiles at the altar in the hope of destroying the dangerous tome. But as he took aim, there came the whine of a projectile in flight and two of the monsters in the rear exploded.

"Jane!" he cried, ready to warn the doctor to flee the unnatural army. But the one who had fired was considerably hairier than his adopted niece.

Monsieur Balaoo came further into the room, carrying a rifle made for his longer arms. He was followed by Lestrade, Sir Denis, and finally, Jane.

Holmes expected that some of the creatures would turn toward the invaders but, following their mistress's order, they continued to advance toward him.

Lestrade and Balaoo raised their weapons and prepared to destroy more of the creatures. Jane took aim at Rossum. Even as her creations closed in on him, Holmes noticed that Sir Denis, though armed, was reluctant to fire. He knew the reason why.

The creatures were closer. Holmes could feel the heat coming from their bodies. He prepared to fire into their midst, to destroy as many as he could before they did for him, trusting Jane and Lestrade to do the right thing, hoping that Sir Denis would allow them to do it.

He had almost pulled the trigger when Rossum shouted, "Halt!" The creatures stopped.

"My husband's life work will not be destroyed. It's not what he would have wanted. It's not what I want."

Holmes approached her, the others standing back, weapons ready should she change her mind.

"I only wanted the book. Those in the flat resisted. They were not meant to die."

"Nevertheless, Mrs. Rossum, you are responsible for their deaths." Knowing it was a useless gesture, he signaled to Lestrade. "Inspector."

But even as the man from Scotland Yard moved to take her into custody, Sir Denis spoke. "Hold up, Inspector. Mrs. Rossum, could you continue the work of your husband and father-in-law?"

"I have their notes. Given time, a proper place to work and the . . . freedom to do so, I believe I could."

"Then on my authority granted me by His Majesty, I give you pardon on the condition that you do continue their work, under my supervision of course."

Helena Rossum's "Of course," was barely heard over Lestrade's "This woman is a murderess," and Jane's "This is not right. You have not the authority . . ."

"Quiet!" Holmes's voice silenced them. "Right or wrong, Sir Denis has the authority. In fact, he has the King's authority. And I am sure that under his supervision and strict control these creatures will make a proper . . . Praetorian Guard in defense of the Realm."

"Thank you for your understanding, Mr. Holmes. You are correct, as you usually are. An army made of such as these will protect our shores and cause dismay among our monstrous enemies, especially if those damned Martians return. And combined with the knowledge that is no doubt in that book . . ."

There was the whine of a projectile in flight, then the book and the altar on which it lay disappeared in a cloud of powdered granite.

"Sorry, Sir Denis," Holmes said without a trace of remorse, "my finger slipped." He lowered his weapon. "My understanding has its limits. Stay away from that which you do not comprehend and cannot control, or you will doom us all.

"Now then, as I am sure that you have arrangements to make with Mrs. Rossum, we will take our leave."

There were four of them on the train back to London. The trip was uneventful, save for the conductor insisting on Balaoo riding in the baggage car. However, after Holmes made several deductions about the man's personal life, not the least of which was a possible relationship with the baggage master's wife, the pan sapien was allowed to remain in first class.

It was during a game of whist that Holmes commented, "You are correct, Lestrade, it is neither fair nor just."

Having grown accustomed to Holmes divining their thoughts, neither the inspector nor Jane asked Holmes what had prompted his comment. Instead, Lestrade remarked, "Are you referring to how the monkey deals the cards, Mr. Holmes?"

Balaoo gave an aggrieved look as Holmes answered, "That too, but I meant the outcome of this case."

"I have learned, Mr. Holmes, that when the government becomes involved there is usually no fair or just outcome. Give me a common murderer or an honest thief any day."

"There is one thing I do not understand."

"Just one, Jane?"

Ignoring Holmes, she turned to Lestrade. "Uncle Gregory, how did you know to come after us?"

"Mr. Holmes here sent this telegram." Lestrade produced the form which read,

Will need your help in Bancroft. If convenient come at once. If not convenient, come anyway.

"Balaoo and that Sir Denis were still there so I brought them along. We traced you to the inn then Balaoo here tracked you the rest of the way."

"And I am grateful for your assistance. Lestrade, take care in your dealings with Sir Denis. He is an honest man doing the devil's work in a noble cause. Monsieur Balaoo as well as he serves the same duty for the French, No good can come of it. However pure one's motives, dark deeds lead to hell. Or darker dimensions. But that is for the future. For the present, let us resume play, my skill against yours, and we'll see who is the richer when we arrive in London."

Excerpt from a letter from the Protector General of the Sway:

Victor Frankenstein was brilliant enough to defeat death and is responsible for the creation of one of the most persistent and dangerous monsters of which we are aware.

Frankenstein's crime is not even close to being balanced by his creation of the elixir of life which has allowed many, including our founder, to survive for centuries.

There have been times when humanity itself spawns evil that far outstrips those of the monsters. It is worth noting that on a few of those occasions, Frankenstein's monster has defended humanity from great depravity. These acts will not stop the Sway from one day exterminating the beast, but perhaps it will earn him a quick death.

Spawn Of Lightning

A tale of Adam Frankenstein

Patrick Thomas

A monster made from the resurrected dead should have a difficult time passing himself off as a man, but Adam Frankenstein had long ago learned to copy the mannerisms of those around him. He did this so well that even his appearance didn't prevent him from mixing with humanity. Still, it should have been far more difficult for a creature such as himself to gain access to a security-conscious Nazi concentration camp. Adam Frankenstein not only got into Maly Trascianiec but was given a guided tour of the facilities. He was aided by his history. The resurrected man had lived relatively uneventfully among the German people since the end of WWI after serving Germany as a decorated fighter pilot. The unusual condition of his skin and his many scars were now passed off as war wounds. These days, Frankenstein's scars seemed far tamer than the ones the people of Germany were seeing firsthand.

Because of his triumphs as a pilot, Adam Frankenstein had been recruited to help train the new generation of German air wolves. Even from the early stages of the Nazis' rise to power, Adam had been repulsed by them. Understandable, since they had risen to power on a platform of blaming those different than themselves and few were more different than the creature who now lived as a man. His earliest memories were of being chased by those who thought him a monster because he was not like them. He had spent years barely escaping death at the hands of others and the Nazis' rounding up of the Jews and Roma brought flashbacks of his past, and he was torn between standing up to help them and finding a cave to curl up in.

Knowing he could not stop the roundups alone and being unwilling to go back to an existence of running and hiding, he took the military commission pressed upon him, but worked with the German resistance to fight back. Adam Frankenstein's latest assignment brought him to a pilot school outside Minsk, Belarus to train German pilots to fight the Russians. The airfield was less than an hour's drive from Maly Trascianiec and the officers there were only too happy to oblige a holder of the Iron Cross with a tour of their camp.

Adam had no desire to see the horrors within. There were rumors and very loud whispering about what was happening in the many camps. Medical experiments that boggled the mind: torture, rape, and even worse atrocities. Those in the camps wearing their brightly colored single or paired triangles being readied for slaughter en masse.

Adam Frankenstein was only one man—he knew he could never single-handedly free an entire camp. Even if he did get them out, what could he do with hundreds or thousands of people? He didn't have the resources to transport, house, or feed them. However, he knew those who might. Earlier in the struggle, he had saved some individual families before they arrived at the camps and gotten them away from German-controlled lands. Besides, it was too late for those brought to the camp. They had all been slaughtered earlier in the week. A new shipment of prisoners was due in a few days. Once in the camp, it would be too late for them, but before then… there was still hope.

What had made him force himself to view firsthand the latest horrors that men had wrought was the tale of a drunken scientist who swore they were piecing pieces of Jewish corpses together in an attempt to infuse them with life. It sounded like the process that had long ago birthed him in his reluctant entrance into the world, albeit twisted by the movies and books based on Victor's lies and the legends that had grown in the telling about the monster spawned from lightning.. Despite Adam Frankenstein's acceptance among men, he had never truly been one of them. Adam sought to spare this new creation the same hard fate of his terrible beginnings. If he happened to find a friend or even a brother in the process, so much the better.

The tour of the camp was designed to take him only through the sterilized areas of the camp. Nothing too bloody, nothing too horrible, nothing that would churn the stomach of a seasoned veteran. From a distance he could see ash rising from the ovens and even had he not come here forewarned of the mass murders, he would still know. Adam suppressed a shudder. The masses that once chased him would only have burned him. How much worse would it have been to have suffered these tortures first?

"So what do you think of our camp, Captain Frankenstein?" asked the lieutenant who had served as his tour guide, trying to hide his intimidation at the giant of a man who strode beside him.

"Very efficient," Adam said, keeping himself aloof as any good officer would to a lesser rank. He knew the reputation of the camp. No one had ever escaped Maly Trascianiec.

"Would you like to dine in the Officers' Mess?" asked the lieutenant.

"I'm actually far more interested in things I have heard. I am told that there is the most amazing medical work being done here. Things that will save soldiers' lives. Or perhaps…." He let the word hang in the air. "Create them."

The soldier grinned knowingly. "Oh, you mean Private Blitzkrieg, our jigsaw soldier."

"Stop speaking!" shouted a major who had been approaching, hoping to greet the holder of the Iron Cross personally. "That is classified, even to a war hero such as Captain Frankenstein." The major looked at up at the pilot, an apologetic look on his face. "I'm sure you understand that some things are too important to the Fatherland to come out too early. I will have to insist that you stay away from building 22."

Adam bowed his head to the superior officer, to hide a smile at being so easily given the location of what he was looking for. "Entirely understandable. I hope you will forgive my curiosity as such a thing would certainly assure the Fatherland's victory against its enemies."

The major laughed and slapped the reanimated captain on his back. "Yes, I understand, but be patient. All of Germany and the world will see the fruits of our labors soon enough."

"Excellent," Adam replied. But I am famished. May we your Officers' Mess."

When the meal was over, Adam was shown out of the camp. He drove a few miles away, hiding his Kübelwagen on the side of the road, and waited for night. Under cover of darkness, he made his way back to the camp. He had noticed a gap in the sentry's patrols that would not do anyone trying to get out of the camp any good but was perfect for someone foolish enough to break in. He scaled the twenty-foot fence in a matter of seconds and was over and hidden behind an outbuilding before the sentry passed him again. He easily made his way slowly and stealthily. Despite his size, he was quite agile. Still, he knew that luck was a fickle mistress, just as likely to offer her favors to his enemy as to him. One row over from his destination he felt the barrel of a rifle pressed against the back of his head and knew that Lady Luck had moved on to a new lover. *The whore*, he thought, *just like my former bride.*

"Stand and place your hands behind your head," said the soldier.

Adam stood slowly and as the soldier watched him rise to his full height, Adam said, "I am sorry."

The soldier mistook the apology as the start of an excuse as to why he was there and the beginning of a plea for mercy. It gave him a false sense of superiority, assuming the gun made him top dog, so he was quite shocked a moment later when the huge man's hand shot out to grab him around the neck and snap his spine like a twig.

The body of the dead German soldier would raise alarms. Adam stripped the soldier of his clothes and dragged the body to where a pile of rotting corpses lay outside the crematorium. He threw it in the center of the pile then realized it stood out. It wasn't wasted away and malnourished, so it looked more like a man while the other corpses seemed to be bags of skin with some bones inside. The reanimated man threw a few more corpses on top to better hide it.

After disposing of the soldier's uniform, he made his way back without being noticed until he stood outside of building 22. A pair of armed soldiers stood sentry duty. Adam had learned much about human nature in his more than two hundred years. He especially knew soldiers. As a captain, he outranked both of sentries and so marched up to them as if he belonged. They both moved to stop him but did so differentially.

"I'm sorry, sir, it's by invitation only in there and everyone on the list is already inside."

"I understand." Adam pulled a sheet of paper out of his pocket. "I have a message from Himmler for Colonel Gustave." Invoking the head of the SS, was a risk, as was assuming the colonel was inside this building, but something this big would demand the involvement of the camp's commandant. "If you could deliver it to him, I'm sure it would be appreciated."

After he handed the paper to the soldier who had spoken, the man nodded and turned to go inside. In that instant, Adam hands wrapped around both men's skulls and squeezed. During the First World War, he had heard soldiers brag how they had crushed skulls and they had made a sound like a melon popping. Adam knew them instantly to be liars because a shattered skull makes a unique sound that's as close to a melon popping as a bullet is to heavy artillery fire. At this point he assumed he would be discovered as soon as he walked through the door, so he didn't worry about body disposal.

Adam stepped inside and what greeted him stopped him in his tracks. Despite the many embellishments on the story of his creation over the years, the truth of the matter was he was brought to life in an apartment in Ingolstadt near the university, with a wire that was attached to a lightning rod on the roof of the building. Others had spread the rumor that he was birthed in a castle.

The Nazis had their creature laid out on a concrete slab and dressed in a private's uniform, but the shirt was unbuttoned. Adam could see where the various parts had been sewn together. The stitching was much more delicate and neater than his own. The Nazi scientists weren't bothering with anything as risky as a thunderbolt. They had a very large generator, easily the largest he had ever seen with a turbine of some sort, its wires hooked up to their creature.

The assembled officers and scientists were so intense in their quest to create life in the ultimate soldier that none of them even noticed the original creature enter and stand in the shadows. Adam was faced with a dilemma—either stop the Nazis or allow another creature such as himself to be brought to life, to know the same pain and loneliness of forever being an outsider. In the end, the decision was taken from him as the generators sent their man-made lightning to course through the patchwork corpse they had assembled.

The Nazis' creature was strapped down to the table with thick pieces of leather that would have easily held any typical man, no matter how strong. The scientists just did not realize how strong a thing made of corpses and born of lightning would be. They may as well have tied their jigsaw soldier's wrists, ankles, and chest with twine for all of the good their leather shackles did.

At first nothing happened, Then the creature awoke. Over cries of "It's alive!" he broke one arm free, then the other. Both legs burst their bonds simultaneously. One scientist mistakenly moved forward with a full syringe in hopes of quieting their super soldier, but it was too little and too slow. Drugs did not work the same on those with the elixir of life coursing through their veins. Even if the scientist had managed to jab the needle in, it would have done him no good. He was flung across the room to smash against the wall. A second scientist, faster than the first, but still far slower than their monster, picked up the syringe and jabbed it in the back of the creature's neck. It was a mistake. That scientist had not yet been seen by the creature and could have probably escaped. Instead, the pain caused by the jab of the tiny piece of metal enraged the spawn of lightning. That scientist's neck was snapped with a backhanded slap.

The soldiers in the room lifted their rifles and pointed them at the creature, but the colonel shouted, "Nein! Private Blitzkrieg is not to be harmed."

There was a mistake. Enough bullets might have destroyed him and saved them.

A half a dozen soldiers waded in trying to use their rifle butts to beat the creature into submission. It was clear the newly born creature felt the blows, but the battering seemed to anger more than hurt him, merely throwing him off balance.

Adam remembered the pain of his birth. The searing and burning of the untold volts of electricity that coursed through him stayed with him long after the lightning had stopped, torturing the very flesh it was animating. Because his brain had once belonged to another, Adam had inherited some basic motor control and language capacity but was without memory. He imagined it must be the same for this new creature. He was not striking out in hate or violence. He was in searing agony, his main desire to be left alone.

The half dozen soldiers were tossed about the room like so many rag dolls. Adam was impressed. This new creature appeared to be even stronger than he was at his creation. Of course, the corpses that made up his jigsaw of parts were fresher than the body Victor Frankenstein had used , so the serum may have worked quicker on fresher tissue after the man-made thunderbolt strike. The muscles grew before his eyes, increasing in both mass and size.

The original revived man still stood in the shadows, careful not to even breathe, not wanting to alert anyone in the room to his presence. Luckily, the soldiers and scientists were far more concerned with their own creation. Colonel Gustave decided to try and reason with the creature.

The commandant stepped forward, his arms outstretched to his side in a non-threatening posture.

"Please. We mean you no harm. We are very pleased that you have joined us, Private Blitzkrieg."

No one else in the room made a move, more than content to let the colonel have his try, not to mention be the focus for the next attack. The creature did stop, looking up at Colonel Gustave.

"What did you call me?" The creature's vocal cords had not spoken for some time and it was obvious that just speaking was an effort. The jigsaw soldier's voice was slow and gravelly with a stammered Yiddish accent. The memories of motor control were due to their choice of taking a brain from a very learned rabbi. It seemed an odd choice by men who were attempting to exterminate the Jewish race, but it was based on the assumption that a brighter mind would help their Private Blitzkrieg serve them better. He was envisioned as the first leader of their jigsaw corpse troops. "Why do you call me that?"

"Because it is your name. I am your creator," lied the Colonel, but he knew full well that the scientists who had done the actual work were in no shape to dispute his claim.

"Why have you created me?" asked Blitzkrieg.

"Because you will save us from our enemies. Come, let us retire to someplace more hospitable. We will go to the Officer's Mess. And although you are just a private, I think we will make an exception this time," said the Colonel with a chuckle, extending an arm towards the exit. Adam had already backed out the way he came and thrown the bodies of the slain sentries on a neighboring rooftop so they would not be found by the exiting men.

The colonel led the creature born of Nazi-generated lightning across the camp, chatting with him about simple things, speaking of the greater glory of the Fatherland. Blitzkrieg half-listened, looking around him, not only at the men who followed but also at the camp itself. He had literally just been born and everything was new to him. Colonel Gustave tried to lead him down certain rows. The sewn together bits of corpses of the jigsaw soldier had made him slightly taller than the average man, but the reanimating process had increased his size to almost seven feet tall. They had planned well with his uniform for it was strained by the muscle beneath only slightly. His high vantage showed him the one building that stood higher than the others in the camp.

"What is that?" he said, pointing to the gas chambers.

"It is nothing. Come with us. We will feed you well, then we shall all drink and make merry," said Colonel Gustave.

Blitzkrieg was having none of it. Something about that building disturbed him, but what exactly escaped him. Without conscious thought, he turned and walked towards the gas house. A soldier made the mistake of getting in his way and was swatted aside for his trouble. The colonel looked nervous but waved at the other soldiers to stand down as they followed slowly in his wake.

Adam followed as close behind as he could manage without risking discovery.

When Blitzkrieg arrived, he stopped short and stared at the building. Reaching for the door, he found it locked, so he simply pulled the door off its hinges. After stepping inside, he was greeted by mounds of sorted clothes and a large pile of shoes. The jigsaw man moved further in, opening the next door and setting foot inside the chamber of death. The colonel and his men went as far as the outer door and looked inside after their creation. When Blitzkrieg turned to face them, tears fell from his eyes. Memories were assaulting him with the force of bullets.

"I know this place. People died here. People were killed, I was killed, our breaths choking us until we breathed no more." Blitzkrieg's posture changed. Where before he was hurt and confused, now he was filled with anger. His hands balled into fists and he turned to Colonel Gustave. "You must have done this."

"They were enemies of the Fatherland. It was necessary," said Gustave. "For the greater good."

"There is nothing good in this. It must be avenged."

There were no more words; the creature's rage spoke volumes as he charged for the colonel who was smart enough to slam the heavy doors. The creature smashed into them, pounding them with his fists until even the heavy metal looked like it might buckle.

Colonel Gustave, his face blanched white with fear, knew it would not be long before his Private Blitzkrieg waged a war upon his own creators, so he gave the only order he could.

"Release the gas!"

"But sir, you said he was not to be harmed," said one soldier.

The colonel hit the private in the back of the head. "The gas will just kill him, but leave his body intact. There is more serum left. We can take him far from here into the Blagovshchina Forest and revive him again. We did not realize that the brain we gave him would have remnant memories that would be triggered by these sights." The gas poured in. Even the monster needed to breathe and he began to choke, but it did not stop him from trying to bust down the door. "We will do it again and we will do it better. We will learn from this mistake."

The pounding made Gustave more nervous than he wanted to show in front of subordinates.

"We will adjourn and meet again tomorrow morning to discuss how to better handle things the second time. You two will tend to Herr Private." Colonel Gustave singled out two privates for this possibly dangerous duty.

"Colonel, if he should escape from the chamber, can we shoot him?" asked one of the privates.

The colonel knew that the creature was valuable and should not be harmed, but the pounding at the door made him realize that if he escaped, the creature would be coming for him.

Gustave gave a curt nod. "Do what is necessary."

Adam had been a soldier, a wanderer, a farmer, a criminal, and even a killer, but still, he could not take life lightly. The men, he hesitated to call them soldiers, who worked in this camp turned a blind eye to the atrocities committed here, cloaking themselves in the protection that they were only following orders. It made them just as guilty as those who did the actual killing. It mattered not if they justified it by saying the majority were Jews and Russian prisoners. German, Jew, Roma, or patchwork creature, all deserved life, and those that took it had no moral protection against losing their own. Adam knew he was in their number, but at least he fought for life. He knew that would hardly matter when his time came. It didn't stop him from hoping.

Despite his great capacity for violence, Blitzkrieg was virtually a newborn and thus by Adam's reasoning not yet fully responsible for his actions. So it was hardly a difficult choice when he stepped out of the shadows behind the two soldiers who were looking inside the gas chamber with a mix of apprehension and glee then smashed their skulls together.

Quickly Adam maneuvered the door open, but the gas had taken its toll. Even though Blitzkrieg was still banging on the doors he was doing it from his knees. The two century plus spawn of lightning took a deep breath and stepped inside to pull out his fellow creature.

Adam remembered his own unusual birth and knew how strongly he reacted to small acts of kindness. It was plain in the eyes of his brother creature that he felt the same way.

"You saved me," said Blitzkrieg. "Why?"

"Because I am like you." When Blitzkrieg looked at his German uniform Adam pointed to his head to show Blitzkrieg his own scars. "I only wear these clothes to give me an advantage should we be discovered. I also use them to fight these monsters from within. They think they have created you, their monster soldier, but they are the true monsters. We will get you out of here."

Blitzkrieg had been gulping air greedily, pushing the effects of the gas from his system. Slowly he rose to his feet.

"This place shall not stand. It has caused too much death for my people."

Adam brows rose. "You can remember a time before the machine's thunderbolt?"

Blitzkrieg shrugged. "Not quite remember. Not as if I was there. I see things as if I was watching from a distance. The horrors they did. Laughing, enjoying the savagery. We must free the prisoners."

Frankenstein frowned. "There are no more living prisoners inside the camp. Except you."

"I have to make sure they can't do this again," said Blitzkrieg.

"There is more to this than just those here. There are hundreds and thousands of them with weapons that can destroy either of us. The fight must be done in stealth," urged Adam Frankenstein.

"Perhaps, but first I will find and make the colonel pay," said Blitzkrieg.

"It is more important that we get you out of here," said Adam laying his hand on Blitzkrieg's shoulder, forgetting what it was like to be touched so soon after riding the lightning.

Blitzkrieg lashed out with his arm, smashing Adam first into a wooden wall and then through it. Beams collapsed on top of the older creature. Blitzkrieg made his way out into the camp. He had not gone far before more soldiers attacked him. They fired at him, trying to contain their bullets to his extremities. The lightning and the chemicals that brought the bits of corpses to life were still doing their work. The flesh mended itself back together, ejecting the spent bullets as it did so. Those that were daring or foolish enough to try for hand-to-hand combat were crushed, battered, or torn apart.

Blitzkrieg lifted a young soldier who most likely lied about his age to get into the army. Holding him by the throat so that they were eye to eye, he demanded, "Where is the colonel?"

Being brave while surrounded by fellow soldiers and carrying a loaded gun is hardly the most difficult thing in the world. Maintaining that bravery, that willingness to accept even a painful death for one's cause can be overwhelming for some when they find themselves facing death in the eyes, even if the orbs were mismatched and different colors. It is especially hard when that death was squeezing one's windpipe closed.

The soldier had difficulty speaking with his semi-crushed larynx so he merely pointed with his left arm. Blitzkrieg turned in the direction he indicated and walked. He hadn't intentionally planned to use the young soldier as a human shield, but that is how it worked out. The other soldiers were hesitant to shoot one of their own, so followed at a distance.

Finally, Blitzkrieg arrived at the colonel's office and dropped the soldier who gave him directions, battered but alive. The two soldiers that were posted at the door only got one shot off each before their necks were snapped. Blitzkrieg didn't even bother to try opening the door, merely smashed it in. Colonel Gustave had climbed partway out his window but was half a second too slow. Even with mismatched legs that were slightly different lengths, Blitzkrieg still moved too fast. The colonel was caught by the ankle and dragged back inside.

"Let go of me, I order you," yelled Gustave, pointing his finger at the jigsaw man. Blitzkrieg took the colonel's right hand in his left and crushed it until the bones became fragments. Gustave collapsed sobbing.

"Please, do not hurt me. I am your father. I gave you life."

"But what of all those lives you have taken? What of their fathers?

Or children? Did you think you would never answer for them?" said Blitzkrieg.

The colonel dismissed the murders of tens of thousands with a twitch of his face. "They were Jews, Russians, Gypsies, Jehovah's Witnesses, homosexuals, and communists. They did not deserve life and from their ashes, a new German army will rise with you at its head." Colonel Gustave swelled up with pride as he spouted his beloved propaganda. "Not all the bodies were put in the crematorium. The strongest were put aside and hidden. Ready to be sawed apart and put back together, Herr Blitzkrieg. Together we will conquer the world for the Third Reich."

"There is no *we*. I will have nothing to do with such horror," said Blitzkrieg.

Colonel Gustave smiled. "Ah, but you will. That is the next part of the plan, one we should have had ready to go immediately. You will be indoctrinated to be the perfect Nazi soldier."

Before Blitzkrieg could respond, a potato masher grenade flew inside the office. Blitzkrieg could tell by the look of horror on Gustave's face that it was a deadly weapon of some sort. The jigsaw man threw the colonel atop it. Gustave's body blocked and absorbed much of the force of the explosion and the resulting shrapnel. Blitzkrieg bent over to examine the pieces of the colonel. He was quite thoroughly dead and dismembered. Part of him felt robbed of the killing, but the rest of him was satisfied that it was done.

Before the smoke cleared, a group of soldiers eased their way in the doorway still pointing their rifles ahead, each covering the one in front who held another grenade. The soldier armed the grenade and threw it. Again, the creature was too fast and plucked the explosive out of the air as if it were a falling handkerchief. Blitzkrieg stepped up to the first soldier and rammed it into his chest, tearing through bone and muscle. The jigsaw man lifted the soldier and threw him out the door into a group of other soldiers who were waiting to come in. Before the explosion, Blitzkrieg managed to rip the throats out of the two men who hadn't had time yet to fire their rifles at him.

The blast wounded more soldiers, using the thrower's bones as shrapnel. Watching one of their own turned into a bloody and deadly weapon was reason enough for the rest to retreat, dragging their wounded comrades behind them. Switching to a new tactic, a few ran to look for gasoline to burn the building down. The rest stayed, determined to keep the creature inside until they could incinerate it.

Rifle fire pummeled the wooden walls of the office slowly, turning the boards to kindling and Blitzkrieg realized he was trapped. There was a loud crash, barely heard above the incoming gunfire as Adam smashed through the wooden back wall of the office.

"Hurry! We have to get out of here," he said. "They are going to burn this place down."

Blitzkrieg nodded when his eyes caught sight of something on the colonel's desk. Instead of leaving through the gaping hole, Blitzkrieg walked to the desk.

"What are you doing?" questioned Adam.

"These papers here—I know they are important." Blitzkrieg was looking at Jewish holy books, scrolls of the Torah and Kabala. "They should not stay here to burn. They should be saved."

Adam walked to the desk as Blitzkrieg gathered up the holy writings. He saw familiar notebooks and papers and recognized the handwriting as that of his creator Victor Frankenstein. He rushed over and picked those up and clutched them to his chest.

"Are those holy documents too?" asked Blitzkrieg.

Adam tucked the papers in his jacket with great care. "For us they are. They contain the secrets of how we came to life."

As the outside walls and roof began to smolder, the two reserrected men ran out the hole in the back wall, straight into a group of soldiers who had moved to cover the rear of the building. The battle was short and very one-sided. When it was over the two men, who some would call monsters, escaped the camp by pulling down a guard tower and running over the rubble into the night.

They did not stop running until well past the first light of morning. They found the Kubelwagen that Adam had hidden the night before and they rode to a shack Adam had set up in the Blagovshchina Forest. He had the foresight to have forged papers ready for Blitzkrieg that passed him off as another war veteran. It would help explain the scars.

"What am I to do now?" asked Blitzkrieg.

"The German resistance could use someone with your strength. It would help you to destroy that which you have come to hate."

"Is that what we do? Destroy what we hate?" asked Blitzkrieg.

"No, not always. Sometimes we destroy that which we love. There are even times when we don't have to destroy anything at all. But tonight won't be one of those nights," promised Adam.

Blitzkrieg was fed and given a change of clothes. They were too small even though they were tailor-made for the elder creature. Next Adam took Blitzkrieg on a motorbike with a sidecar through the forest until they came to a large clearing covered with camouflage netting.

"What is this?" asked Blitzkrieg as Adam cleared away the camouflage as the sun went down.

"A trophy from the last war. I defeated the French pilot known as the Phantom. I managed to get his plane down intact. I decided not to give it to the military, but to keep it for my own. The newer planes are much faster, but they don't have the Nieuport's maneuverability. And I've made some additions of my own, including a newer engine and a second cockpit. Helpful when I need to smuggle someone out. The black paint helps hide me at night. It was a challenge to bring it to Belarus with me, I'll tell you." Adam got Blitzkrieg situated in the rear cockpit and then loaded him up with three bombs, each the size of a small child.

"What are these?" Blitzkrieg asked.

"Remember the grenades from the camp?" Blitzkrieg nodded. "Each of these is a hundred times more powerful. We will use them to destroy the camp."

"We will drive this to the camp? Won't they see us coming long before we get there?" asked Blitzkrieg.

Adam grinned widely as he climbed into the front cockpit, putting on his aviator cap and goggles. "No, my friend we will not drive. We will fly." He then hopped out and quickly spun the front propeller around until the engine coughed to life. Moments later they were careening down the dirt runway until they took off into the air.

"What should I do with these?" Blitzkrieg asked indicating the bombs.

"Be careful not to jostle or drop them," Adam warned. "When we get over the camp you will let each one go as we go over a target and they will blow it to kingdom come."

It was much faster to fly than drive, even keeping to just above the treetops. Adam kept his plane too low for anti-aircraft artillery to accurately get them unless he was foolish enough to fly directly over them. He wasn't that foolish. As a teacher in the flight school, he knew where the artillery was located so his pilots could avoid them during their training and so he could do the same on his night missions.

Their first target was the gas chambers. What Blitzkrieg could not do with his fists the night before, one bomb accomplished in an instant. Next was the crematorium where the Nazis were storing the bodies they were saving to build their army of jigsaw soldiers. The third explosion took out the armory, which in turn caused a larger explosion, which damaged the road leading to and from the camp, making a rapid land pursuit of the aerial bombers difficult. As chaos rained beneath him, Adam pulled up into the sky tipping his wings once in a salute, not to the butchers that called themselves soldiers, but to the dead he could not save. His respects paid, he took his new brother up into the night sky. A lightning bolt flashed through the darkness and Adam smiled at the good omen. Tomorrow he would tell Blitzkrieg of the trains headed for the camp with new prisoners and his plans to make sure it never gets there.

From the writings of Abraham Van Helsing, founder and Lord Protector of the Sway:

The single greatest threat to humanity is the count who has declared himself King of Transylvania. It was bad enough when he contented himself with a small province of the once vanished country. He had forgotten his warrior ways. His defeat and death at my hands made him remember. To my eternal shame, he managed to resurrect himself to again plague the human world. In response, I founded the Sway to defend humanity from the monsters.

In 1916, the vampire joined in the Battle of Transylvania against both the Germans and the Romanians. In his fury and cunning, the beast defeated both armies. He then claimed his former lands as spoils of war. Transylvania was a country once more and Dracula its king.

This still left him as only a minor player on the world stage, but then he took up arms during the second Martian invasion and, with an army of monsters, defeated the alien invaders. This time he claimed their war machines as spoils and became the most dangerous creature in our solar system.

The Dolingen Gamble

A tale of King Dracula

Robert E. Waters

Near the Borgo Pass, 1950

Baba Yaga stood at the front window of her chicken hut, peering through the white fog of early morning. The hut's thin, though powerful, legs worked their way up a steep incline of sharp rocks, rotting stumps, and choking weeds. Somewhere in the hazy distance, a wolf howled, and Baba wondered if it were the king. *King, indeed!* The thought of that pale, over-dressed, arrogant creature being anything but a *beast* offended her. But she was in his country now, and it was best to play safe. *I love the king,* she thought to herself, in case anyone was listening to her thoughts. And soon, she would show him just how much she loved him.

The spurs of her hut's webbed feet struck the impacted dirt of the long, winding road to his castle. The king had several castles, in fact, but Baba's intelligence report confirmed that he was staying at the moment in Bran. The hut pulled itself up onto the road, and Baba breathed a sigh of relief, happy that her journey was almost over. If it had been her, she'd have simply attacked the castle with every plane and rocket in Russia, but she was a mere messenger for the Premiere of the Soviet Union. Stalin was expecting an answer, and Baba intended on getting one.

Through the fog, she could see the black spires of his castle reach into the heavy sky like dead fingers. It seemed so close, yet the empty road before her, twisting its way through the Borgo Pass, might take another hour to travel. But she had been lucky so far, with nary a whisper or hint of danger. *They fear me,* she thought as her hut straightened itself onto the road and began walking. *As they should.*

A high-energy beam struck the escarpment left of the hut. Rock and dirt loosened and cascaded down into the road, blocking her path. The hut almost lost its balance as it navigated its way through the cascade. Baba held onto her mortar to keep from falling. She spit curses into the air and desired the heads of the gypsies who had committed such an offense. But then, it might be Jews or Armenians, or whoever. These days, the "king" harbored many groups who had fled the ravages of The Great Patriotic War. It could be anyone in those ghastly machines from Mars.

A tripod rose out of the valley below, its turtle-like head pulsing a low humming, red light. It looked at her through a visor of deep crimson. It raised an arm that served as a cannon. It was ready to fire once again. Baba stood her ground and shouted at the iron thing from her modest doorway.

"You fools! Do you know who I am? I am Baba Yaga, and you will show an old lady respect, or I will rip that carapace off and cook your bones. I am here to see your mast—"

"Baba Yaga," said a booming voice from the Martian tripod, "by order of the king, I will escort you to Bran Castle. Come out of your hut and follow."

Nobody interrupts me! But Baba stilled and tried to calm herself as she eyed the cannon leveled at her. "And what will become of my home?"

"It will remain here, where it will be protected, as ordered by the king."

She nodded. "Very well."

She ran her hand over the course, chipping wallpaper of her hut to give it comfort. She whispered to it careful instructions if she were not to return. Then she crawled into her mortar, took her long pestle staff into her frail hands, and pushed off through the door as if she were guiding a boat down the Volga.

"You will walk, Baba Yaga," said the voice through the red visor.

Baba flashed her weakest and most feeble visage. She appeared before the tripod as a grandmother, with a sweet, rosy face, and a smile to match. "Aww, surely you will not force an old woman to walk fifteen miles, will you? Such a journey would kill me, and your master would be most unhappy with that." She cleared her throat and nodded. "I will agree to leave my mortar and pestle behind, sweetie, if you will carry me yourself?"

Oh, to see the inside of that tripod! Stalin would be most pleased with information about Martian technology, and she half-hoped that the hapless pilot therein would agree. But the pilot did not hesitate. He (or she) simply turned its tall, lanky body and said, "Follow me, then."

Some battles you win, and some you lose. Baba Yaga had lived forever, it seemed, and she knew the fickle ebb and flow of fortune. She would not get to see the inside of that alien tech today, but she had her mortar and pestle. And with those, she knew, she could turn herself into anything King Dracula desired.

Baba Yaga followed the tripod in her mortar while she smiled and hummed the old Russian folk song, *Ah Vy, Seni, Moi Seni.*

Bran Castle

Baba Yaga brought her mortar to a halt at the stone steps of Dracula's castle. The creature was already there to greet her.

"Welcome, Baba," King Dracula said. "How have you been?"

He was tall, slim, and covered head to toe in black, the collar of his cape cradling his egg-shaped head like a bird's nest. His thin blood-red lips curved slightly upward in a smile that Baba could tell was more perfunctory than sincere. His right hand opened its long, pale fingers, revealing sharp nails that seemed to lust for her throat, as did the fangs he failed to hide.

"As well as can be expected, Count," Baba replied, "given the situation. Better than I have been in the past, as you well know."

Dracula nodded, and Baba could feel the vampire reach out with his mind. She, in turn, gave him a look that would melt a mortal man, and her face changed from coarse and taut to supple and smooth. Perfect teeth. "Do not waste your time trying to seduce me with your illusions, Baba," Dracula said, a flash of fire crossing his eyes. "My whole castle is filled with beautiful women. As pleasant as they are, I do not need another. Won't you come in, though, so that we may speak about why you are here?"

He stepped aside to allow her admittance. Baba shook her head and sent out a tentacle of persuasion herself. "Right here is fine, Count. I know how you protect your home with psychic energy. If I enter, you have the advantage. Besides, what I have to say can be said in the light of day."

The sun was finally rising, and though they stood beneath the canopy that shielded them from direct sunlight, she could see that Dracula was agitated, and longed to take a few steps backward. He had too much power for the sun to burn it away, but the daylight weakened him. But he endured, sighed, shook his head, and said, "Very well, speak your mind then, so that I may return to more important matters."

Baba cleared her throat and wiped a line of nervous spittle from her mouth. Dracula's mental control was so strong… "It is my understanding that you house the sorcerous Circe, daughter of Helios and Hecate. She has broken her promise and pledge to the Premiere of the Soviet Union, Joseph Stalin, an oath that he—that *we*—take very seriously. She made promises that she has forsaken, and I have come to ensure that she returns to Russia to fulfill those promises."

"You?" Dracula asked, a touch of mirth and disbelief flashing across his face. "You alone can compel a Greek goddess to do your bidding? You are good, Baba, but not that good."

"Circe is powerful, yes, but she is not a goddess, not in the strict sense. She is a mutant, with incredible powers indeed, but no goddess. And I am not alone in this endeavor!" She barked, more harshly than she wanted. She calmed, smiled, and said, "I am merely a messenger for a greater power than even you, Count."

"I am no longer a count, Baba," Dracula said, showing his anger. "I am now a king."

She huffed. "As you say, but a greater title does not automatically make you a better man, or a more important one. Centuries of shifting political fortunes have brought you status and prestige across the world, but you are still the same, simple vampire I met three centuries ago, and in my eyes you always will be. Your power has limits too, *King* Dracula. Don't forget that."

Baba could tell that he was about to blow, his anger bringing rare color to his face. If he were to shift right now into a bat or wolf, perhaps she'd have a chance in taking him, her pestle not just for pushing her mortar through the air. The shiny, silver cudgel at its head was ready.

"State your offer, Baba," Dracula said, his sallow complexion returning. "Quickly."

"Turn Circe over to me," she said, "and the Premiere of the Soviet Union agrees to never attack or harass Transylvania, so long as he is in power."

It was Dracula's turn to huff. "An empty threat. I already have an agreement with the Premiere that we signed in blood at Stalingrad those many cold nights long ago. Atop a pile of German soldiers, if I recall correctly." Dracula licked his lips. "Bavarian blood is best in the winter."

Baba Yaga blanched, her stomach turning. "Times are changing. Russia needs new conquests, new land, and past agreements weigh heavily and inconveniently on her mind. Stalin will tear up that agreement, King Dracula. You can count on it, now that he has the atomic bomb." She reached out with her thoughts and sensed fear. "Oh, you were not aware that we have one, were you? Really, my good fellow, you should read the papers more often. Like America, we have it now, just sitting and waiting for the proper target. I would hate for that target to be Bran Castle, my good king, but rest assured, if you do not hand Circe over to me, the skies will rain fire, and there is no magic, no sorcery, no science, that will save you and your kin from such a fate."

There was a pause as both tried once more to penetrate the defenses of each other's mental shield. Dracula's was strong, the strongest that Baba had ever tangled with. But so was hers, and she kept up her shield despite withering fatigue that gripped her legs.

Finally, one of Dracula's renfield thralls came up behind him and whispered something in his ear. Dracula nodded, touched the man lightly on his head, then sent him away. He turned back to Baba Yaga, and said, "Thank you, Baba, for traveling so far and for tendering your offer. But Circe is a guest in my home, and she may stay here for as long as she wishes. Please convey my answer back to your masters… and I bid you farewell and safe travels."

King Dracula stepped back three paces. Before he turned his back to her, Baba Yaga asked, "Dread king… is that your final word on the matter?"

Dracula paused, smiled, and said, "Baba, every word I utter is the last."

He disappeared into his castle, and Baba Yaga lifted her mental defenses and collapsed in her mortar, exhausted. One of Dracula's beautiful thralls stepped up to assist. She waved the little waif off with her pestle, regained her strength, and stood. "Take me back to my hut. Now!"

I've done everything I was asked to do, she thought as she once again followed the Martian tripod down the road. *Now it's in the hands of the Countess.*

Kremlin Senate Chambers, Moscow

Countess Dolingen of Gratz stroked the head of the male thrall as he laid gently across her lap. He was older than she usually preferred, much older in fact, but she did not mind. Where he failed her in duties that she required from all of her male pets, he more than made up for in devotion and knowledge. For right now, knowledge was what she needed, and as long as he served her well in that capacity he would stay alive.

"You seem nervous today, Baba. Agitated." Dolingen let her long fingers tickle the man's bare cheek. Her sharp nail cut the skin. Dolingen scooped up a droplet of blood and let it fall onto her tongue. She shivered in joy and felt a surge of renewed energy. "Why do you rock back and forth on your bare heels with so much impatience?"

"The matter is serious," Baba said, "and you're wasting time playing with toys."

Dolingen giggled, and on cue, so did her thrall. *What a devoted toy!* "I never play, Baba. I'm securing my investment. Do not fret, my aged friend. My plan is sound. My plan will succeed."

Baba sighed, shook her head. "It is my responsibility to convey your plan to Stalin. He is not a patient man, nor is he resting euphorically on your lap like a puppy. But he is waiting, and so, I ask you again, let us discuss your plan. Or do you wish to explain it to him yourself?"

The thought of having to be in the same room with that oaf again disgusted her. She found the very nature of Joseph Stalin revolting; the thought of his blood in her mouth abhorrent. She could care less about Soviet desires or the Premiere's personal agenda. If it were up to her, she'd kill the tyrant where he stood and walk away smiling. But in this particular endeavor, their desires crossed. Stalin wanted Circe; Countess Dolingen wanted the king.

"Very well." She uncrossed her legs, and her pet sat upright. "Go, my sweet," she said softly, "while the adult women talk. Fetch me that *stick* you showed me the other day."

The man nodded a profuse number of times, much to Baba's chagrin, then left through a tiny side door. Dolingen clapped her hands twice, and two lovely girls came forward with a large map unfurled between them. They laid the map out on the large mahogany table, bowed, and stepped away. Dolingen stood and seemed to float to Baba's side.

Bran Castle lay on the map, a full blueprint of every bend and corner in the dread estate, every turn of stairs, every locked and unlocked door that Dolingen could remember. And her memory was excellent, even after so many years. She remembered everything.

She leaned over the map and pointed to a small, wooded section on the east side of the castle. Beyond that lay a field of knee-high grass and red pipac flowers. "Irina Sebrova will instruct her Night Witches to put their *Polikarpovs* and their An-12 transport plane down in this field. *Polikarpovs* fly low and slow, but their wood-and-canvas construction is near impossible for Martian radar to detect."

"And you will fly in with them?"

Dolingen nodded. "When we get closer to the target, yes. Alongside their forward plane." She pointed to the river hastily scribbled onto the map, which flowed near the foot of the rocky escarpment on which Bran Castle lay. "I will touch down here, near the river, so that I may conduct reconnaissance to ensure their safe approach. Once I've secured the perimeter, I'll call them forward, through these trees, which will give them additional cover, and then we'll enter the castle."

"Just like that, eh?" Baba scratched the red bandana wrapped across her sweaty forehead. Her expression wavered between exasperation and doubt. She looked like she wanted to use her psychic abilities on Dolingen to make the countess do something stupid or embarrassing, just to relieve her nerves. "I will remind you, Countess, that Dracula has a psychic shield wrapping his home. That is why I refused to enter during my engagement with him four days ago. You cannot just simply waltz through the front gate undetected."

It was Dolingen's turn to be annoyed. "Who do you think you are speaking to, Baba? I lived in that castle for years, for centuries."

And indeed she had, with two other women—her blood sisters as she used to call them—brides and devoted servants to his majesty, King Dracula. But how dare they rebel and consider living lives of their own and making decisions which were often incompatible with what the "Count" wanted. He had been only a count then, and his wrath and dissatisfaction swift and terminal. He had tried to kill them all, to walk away from their lifetime of devotion and service. His needs, his desires, no longer required her and her sisters. The other two were dead. But she had escaped such a fate. Now she was returning home.

"Trust me, Baba, I know a way into that infernal place that the good king knows nothing about and that his shield does not cover. Trust me."

Trust was not in Baba Yaga's nature, especially when it meant having to accept the plans of a woman that, Dolingen knew, she did not trust. Baba was powerful, and she'd be formidable in a fight. But there would be no fight today. Whether Baba trusted the plan or no, it was not her decision. Stalin had given the mission to the countess, and that was all Baba needed to know.

Baba cooled, calmed her breathing, and nodded. "Very well. But it is imperative that once you find Circe, that she not be harmed in any way. She requires her full strength to fulfill the promise that she gave Stalin a simple year ago. He needs her strong and healthy so that she can turn all those men who rot in Gulags into feral beasts that he can throw against Germany. He wants the entire country, not just half. Stalin believes that the only way to achieve that is through a battalion of beastmen that can fight twice as hard and three times as long as any normal man. He wishes to try reacquiring Circe through subterfuge and not through the application of the atomic bomb, which would undoubtedly kill her. And, of course, using atomics would bring too much attention to his country from actors that he prefers to keep in the dark for now, until such a time as Russia is ready to strike in a more forceful manner. His options are few, and his patience grows shorter by the day. So I beg you, Countess Dolingen. Bring Circe back alive and unharmed, and save us all a lot of grief down the road."

"If the serum you supplied my Night Witches works," Dolingen said, "then Circe will drop into a peaceful sleep, and she'll be as easy as a pillow to port. Assuming it works."

"It will, and you can trust *me* this time. All my potions work."

Dolingen nodded. "Once we have Circe, we will exit and make our way back to the planes. We'll load up and be out before he can rouse his tripods."

Baba nodded and kept nodding for several minutes. She didn't want to approve, Dolingen knew, but she had no choice. As she had said, Stalin was waiting.

"Very well," Baba said. "I need radio contact as soon as you're outside Transylvanian air space. I'll be waiting for your signal in Belgrade."

"Don't worry, Baba," Dolingen said, this time putting on her charm. It was unlikely to work on the old crone, but it was always worth a try. "Stalin will have his sweet little Greek goddess back very soon."

Baba Yaga left. Dolingen called in Irina. The young commander entered, the red fang marks on her throat healing nicely. "Rouse your Night Witches, sweet girl. Tonight, we prepare our force. Tomorrow, we strike."

Irina nodded and left. A few minutes later, the male thrall returned with his stick.

He held it in his teeth like a rose. He offered it to her by going to his knees and lifting his chin as a dog might do for his master. Dolingen smiled pleasantly, caressed the man's left ear, and then accepted the stick.

Not a stick, really. More of a dagger. A sharp, thin one, eight inches long and forged from kilns used by the Sway to make blades to kill all manner of scary beasts. But not this man before her. He had once been a member of the Sway. Now, he was hers, and he had given her the most important commodity in this rapidly changing world: knowledge. Knowledge of technologies that would be most useful in the wars ahead. Knowledge most useful to her plans.

Her plan was not the plan that she had just conveyed to Baba Yaga. The Night Witches could have Circe if they wished, and best of luck to them. Her plan was very different, but simple.

Enter Bran Castle... and kill *King* Dracula.

King Dracula's Domain, Bran Castle

Members of the former Soviet 588th Night Bomber Regiment, also known as the Night Witches, huddled quietly in their transport plane as it flew low in formation with its *Polikarpov* escort. The wooden frame of the plane creaked and groaned beneath their boots, but so far, the flight had been quiet and uneventful. Countess Dolingen was pleased with that as she huddled with her girls. Soon, she knew, that would all change. They were flying into Transylvania, where nothing ever stayed quiet or pleasant for long.

She had each member check her weapons and equipment. Each carried an AK-47 and five fully-loaded clips with a mixture of regular and silver-laced ammunition. Each had a knife, and each had three darts in a belt pouch filled with Baba Yaga's special yellow serum for Circe, so that if any one of them had a clear shot on the goddess at any time, they could take it.

Dolingen was proud of them. These Russian ladies had flown tens of thousands of bombing sorties for the Soviet Union during The Great Patriotic War, but had transitioned quickly into shock commandoes that now served her and whatever duties she required. Irina Sebrova was their field commander, and she had been one of the most successful pilots during the war. Irina had shaped them into one efficient fighting force, at the direction of her new mistress, and now she would be leading them on one of their deadliest missions. Dolingen had a notion to go to each of them and sample their blood in recognition of their service, but not today. Today, their minds had to be fixed on their orders.

"Get ready, sweet ladies," Dolingen said over the hum of the transport plane, as she stood and prepared for flight. "Remember your training, and remember your duty to Mother Russia. Keep it tight at all times. Noise discipline. No unnecessary risks. You follow me, and Irina and I promise glory at the end of the day. Cut the engines!"

The engines of the An-12 transport stopped, and now only the sound of the wind could be heard whistling through its frame as the pilot navigated her descent over the tree line. Dolingen opened the transport door. Irina clung to her leg.

"Don't leave us," Irina said, holding on to her like a child. "Land with us in the field. Stay with us so that we may protect you."

Dolingen leaned into the wind. She did not require fresh air but she so enjoyed it on her smooth, sallow skin. And it had been so long since she had enjoyed the sweet breezes of her home. She reached down and patted Irina on the head. "Bless you, child. We will not be apart for long. Guide your women and keep them in order. You know what to do." *And when the time comes, you will serve me well...*

Irina nodded, kissed Dolingen's leg, and then scampered back to her witches.

Dolingen leapt out the door.

She flew at pace with the forward plane, listening intently to the whistling sound of the wind through its frame, the sound that the Germans described as one that a witch makes riding her broom. But these planes were neither carrying bombs nor brooms today. They required more speed and lift for, once Circe was in their care, they had to launch quickly and be gone before any Martian tracking technology could be employed. Dolingen was under no illusion that all of these planes would make it back to Belgrade unscathed. Perhaps none of them would, and how would they get Circe back then? Plan B would have to be employed, and how successful would that be? Questions that must be asked and must be answered in time. But for now, her mind was fixed on the river.

They cleared the tops of the trees, and Dolingen pointed to the clearing where they were to set down. The forward pilot nodded understanding and veered to the right, guiding the rest of the squadron with her. Dolingen kept flying forward.

The river was near. She could smell the water even though the wind flowed left to right. It had an organic, wholesome smell that she recognized and missed, for she and her other two sisters would often come to the river on moonlit nights and feast on a stray deer or an unsuspecting peasant girl who had not heeded the advice of her wise mother. What glorious times they were. The river had given them solace and comfort. The river, in the end, had betrayed them. But in the witching hour, the river would redeem itself.

She touched down in the weeds that lined the bank. She crouched low, listening intently to all the sounds swirling around her. The rustle of the wind through the weeds. Mice fighting for bugs. Squirrels scratching through loose bark. The creaky joints of a Martian tripod on the far side of the castle. The touching down of each plane, one by one, in the field two hundred yards to her right. The casual flow of the river. There were no guards circling this side of the castle, perhaps because this portion of it was the steepest and most difficult for anyone to try and scale its walls. Dolingen had no intention of scaling those walls, nor would she allow her witches to risk their own lives doing so. They would enter Bran Castle a different way.

She reached out with her mind and found Irina waiting for guidance. Telepathic communication was best under the circumstances, though Dracula or his renfields could be listening. It was better, however, than regular radios which could be tracked by his Martian defenses, and Dolingen had no desire getting into a scrap with them. The creaky tripod on the other side of the castle could stay right where it was. She would use her own strengths to make this mission succeed.

Come to me, my sweet ladies. It's time…

Like phantoms and one by one, the Night Witches crept out of the tree line. Some of them had stayed behind to help the pilots guard the planes, but their numbers were still formidable. Certainly enough to storm this old, decrepit castle and take Circe away. Maybe. One by one they crossed the small distance between the wood and the weeds in which Dolingen waited. Irina crouched low at her side, ready for action. Dolingen spoke telepathically.

Hold your breaths, ladies. We're going for a little swim.

Irina and the rest followed Countess Dolingen like a trail of ducks down the rocky bank of the river and into the deep water. One by one, they took a deep gulp of air, held it, and disappeared below the surface.

The cave entrance beneath the river was unknown and unprotected by Dracula's psychic shield. It came up through the bowels of the castle and opened into a small inset chamber also unknown by the so-called 'king'. It was the one place, the one avenue of ingress and egress that Dolingen and her sisters could rely upon to get away from Dracula's wrath when he was raging about this thing or another, which was often. Often enough, at least, to still find solace in the stark, cold stone walls of the tiny place that offered passage into the larger castle. She paused and waited until all of her witches were safely out of the water and had crawled to her side. The room now was cramped and uncomfortable housing all these wet and dripping women. She ordered them to check their weapons. They obeyed. All was well.

"When I push on this wall," she whispered in the darkness. She could see the outline of their body heat, the blood coursing through their rapid hearts and throats. "There will be no turning back. Are you ready?"

Each nodded in turn, then Irina said, "We serve and have faith in you, Mistress. Guide us in."

Dolingen nodded and placed her hand on the wall. She gave a shove. The years had oxidized the seams. It took more of her strength than it used to. She pushed again, and finally the old stones gave way.

The foul scent of rotting corpses and a lifetime of musty coffin soil wafted through the room. One of the witches vomited on the boots of the one next to her. Dolingen laughed. "Get used to it, ladies. I daresay these catacombs are filled with a century of bones and dried sinew. There are probably still skeletons down here from my own kills." She pushed the remaining stones away to give them just enough room to file through. "Follow me."

They followed her in a tight column. Irina walked among them, giving orders, bolstering their resolve, threatening a shot in the back if they failed in their duties. Dolingen smiled to herself. After the war, Stalin had wanted to make Irina a Commissar, but Dolingen refused to give her up. Now she was glad to have made that decision. These witches, as tough as they were, needed strong guidance. They had been on several dangerous missions before, but nothing like this.

Left and right, left and right. Dolingen remembered the path through the catacombs as if she had walked it just yesterday. One never forgets the paths one walks in youth, and she had done so hundreds of times as Dracula's wife. Left and right, left and right. One more left, and finally, they were there. She placed her hand on the double-wide, two-inch-thick, iron-banded door that separated them from pain and death.

Dolingen closed her eyes and focused. She reached out with her mind and searched the entire castle from top to bottom. Dracula's psychic shield was active; it was hard to decipher shapes and sounds through the morass of his chaotic mind and thoughts. But slowly,

slowly, a picture began to form, a pattern. A guard here, a junior vampire there. Dracula's new wives… there, there, and there. Gypsies, Jews, Armenians there and there. But the largest gathering of heat and blood flow was in the very middle of the castle, where the main dining room lay and where there were older, yet still functional, living quarters. Dolingen smiled, despite the gathering threats on the other side of the door.

She removed her hand, turned, smiled, and waved to her witches. Then she pointed her long finger up. Irina and the first rank nodded and lifted their rifles.

Dolingen lifted the latch on the door and pushed it open. She dropped, and the Night Witches opened fire.

The guards on the other side of the door were caught flat-footed. They returned fire, but sparingly. Only one witch fell dead. The others emptied half their first clip into Dracula's shocked defenders. When the bullets stopped flying, Dolingen went through the corpses and cut each throat in turn, ensuring that none of them would ever rise to harm them. None of the bodies were vampires. *Too bad*, she thought, as she took a brief moment to sample the throat of one of the Armenians. She drank cautiously, sparingly, then cast the body aside. "Come," she said, savoring the last drop. "Circe is not far."

Up a winding flight of stone stairs. Dolingen remembered flowing down these steps once in a long, white gown to the joy and amusement of Dracula as he hosted a delegation from Brussels. The poor delegation never left the castle, of course, but it was a glorious evening of feast and drink. Happier, simpler times. Now, her way was paved with bloody footsteps as apparently, the witches had not gotten all of the guards. Someone had escaped and was most assuredly alerting the rest of the castle to her approach. *Let them come*, she thought, as she reached the top and quickly dispatched a simple servant who thought he'd make a mad try to plunge a silver letter opener into her chest. She stopped the sharp end mere inches from her sternum, grabbed the foolish butler by his neck, and snapped it quickly.

They were greeted again by a mass of guards. This time, however, they came better prepared. Each held Martian blasters. They opened fire and immediately incinerated two witches that stood near Irina.

The witch leader received flash damage that singed her uniform and burned her neck and left shoulder, but Dolingen pulled her to safety. The rest of the witches opened fire.

The echo of the exchange ricocheted through the great hall and into the joining room, as both sides scrambled to find shelter behind overturned tables, full suits of armor from the Turkish Wars, and chairs and desks and dead and dying bodies. Dolingen kept her head low and tried focusing again on where Circe was waiting. Somewhere around here for sure, but exactly where she could not put a finger on it. As she concentrated, the battle raged and raged.

A young vampire struck her in the face, a quick slash from behind that propelled Dolingen forward and across the messy battle room floor. The creature wasted no time, coming at her again. Dolingen recovered, turned, and took the young girl in the chest with a swift kick, sending her up, over, and into the morass of battle. Witches put silver, exploding rounds into her belly, and the pretty vampire burst into flames. The fire spread to other bodies among the dying. A nice burning ensued and a choking smoke and stench filled the room. The remaining defenders withdrew behind the billowing smoke.

Dolingen found Irina among her wounded. "He's throwing wave after wave of useless swine against us," she said. "He's forcing us to expend our ammunition before we reach Circe. He's forcing *me* to waste my power."

"Where is she, my mistress?" Irina asked, helping a witch to her feet. "Where is Circe?"

Dolingen shook her head. "Not sure. I need a conduit through which I can gather more strength and reach out through Dracula's shield."

Irina motioned to the dead bodies around them. "There are many to feast upon, my Countess."

Dolingen shook her head. "Not good enough. All of them are thralls to the *mighty* king. If I feast on them too greedily, if I draw the power from them that I need, then he may gain a connection to me, and learn of our progress, and of my waning strength."

Irina offered her throat. "Then use me, Countess."

Dolingen paused. "If I do, you may die."

A tear welled in Irina's eye. It fell across her cheek and cut a path through her own bloodstain. "I serve to die, Countess. I serve you. I serve the Motherland."

Dolingen knew that this might be Irina's last mission. But not so soon, and not because they had miscalculated the amount of fodder that Dracula was willing to cast against them. She had hoped that Irina's last stand would come later, when it really mattered. Taking her life now seemed defeating, and yet, if she did not, then the mission might have to be aborted. She could care less whether or not they secured Circe, but she was not about to give up the fight now, not when they were so close. So close to what she desired, what she needed. That, more than anything, is what mattered now.

"You have served me well, sweet love," Dolingen said. "I will see you soon on the other side."

She took Irina into her arms and sank her fangs deep into the woman's soft throat.

She drank, and drank, and drank, and as she did, she reached out again into every corner of the castle. No place in its cold, unforgiving emptiness was denied to her. She saw everything, could hear and see every movement. Irina's pure, uncompromised blood gave her strength that she hadn't felt in a long, long time. Dolingen reveled in it and now felt that she could take on anything, could achieve any goal in this life or the next. She drank every drop until right before Irina breathed her last. Then she let her go, laid her down gently, and closed her eyes for the last time.

The witches nearby stared in fascination. Dolingen could sense their fear, and some were angry. But that would pass, she knew, for she would now bring them glory and success. She knew exactly where Circe was and how many awaited them. Just three rooms away.

"Come," she said to the remaining witches. "Our goddess awaits."

Circe's powers and stature made those around her *treat* her like a goddess—in name, in birthright, and in beauty- even though, as Baba Yaga had indicated, she was just a very powerful mutant. But regardless of the truth, Dolingen feared her. Anyone with good sense would do so. Mutants with Circe's power were unpredictable, and like a cornered animal, who knew what schemes or tricks she might have up her lovely, silken sleeve.

With Dolingen in the lead, the Night Witches burst into her room, and immediately, Circe's protection was on them. Beastmen—Gypsies and Jews mostly, Dolingen figured, culled from Dracula's refugee population—held the doorway like a chokepoint against the incessant barrage of AK-47 rounds and pistol shots. These feral men that Circe had created through her powers had one sole purpose in life: protect their mistress. The Night Witches' mandate was not much different, and they huddled around *their* mistress and took the wave of slavering teeth and bloody claws gladly and answered with silver bullets.

The bodies piled up in front of them, making entrance to the room difficult. Dolingen herself had to push bullet-riddled carcasses out of the way to let her ladies enter, and once they did, beastmen were on them, shouting and roaring and tearing at their uniforms and tender skin. Dolingen flew into them with abandon, allowing her reflexes, refined through centuries of action, to take each down with swift cuts across the throat or jabs to their chests. Dolingen's deadly punches had been perfected through the Russian marital arts of *samozashchita bez oruzhiya*, SAMBO for short, and she did not waste a moment's training with these wild men, slamming and kicking and punching them until they lay sedate and docile at her feet.

Night Witches were going down as well, much to Dolingen's sadness. There were too many Beastmen to be contained in full, and they had encircled the small cadre of lady fighters and were trying to simply overwhelm them. It was working, at least partially. From where she stood, Dolingen could no longer count the number of witches she had left. The numbers of beastmen now were lower too, and the powerful scent of spilled blood was overwhelming. She wanted to dive into the thickest smear on the floor and drown in it. Beastmen blood, Night Witches' blood… it did not matter. But no. She could not be distracted from the mission. The mission was to find Circe, and where was she in this chaotic melee now raging in her private room?

There she was, on the other side of the fight, as beautiful and as young as if she had been born yesterday. Her long silky black hair, her red lips, her supple form, her flowing countenance belied by a devilish determination in her face, her glare. She bared her teeth, like a beast herself, and directed another three beastmen to join the fight. She held a staff in her hand, and she was trying to resurrect witches that had fallen. She was failing.

With one leap, Dolingen hurled herself over the bloody hand-to-hand and came down in front of the goddess. Circe recoiled. She raised her staff and then brought it down like a cudgel against the vampire's shoulder. Dolingen caught the staff before it struck and snapped it in two.

Circe roared. Dolingen laughed. "You cannot make women your beasts, Circe. Or have you forgotten your own powers?"

Circe flung the staff down. "Watch your tongue, you bitch from the grave! I am Circe, daughter of—"

"Spare me your backstory," Dolingen said, catching Circe in the throat with powerful fingers. "You are defeated. You will come with us willing or unwilling, I care not which, and fulfill your promise to Mother Russia."

Circe struggled under the vise grip of iron claws. "I will do no such thing. I—I'm a guest of—of—"

"Of King Dracula?" Dolingen snickered as she tightened her grip. "And where is your host? Hmm? With his fangs inside another woman, no doubt. A word of advice, sweet goddess: never trust the father of lies. Never trust Dracula. I did… and it nearly killed me. Now, I will have my revenge."

A snarling, ravenous beastman, with claws like a wolf and fur covering his chest and arms through a torn and bloody half coat, slammed into Dolingen's side. The strike tossed her left, but she quickly recovered and ripped the beast's head clean off his neck. Circe scrambled to find her broken staff. She found it, held it up, and skewered a Night Witch who was racing toward her with a syringe of Baba Yaga's serum. Another witch tried the same move. Circe caught her in the shoulder with her bloody staff, and then knocked her silly with a swift smack against the head.

Dolingen moved. She found the syringe of the fallen witch,

scooped it up, and then jumped onto Circe's back. Circe tried tossing the vampire away, but she exposed her left breast. Dolingen longed to sink her fangs into that tender flesh, but instead, she pushed the needle of the syringe deep until all the serum was sucked into Circe's veins.

Another witch struck, then another, and another, until four syringes were sticking out of Circe from her legs to her chest. She wavered in place, tried fighting off another witch who came up to inject a fifth syringe. Dolingen then stepped in. "Enough! We want to sedate her, not kill her."

Was it ever possible to kill an alleged goddess? A question for another time, perhaps. For now, Dolingen stood there, watching as Circe grew more and more unstable as she tried finding a way to flee. But they kept her boxed in until finally, she fell.

Dolingen caught her and laid her down gently. "I'm sorry, my goddess," she cooed softly as she stroked Circe's brilliant hair. "I mean no personal offense. May you, at last, find peace somewhere in the world."

The rest of the beastmen, seeing their mistress fall, broke away and tried to run. The witches were unforgiving, shooting them in the back or bludgeoning them to death before they could escape.

The battle was over. Circe was theirs.

A wolf howled in the distance beyond the castle's stone walls. Dolingen tried to resist, but the call was too strong. She couldn't resist. She didn't want to resist.

"Take her," she said, handing Circe over to the nearest witch. "Take her and go."

"My lady, come with us. We cannot escape without—"

"Do as I say," Dolingen snapped. "You know the extraction plan, you know the way out. Go and leave me. Get Circe out." She stood and drew the dagger sheathed on her thigh.

"Where are you going?" The Witch asked.

Dolingen turned and smiled. "When the master of the house calls, you answer."

She found him waiting in a small courtyard off the west side of the castle. She was surprised about that because the sun was rising fast and even now, small lines of light cut across the cobblestones of the courtyard's short wall. Within an hour, the entire plot would be covered with light. Perhaps he was confident that the entire engagement would be over quickly. Perhaps he was just arrogant and overconfident. Perhaps both.

He stood there like a stone in the center of the court, the full length of his cape and black clothing serving as a shield to the cool wind and slips of fog swirling through space. He was tall. He was marvelous, his gaze, even now, stirring emotions that Dolingen had not felt in a long time. She had learned to control those emotions, to fight against nostalgic memories that weakened her resolve. For everything in her existence since leaving the Count—the King—had given her strength and resilience. But his face, his eyes, the quiet intensity that she so loved about this beast before her, his radiant charm, made her weak in the knees. And for a moment, she considered submitting herself, like she had done many times before. Then the memories of fire and the screams of her and her sisters, the double-cross, the deception. Those memories were just as strong as the good ones.

"Dracula," Dolingen said, ignoring his formal title. She gripped the dagger tucked beneath her sleeve. "They say you grow annoyed when you are not greeted with the proper respect, in the proper manner. A man of your... position, should not concern himself with such trivial details. Then again, perhaps you are not so important, so strong, after all."

"Details, fair Dolingen, are the hallmark of good decision-making. Without detail, without precision, there is chaos." He dared to take a step toward her, the bottom of his cape swishing against his dark breeches. "I left you dead on the bank of the river. How is it you are still alive?"

Dolingen huffed and took a step to the left. She kept a firm grip on the dagger. "You walked away too soon. My sisters lay there all night, burning, crisping, receiving the final death. I managed to crawl to the water and find worms and a fish and whatever else I could manage. They saved me. They gave me my life back. You walked away too soon.

Your arrogance, your over-confidence made you miss that little detail."

"And now you've come back to exact your revenge, is that it?"

Dolingen nodded. "I've come back to right a great wrong, yes."

"You and your sisters, as you call them, were a threat to me. A threat to this kingdom. A threat to my home. A threat to my subjects."

Dolingen now took a step forward, ever careful to stay out of the growing rays of light. "Women speaking their minds, having their own thoughts, their own ideas… how *dare* they!"

Dracula shook his head, and Dolingen could see his prominent veins begin to stretch across his smooth forehead in a V shape that belied his cool demeanor. He flashed his own growing fangs, and said, "That is not the reason, and you know it in your heart. As a count, I could overlook the killing, but a king must protect all of his subjects, even the human ones."

"I know nothing of the sort," she said, "but I have learned a lot away from you, great King. A lot about myself, a lot about the changing world. The Night Witches have taught me a lot about how to be strong, how to face the patriarchy—you, its greatest spokesman—how to stand against it and prevail."

"And yet here you are," Dracula said, opening his clawed hands and holding them open as a gesture of goodwill. He took another step towards her. "Breaking into my home. Killing my servants, my guards. All for the purpose of delivering a woman, one considered a goddess, into the hands of a brute, so that he may have his way with her. Tell me, sweet lady Dolingen, how do you sleep in the day cloaked in such hypocrisy?"

Dolingen lowered her head, her shoulders. She was not happy about it, but what could she say? "It is a means to an end."

"Then let it end now."

Dracula whisked his cape around like a ballerina and dropped like a stone. Light, which had covered his back, now fell across Dolingen's face. Suddenly, she felt weaker. She shook her head against the growing fogginess. The sun was not as strong as a sun fully risen, but it was draining her power, enough at least, to force her to fall back and to the right.

Dracula struck midriff and pushed her backward until she slammed against a dead tree. The force of the blow cracked the trunk. Dolingen screamed; not so much from the pain but from her stupidity at not anticipating the strike. There was pain, indeed. Dracula was one of the strongest vampires in the world. Such a strike against a mortal would have killed outright. But she was not mortal.

Dracula reached out with his sharp claws, trying to find her face. Dolingen grabbed his arm with her free hand and made her body go limp. Her deadweight caught Dracula off balance, and he stumbled forward, striking the tree himself. Dolingen kicked up and caught Dracula in the groin. Then she rolled away and came up hefting the dagger.

Dracula recovered and looked at her as if she were holding a hairpin. He huffed. "You think that little blade will harm me? You've forgotten my power, Dolingen."

She nodded. "We'll see."

He attacked again, but this time, she was ready. She blocked a strike and drove one of Baba Yaga's syringes into his thigh. It wouldn't cause much damage, she knew. The formula was not made for vampires. But perhaps when he felt it coursing through his veins like hot lead, he would pause and wonder.

He did, and just enough to allow Dolingen to strike him with the hand that held the dagger. She did not strike out with the blade; it wasn't the right time yet. She drove her fist, wrapped around the hilt, across his chin. A tooth flew out of his mouth. That, more than the serum, shocked him. He fell back, made a feeble attempt at a counter-strike, but Dolingen delivered blow after blow after blow to his face, his head, his neck. Dracula fell back, tried protecting himself, tried blocking her assault. *It's happening*, she thought, striking him once again to ensure that he was down. *I've got him.*

She lifted her dagger and focused on a soft spot on his chest, right between the snaps on his shirt, the part that exposed his pale flesh. *Right there.*

She thrust, but he grabbed her arm and her throat. His grip was iron, and she almost dropped the blade. His grip on her throat made her faint, and the intermittent sunlight on her body kept her from focusing her strength. She struggled against his grasp, but nothing she tried broke the seal.

Dracula shot into the sky, still clutching her arm and throat. His face was curled into a maniacal grin, a terrifying grin that Dolingen had only seen twice before: once while fighting the Turks, and again alongside that riverbank as she and her powerless sisters burned. It was his death face, and soon, she too would be dead.

He threw her down, like God casting Satan from Heaven, and she struck the ground of the courtyard so hard, the shock-wave rattled the stone wall. Dolingen felt every bone in her body snap. She felt her skull crack like ice across a frozen lake. She had never felt such pain. It was like a volcano burst. Every nerve ending in her body screamed for release. It was even more painful than when her body had burned on the riverside, and it felt as if she would never recover. This was indeed the end. Dracula had won.

But he lingered there before her, waiting for her own immunity to revive her enough so that he might gloat, to stare into her eyes once more to let her know that it was he, King Dracula, who had decided her fate. His smile was still devilish, but it no longer possessed the danger, the rage, that he had shown a moment ago. He was calm, happy. He thought he had won.

But Dolingen still held the dagger, despite her concussive strike on the ground. Dracula lingered. He let her body recover, just enough so that she could see his face, his chest, and reaffirm her grip on the blade.

Dracula leaned in, smiling. "It was nice to see you again, my sweet Dolingen. I am sorry that we cannot chat longer, but my kingdom awaits, and I—"

Before he finished, she lurched forward and drove the dagger into his side, right between ribs four and five. She pushed the blade up to the hilt, and then snapped the handle with a quick flick of her wrist.

It was like lighting a match, and the sunken blade burst into fire.

Dracula fell back and roared. He reached for the blade, but it was lodged too deep and its flame too strong. "Aaaaaah... what is this devilment?"

Dolingen sat up and pulled herself out of the indentation that her body had caused. "It's a magnesium blade, King Dracula, given to me as a gift from a member of the Sway, a little boy puppy, but more a man than you will ever be. That is the advantage of living in the world, my king, instead of cowering in your castle. You learn things. And so now you will die… and may the devil take you."

Dracula twisted and turned in pain, in agony. He kept trying to pull the magnesium blade out of his side, but his hands were now burning as well. Dolingen walked up to him. Dracula reached out to her with his burning hands, in peace, as he had done earlier in their engagement, but she did not take them. She stood there, watching, as he had watched her those many years ago beside the flowing water. She watched him in his death throw, and a flicker of regret crossed her mind. Not enough to save him from his fate, but enough to tease a tear from her eye. King Dracula had once been a giant in her eyes. He had once been her bright diamond, a jewel of incalculable worth and glory. Now, he was nothing but a burning husk of a man. He was nothing… worthless… he was…

Dolingen did not notice the man sneaking up behind her, until she heard his shoe snap a twig. She turned, and the last thing she saw and felt before dropping to the ground was a sharp wooden stake being driven into her chest and through her back.

Gregor Renfield's fingers felt like worms working their way through the chest. The man screamed and screamed and screamed as he dug through the fire, boiling blood, cooked flesh, and scorched bone to find the magnesium blade and pull it out. He found it, screamed once more, and yanked it free.

Immediately, the fire subsided, the burning stopped. Dracula was weak, so weak, weaker than he had ever felt in his life. Death had been so close. Dolingen had tricked him, surprised him, and he had almost paid for it with his eternal life. But now his strength was returning. He could see clearly again, could focus on the moment. He was alive.

He stood, slowly, carefully, lest he embarrass himself in front of his thrall. Dracula looked down. Gregor Renfield sat on the ground, rocking back and forth like a wounded beast, nursing the burnt stubs of his hands. He was shaking. "I thank you, Gregor," Dracula said, reaching down to pat the man on the head. "You will be rewarded handsomely."

"Thank—thank you, my… my…"

"Shhhh," Dracula said, letting his command fall to a whisper. He turned his head to the wind. "Are those plane engines I hear?" The sound was growing fainter and fainter as he listened.

Gregor nodded. "Yes…yes, my master."

The Night Witches had gotten away. "Gaah!" Dracula stomped. "Someone will die by fire for this. Someone will lose their—"

Then he remembered Dolingen. He looked down again, and there she was, writhing in pain herself, writhing in her death throe with a long bloody stake sticking out of her chest. "And there is another great thing you have done, Gregor. You have brought the head *witch* to her death. Thank you again, though she is still alive. We must end it now."

"My sword," Gregor said. He motioned to his belt with a stump, and there lay a sheathed short sword, its hilt exposed and ready for a hand. "But I can't… I can't…"

Dracula drew the sword. "Then I shall do it for you. It's fitting anyway for me to be the one."

He walked to her, slowly again because the wound in his side, while healing nicely, still caused pain with each step. Dracula walked forward, letting the sword tip hang down and scrape the cobbles.

Her eyes were wide and bloodshot. Her face sallow though still beautiful. It was a shame to end it now, and for a moment, he hesitated. She had once been a wonder in his eyes, a precious jewel that he had cherished above all others. Now she was nothing but a dying shell, a carcass bereft of joy and vitality. What a shame.

Dracula raised the sword. He positioned himself above her throat and angled the blade so that when he swung, only one stroke would suffice. "My apologies, Countess Dolingen, but this is, as they say, the end. But I think I do agree with you on one thing. I have been languishing too long behind this fortress of cold stone and mortar. The world is changing, and I need to change with it. I will strike out, for America perhaps, or Africa. I'll go out there and learn, as you suggest, how the world is changing."

Dracula brought the sword down, and Countess Dolingen was gone.

Excerpt from a letter from the Protector General of the Sway:

Abraham Van Helsing formed the Sway at the dawn of the twentieth century to stop the monsters from encroaching upon humanity. We operate in the shadows yet are a power greater than many governments. This is the key to our power and knowledge.

Often objects of power that are dismissed as legends are unearthed in our modern world, so it is best to always be on the lookout for sources of knowledge about ancient dangers that may once again rear their venomous fangs.

Horsefeathers

A tale of the Night Witches

David Lee Summers

Baba Yaga didn't scare Captain Yekaterina Savitskaya … much. The ancient woman stood beside a projector screen at one end of a Quonset hut. "The mujahideen have been particularly effective taking out regular air force bombers making runs through the Panjshir Valley. That's where you come in, my Night Witches." She wore a Soviet colonel's uniform—a male Soviet colonel's uniform. Savitskaya wondered about the original owner's fate. No doubt Baba Yaga had killed him. Had she eaten him as well?

Legend described Baba Yaga as a hideous crone. Savitskaya disagreed. True, Baba Yaga's nose was a little too long for her face and her hair, now coiled into a bun at the back of her head, was a bit stringy, but the ancient woman possessed an almost aquiline grace. If anything, she reminded Savitskaya of a hungry eagle.

The slide shifted to a map of the Panjshir Valley. Several red points dotted the valley near the town of Rukha. Baba Yaga stabbed her pointer at them. "According to Soviet intelligence—" she sneered at the word

"—these are the locations of the mujahideen strongholds. You will fly out tomorrow, two hours after sunset, bomb your designated targets, and return. Use your telekinetic powers to make sure your bombs actually strike their designated targets. Each pilot and bombardier will find specific coordinates in sealed orders to be delivered at sunset tomorrow. Are there any questions?"

Savitskaya glanced over to her bombardier, Lieutenant Veronika Raskova. The woman gave an almost imperceptible head shake.

When no one raised their hand, Baba Yaga nodded. "Dismissed."

The Night Witches stood and began shuffling out of the Quonset hut. Baba Yaga aimed her pointer at Savitskaya. "Yekaterina Borisova, I would have a word with you."

Raskova gave Savitskaya a consolatory pat on the shoulder, then followed the others out the door. Savitskaya swallowed, then stood at attention. A moment later the door slammed shut with a stark finality.

Baba Yaga waved her hand at Savitskaya. "No need for military formality here. Relax. We're all comrades in the Soviet order."

Savitskaya forced herself to relax while Baba Yaga retrieved a photographic slide from her breast pocket. She took it over to the projector, inserted it into an empty carousel slot, then advanced it until it was next in line to be viewed.

"Soviet intelligence is not altogether useless," said Baba Yaga. "It turns out one bomber survived the most recent assault on the mujahideen." She advanced the slide. It showed a blurry photo of planes and missiles in the air.

It also showed something misshapen at one edge. Savitskaya crept closer to the projector screen. At first, she thought the dark thing must be smoke from an explosion, but it didn't look right. After a moment, she recognized the silhouette. "Is that a horse?"

Baba Yaga's mouth spread into a toothy grin. "Very good, Yekaterina Borisova. I agree. It does resemble a horse."

"But that's impossible! It would have to be a flying horse!" Savitskaya laughed.

Baba Yaga narrowed her gaze. "Impossible? Really? Given the wonders and horrors you've seen flying with the Night Witches?" The ancient witch folded her hands behind her back and took a few steps away, then turned around. "How well do you know the tales of the One Thousand and One Nights?"

"I read a few of them when I was a girl." Savitskaya shrugged.

"Are you familiar with the tale called 'The Enchanted Horse'?"

Savitskaya thought back to the stories. "A wooden horse that could fly. A gift from a Persian wizard to a king as I recall."

"As recently as two centuries ago, most of modern Afghanistan was part of the Persian Empire, wasn't it?"

Savitskaya shrugged, then dared to release a chuckle. "Still, it's just a story … a story that goes back to antiquity."

"And yet, how many such stories have proven to be true?" Baba Yaga aimed her pointer at the horse silhouette. "Here, we see a horse among planes and missiles and bombs. Whether that horse is the 'enchanted horse' of the Arabian Nights or some other technological wonder, I want it. The mujahideen are too good at shooting down Soviet planes and I think that horse may be the key to understanding how they manage it. The Soviets don't know about the horse. This slide was taken from a short film the general staff sent over. I only recognized the silhouette in a half dozen frames and this is the clearest. Nobody knows about this but you and me. Nobody *will* know about this but you and me. Am I understood?"

Savitskaya gave a curt nod.

"All the Soviets want is for the Night Witches to bomb the mujahideen back into the Stone Age and we will do our best to accomplish that, but I think we may fail despite our best efforts. If that happens, I have a special mission for you." Baba Yaga stepped up to Savitskaya. "Monitor the campaign's success. If all goes as it should you need do nothing. Perhaps this image that resembles a horse is nothing but smoke after all, but I think there's more to it than an optical illusion. If our bombs miss their targets, I want you to eject, infiltrate the mujahideen base, and find out what magic they employ."

Savitskaya smirked at the old word for understanding and manipulating the world's invisible forces and energies. The old woman enjoyed the power such understanding gave her. So did Savitskaya. The smirk fell when she caught Baba Yaga's pointed gaze.

"If the enchanted horse is there, and I believe it is, you will bring it back to me."

Savitskaya frowned. "What of my crew? What of Lieutenants Raskova and Budanova? Surely they will be informed of this plan as well? Their assistance would be helpful infiltrating the base."

Baba Yaga's face darkened and her eyes narrowed. "Nobody will know about this but you and me. You said you understood."

Savitskaya swallowed and nodded. "I understand."

"The best way to avert suspicion will be to use your powers to bring a mujahideen missile directly into your craft. It must be destroyed. If the bombing run goes poorly, your ruse may give them false confidence which we can use against them in a second strike, if needed." Baba Yaga's face softened. She stepped up to Savitskaya and put her hand on the captain's shoulder. "All of you are my students and I don't ask for sacrifices lightly. You are my proudest pupil, more like a daughter to me than most. You will not let me down." The last words held a razor-sharp edge.

"I understand and I will succeed." Savitskaya stood at attention and saluted.

Baba Yaga smiled. "Dismissed, Yekaterina Borisova."

Savitskaya left the Quonset hut. She would find a way to warn Raskova and Budanova in the event she must put her plan into action.

After all, Baba Yaga didn't scare her … much.

Magic, like technology, is just applied science.

However it's characterized, Baba Yaga possessed powerful magic. She could eavesdrop on the Night Witches whenever she wanted. In 1982, such eavesdropping didn't even require especially powerful magic. Perfectly understandable technology worked just fine.

Savitskaya needed a way to warn her crew that they may need to bail out at some point during the operation without giving them any hints about the secret mission. She needed to warn them without making Baba Yaga suspicious.

After the briefing, the Night Witches adjourned to a ramshackle hut on an overgrown, out-of-the-way section of Ayni Air Base. The base in Tajikistan served as a launching point for Soviet air strikes into Afghanistan. The Soviet Air Force granted the Night Witches a cluster of older structures well away from the air field's most utilized facilities.

Savitskaya joined her crew in several hands of durak while they split a bottle of vodka. As they played, the captain reiterated the point Baba Yaga made in the briefing about the mujahideen's missiles being better at taking out Soviet bombers than they should.

Lieutenant Lydia Budanova, the tail gunner, narrowed her gaze. "Do you suppose the mujahideen have people with telekinetic powers like ours?"

"If they do, it will be a battle of wills to see whose power is the strongest." The bombardier, Raskova, took a shot of vodka. Tall and thin, the bombardier possessed an ethereal, fae-like quality that extended beyond the physical. Like the fae of legend, she could be a vengeful creature.

"I know we can push away anything they throw at us." Savitskaya didn't have to work hard to betray her lack of confidence.

Budanova winked and smiled. The woman lifted weights and exuded a quiet calm. Her support gave the captain hope she wouldn't need to pursue the secret mission. The card game continued while Raskova and Budanova speculated about how Afghanis might have gained telekinetic abilities. Savitskaya suppressed a grin. Step one had succeeded. She had placed the idea that the mujahideen missiles presented a creditable danger into the forefront of her crew's mind. Games and drinking continued late into the night.

Savitskaya slept in late the next day. The clock struck noon as she joined her crew in the mess hall for a late breakfast. As they ate, the captain rattled off tasks the crew needed to attend to before flight. "Be sure to check your ejection and escape mechanisms." She tossed it in as though it were routine and, aside from a suspicious upward glance from the bombardier, she thought it might be ignored.

In fact, the Night Witches rarely considered ejecting from their craft. They had grown so competent at deflecting fire aimed at them, they had little need. Neither Raskova nor the tail gunner commented on the new check-list item. If they understood the significance, they were wise enough to stay quiet. The captain hoped step two had sunk in.

Just before sunset, Savitskaya donned her flight suit. A high-pitched yap followed by a hiss captured her attention. On her dresser stood a bizarre creature that could best be described as an American Gila monster's disembodied head on a pair of thin chicken legs. Savitskaya called the creature Tina, after her hero, Valentina Tereshkova, the only woman to have traveled into space. As best as she knew, Tina was one of Baba Yaga's first experiments in genetic engineering, perhaps even a prototype for her famous "hut" on chicken legs. The creature yapped and whined.

"Well, if you're coming along, hop aboard," said the captain.

Tina bounced up and down, then leapt from the dresser and climbed up the captain's flight suit to her belt. She grabbed on with clawed feet and pulled herself close. It would be easy to mistake her for a pouch on the captain's belt. The creature listened well and always seemed to understand the words spoken to it.

Savitskaya joined her crew. They strode across the tarmac toward their plane, an Ilyushin IL-28 which first saw service over Hungary two decades earlier. The ground and flight crews each put considerable effort into keeping the planes airworthy. Other IL-28's flew in the Afghan war—the Soviets had given a few to the Afghani communists—but the Night Witches possessed the bombers with the most flight hours.

"If you see a missile heading our way, and it can't be shot down or deflected, eject or bail out," said the captain. "If anyone bails out, we all should."

The bombardier and tail gunner both glanced at her but nodded. Had they reviewed their escape procedures? She hoped so. She couldn't simply order her crew to escape when the time came. Each member of an IL-28's crew sat in a different compartment. In-flight orders had to be transmitted over the intercom. If Savitskaya ordered her crew to bail out, Baba Yaga would know. Her orders as they strode across the tarmac were risky enough.

As they reached the plane, the crew put their hands together. "We will succeed for Baba Yaga and Mother Russia." The three women tightened their grips for a moment, then they separated. The captain climbed up a ladder alongside the craft into the cockpit while the bombardier entered through a hatch near the forward landing gear. Budanova strode to the craft's rear.

Within half an hour, the twenty-year-old Ilyushin IL-28 roared through the air toward Afghanistan held together by bonds of science, technology, and the magic of sisterhood.

The mission went as Baba Yaga predicted. Bombs exploded far off target. Anti-aircraft missiles came far too close for comfort. Savitskaya feared the mujahideen might even down a plane or two.

"Is that a…" Budanova's voice, normally strong and confident trembled over the intercom. "To port…"

The captain looked to her left but saw nothing but moonlight glinting off another IL-28's nose.

"No, to starboard … sorry." Facing aft, a tail gunner could easily confuse right and left. The captain couldn't remember Budanova being that flustered before.

Savitskaya looked to the right and cursed under her breath. Even in the wan moonlight, she could not mistake an airborne horse, matching their speed. Was there a rider on its back? She had the impression of coat tails flapping in the stiff wind. Was the man crazy? What the hell even propelled the horse? She cursed again. Given visual confirmation, she had no choice but to follow through with the mission. She reached out with her mind and felt an anti-aircraft missile. Another mind worked to deflect the missile. Savitskaya shoved that mind away without revealing herself to it and pulled the missile toward their craft.

The tail gunner's voice came over the intercom. "I was pushing a missile away when something shoved me hard…"

"The mujahideen must have figured out what we're up to," lied Savitskaya. She willed Tina to hold on as tight as she could, then reached out and threw the ejection switch. Air roared as the canopy blew clear. A moment later, all the forces on her body shifted as she shot up into the cold night sky and clear of the craft. All too soon, she reached the top of the arc and began to tumble. She lost all track of her position relative to the bomber. An explosion illuminated the landscape below. Was it her craft or did a Night Witch blow up a missile? The parachute burst forth, yanking her upward again.

Heart threatening to burst from her chest, she looked around. She drifted down into the Panjshir Valley. Something vibrated at her belt. She reached down and stroked Tina, comforting the strange beast. A moment later, Savitskaya thought she spotted another parachute. Her breath caught. She looked around, hoping to see a third, but no such luck.

Four minutes later, she hit the ground. Stunned, it took a moment for training to kick in. She unbuckled her harness, grabbed her survival bag, and disappeared into a stand of trees not far from the Panjshir River. She scouted out her surroundings and took her bearings. She thought about their airspeed and how long it had been since they dropped the bombs. It couldn't have been longer than four or five minutes. Still, that could put her as far as forty miles from the target location. She cursed under her breath, then realized she had landed before the river's headwaters. She was less than fifty miles from the base. Finding a vehicle would help.

Just then, a shadow passed in front of the moon. She looked up. A horse circled above and then came to a gentle landing a short distance away. As she had suspected, a man sat astride the horse, leaning forward, like a jockey at speed. His riding posture may have obscured his presence on the grainy, blurred film footage Baba Yaga had shown her. He climbed off. The bearded man wore a traditional round Pokul hat and a long, leather coat. He dropped his goggles to his neck and drew a sidearm as he looked around.

The horse was not a real animal, but rather a beautiful simulacrum carved from ebony wood. Jewels ringed its neck like an elaborate necklace. The automaton pawed the ground as though impatient to return to the sky. The man patted its neck and the mechanical horse settled.

Savitskaya considered what to do next. She could shoot the man from her hiding place, then the horse would be hers. But what then? Could she operate the flying horse? No doubt a mechanism from ancient Persia would not have the same controls as a modern jet aircraft.

She could try to subdue the man, get him to tell her how to ride the horse. The problem was, she didn't know how well he'd cooperate or how well they could communicate. She'd taken Dari language classes but didn't know if her skills sufficed for horse flying lessons. Also, while she could subdue the man with her telekinetic powers, she hesitated to use them, lest he had friends nearby who could turn the tables on her before she mastered the horse.

As she evaluated the situation, he looked around and spotted the abandoned ejection seat and parachute. He grabbed a radio from his belt and spoke into it. The time had come to act.

She reached out with her mind and gave the horse a nudge from behind. Instead of moving, she felt more than heard a "pwang" that set her teeth on edge much like the sound of fingernails on a chalkboard. She took an involuntary step backward.

The man must have noticed the sensation as well because he turned to face the horse.

She pulled herself together and stepped out from behind the tree, aiming her sidearm at the man.

"Put down your weapon and your radio," she said in her best Dari.

He complied, then stood upright and smiled. "I'm surprised, but pleased, to have downed a plane flown by the Soviets' infamous Night Witches." He spoke in perfect, clear Russian.

Savitskaya narrowed her gaze. "You know who we are?"

"It took much work to deflect your weapons. We found it difficult to keep our missiles locked on target." He shrugged. "Allow me to introduce myself, my name is Ahmad Shah Massoud. And you are?"

She ignored the question. "You use your pet to deflect our weapons?" She indicated the ebony horse with her chin, keeping the weapon pointed at the man.

"And keep ours locked on target, yes," explained Massoud.

"How does it work?" Savitskaya lifted the pistol's muzzle to emphasize her point.

"The same way your tech must work." He shrugged. "It generates and manipulates fields. Gravitational, electromagnetic, strong and weak forces."

Savitskaya nodded, allowing Massoud to believe what he would. "I want you to show me how to fly it."

"I think that would be unwise." He spoke slowly and stood his ground. She began to wonder if he could use the horse to deflect bullets or disarm her. Could he control it remotely? As she considered those questions, she caught the sound of an approaching car engine.

"Step away from the horse." She inclined her head toward the trees. "You can show me later. Get under cover."

He shrugged, then took his time walking toward the trees. Just as they entered the shadows, an American Jeep screeched to a halt nearby. Two Afghani men hopped out and looked around the horse. A third man sat in the back. He held a gun to Veronika Raskova's head. She looked as though she wanted to wrench the gun from his hand and feed it to him. No doubt she could do it if the man didn't have help so close at hand.

"Surrender or I'll shoot her," called the Afghani soldier holding the pistol to Raskova's head.

Could Raskova deflect a bullet at such close range? Unlikely. A better strategy would be to jam the firing mechanism. Still, that might cause a misfire and she might get injured.

Savitskaya considered her options. With odds of four to two, she and Raskova might well escape, but that wouldn't win her the enchanted horse. She needed to learn how to operate it. Better to be captured and learn what she could than escape and disappoint Baba Yaga. "I surrender." She threw out her sidearm. She stepped out from the trees. A soldier approached, then reached down to her boot and withdrew a knife. He withdrew another sheathed on her belt. He reached for Tina.

Savitskaya placed her hand on the small creature and shook her head. "Feminine supplies," she said.

The Afghani soldier withdrew his hand faster than if Tina had bitten him. She let the soldiers lead her to the Jeep.

Raskova opened her mouth, as though ready to ask a question. Savitskaya gave her a brief head-shake. They sat in silence as Ahmad Shah Massoud lifted his goggles, climbed on the flying horse, and ascended into the sky.

The soldiers climbed into the Jeep with the women and sped off in the same general direction as Massoud.

It took about ninety minutes of driving too fast over a rough, dirt road to enter the cave complex where the mujahideen made their headquarters. After the long drive through the dark, Savitskaya blinked under the headquarters' blinding lights. A guard contingent, including two women, met the Jeep. Savitskaya noted that although they wore headscarves, they were not veiled. Before the pilot left the Jeep, Tina disengaged from her belt and disappeared under the vehicle's seat. The two women made a much more thorough search of Savitskaya and Raskova than the male guards had, then escorted the pilot and bombardier deeper into the cave complex.

As they walked, Savitskaya glimpsed Tina following behind, keeping close to the shadows like a rat in search of crumbs. The guards led them to a makeshift room—really just a chamber of the cave isolated from other rooms by a wooden wall and door. Outside the door stood a dented and scratched, golden, mechanical man holding a trumpet. Unlike the horse, the mechanical man had seen better days. Although jewels still surrounded its neck, waist, wrists, and ankles, there were numerous empty settings as though the mechanical man had lost some jewels to antiquity or looters. Savitskaya thought she remembered a mechanical sentry from the tale of the enchanted horse.

The "room" held two chairs and two cots. A portable field potty—a glorified bucket with a lid and a rim smooth enough one could squat on it without being too uncomfortable—sat in the corner. A single lightbulb illuminated the room, powered by a cord strung up along the cave ceiling. Before the guards closed and locked the door, Tina scooted into the room and disappeared under a cot.

Raskova dropped into a chair and glared at the captain. "We are here by your hand, aren't we?"

Savitskaya considered how much to say. She decided to remain silent. Let her friend and partner speak her mind.

"Lydia tried to deflect the missile that downed our plane. She said something pushed her mind away. That something was you, wasn't it?" Raskova's voice dropped in pitch, turning dangerous.

"He said the horse manipulated fields," mused Savitskaya. "He must use it to push bombs away from their targets and to lead missiles into planes." Not an answer to Raskova's query, but she hoped it held sufficient truth to deflect the bombardier's verbal strikes.

"Did you know the mujahideen possessed some ability to make their weapons strike home while throwing ours off target? Is that what Baba Yaga spoke to you about after the briefing?"

Savitskaya walked to the door, her back to Raskova. Guilt over Lydia's death weighed on her along with another feeling. A small part of her mind wished she had not warned Raskova so she wouldn't have to face this onslaught. She turned her mind to the immediate problem. "Finding the flying horse is our best means of escape and getting back home."

"That was your mission all along, wasn't it?"

"I warned you," hissed Savitskaya. "In the only way I could, I warned you."

"And yet Lydia died."

Savitskaya slammed her fist through the flimsy wooden wall in a vain attempt to silence her nagging conscience.

"At least now, we can see whether we have guards." Raskova released a bitter chuckle.

Outside, a trumpet blast blared out. Savitskaya peered through the hole. The mechanical man had raised its trumpet to its mouth, sounding an alarm. Footsteps echoed through the cave.

Moments later, the two women who had searched them plus two men entered the makeshift cell with machine guns. Savitskaya and Raskova raised their hands. A moment later, Ahmad Shah Massoud deactivated the mechanical man and entered the chamber. He spoke Dari to the guards. Savitskaya thought the gist of his instructions was, "leave the room but stay nearby."

Massoud turned to Savitskaya and held his hand toward the room's empty chair, inviting her to sit. She lowered her hands and sat down. He settled into a squat, so as not to hover over the two women. "As you know, I've already guessed you both belong to the Soviet's Night Witch squadron. You are imprisoned because I believe you can help me."

"Help you?" Raskova spat the words.

Savitskaya held up her hand. "Why do you think we would help you?"

"The situation in Afghanistan is complicated, but your people are involved because you want to see the communist faction in control. I won't try to persuade you your goal is wrong, but I also don't believe it can succeed. If it fails, religious extremists gain more control here. They might even be able to take over the country."

"Some would call the mujahideen religious extremists." Savitskaya folded her arms.

Raskova's brow furrowed. "What about the Americans? Couldn't they help you?"

"The Americans do give us some equipment, but they are afraid to get too involved. They don't want to set off a full-scale war with Russia." Massoud sighed and for a moment looked quite old and haggard. A moment later, a smile brightened his craggy features. "First and foremost, I am an engineer."

Savitskaya snorted. Engineer was just another word for wizard.

Massoud continued. "Friends who are archeologists found and brought me the horse and the mechanical man. I was able to make them work again. The technology is incredible. I'm not even sure it originated on Earth. The thing is, I suspect there are other such wonders buried in Afghanistan's mountains and valleys. If the extremists take over, those wonders could be lost forever."

Raskova turned pensive. "These extremists are the same ones who dominate women."

Massoud nodded. "Yes. They believe Islam teaches them women should be subject to men's authority."

"Communist rule would impose equality." Savitskaya folded her arms. "Only the Soviets have put a woman into space ... our valiant comrade Valentina Tereshkova. I became a pilot because I admired her."

"You know that Nikita Khrushchev chose her not because of her skill as a pilot, but because he found her pretty," countered Massoud. "Democratic rule would allow men and women to control their own fates."

"What do you want us to do?" Raskova leaned forward.

Massoud shrugged. "Share with me the technology you use to manipulate bombs and missiles. Work with me to make sure I have unlocked all the powers of the mechanical horse and man. Help me locate other such wonders for Afghanistan."

Savitskaya narrowed her gaze. "What would we get in exchange for this?"

Massoud stood. "Your freedom … from Communist control … from the witch known as Baba Yaga." He backed toward the door. "Think about it. I would like an answer by tomorrow afternoon."

"And if we answer in the negative?" asked Savitskaya.

Massoud shook his head. "I can't afford to hold prisoners."

The guards had taken Savitskaya's watch. She guessed it was somewhere between three and four in the morning. Savitskaya peered through the hole she made in the wall but could not see any guards. All she heard were Raskova's soft snores from the bunk.

Savitskaya summoned Tina and whispered a plan to the little beast. Tina hopped up and down, then yipped a guttural bark. The pilot hushed the little beast, then walked over to Raskova. She woke the bombardier and held her finger to her lips. "If we're going to escape, now is the time."

Raskova sat up and rubbed her eyes. "Must we?"

"Don't tell me you think we should stay."

"I doubt we can escape from the heart of a mujahideen compound." Raskova shrugged. "And I don't think Masoud is wrong. I think extremists could be the ones who benefit most from the current conflict. Perhaps we could do more to keep that from happening if we remained here than if we returned to the squadron."

Savitskaya sensed her old friend's care in choosing her words. "You're trying to convince yourself to stay. You don't want to return."

Raskova's eyes locked on Savitskaya's. "Baba Yaga ordered you to let me and Lydia die. Why would this make me eager to return?"

Savitskaya sat down on the cot next to the bombardier. "Nika, I found a way to warn you and you listened."

"And what about Lydia?" Raskova's eyes shone with unshed tears.

"I warned her, too, the only way I could. She had the same chance as you, but it's much more difficult to escape the tail section. She had to kick out the window and dive straight out. Maybe she did but was too late." Savitskaya's voice caught. She reached out and grabbed Raskova's shoulder, in part to steady herself. "I wanted to save you both. I succeeded in saving you. I want to save you again."

Raskova sniffed, then wiped her nose on her sleeve. She looked up and met Savitskaya's eyes. "What do you mean?"

"If we stay, Baba Yaga will find out and she'll be back." Savitskaya sighed. "Let's see this mission through. Baba Yaga is more likely to forgive us if we bring her what she wants."

Raskova considered the pilot's words for a time. At last, she gave a curt nod. "All right, what do we do?"

Savitskaya summoned Tina, then pointed to the hole. The creature scrambled up the wall, through the hole, and disappeared. The pilot looked from the bombardier to the door. "Open the lock and be quick."

Raskova put her hands to her head and concentrated. Savitskaya stood. As soon as the lock's tumbler's clicked, the pilot pushed through the door. The mechanical man raised the horn to his mouth, but Tina blocked the way, looking as though the little monster gave the automaton an obscene kiss.

Savitskaya darted around to the automaton's back. She felt around the surface and pushed the jewels and the mounting surfaces. At last, a hatchway opened. The pilot reached down and grabbed a rock from the ground and smashed the internal gears and clockworks. She hated to destroy such delicate and ancient magic. At last, the mechanical man fell limp and Tina jumped down from her perch.

When one of the women guards crept down the corridor to investigate the banging and crashing, Raskova leapt from the shadows and knocked her cold before she could raise an alarm. Savitskaya took her pistol then handed the rifle to Raskova. They locked her in the cell, then continued up the corridor. Few guards patrolled the caves in the predawn hours. The cave's shadows proved sufficient cover to elude the sleepy guards who weren't expecting trouble from within.

The two reached a junction in the cave. One path led to the main entrance where they were brought in. Raskova started to move toward the entrance, but Savitskaya waved her back. "There are Jeeps and trucks that way," said the bombardier.

"There are also many more guards and sentries that way," countered the pilot. "This way also leads to the surface. Let's see what we find."

They ascended through a less developed part of the cave. Few lightbulbs illuminated a crate-lined path. Savitskaya began to have misgivings. Maybe this was just a storage area.

At last, the path opened up onto a bigger chamber. Beyond that, the pilot saw a brightening, twilight sky. In the chamber, stood the enchanted horse, polished and beautiful, along with two guards.

Savitskaya sent Tina into the chamber. She ran in and climbed the guard's leg. Panicked, he tried to shake off the strange creature. The other guard put down his rifle and tried to help. The pilot and bombardier ran in, grabbed the distracted guards, knocked them cold, then drug them to the corner and bound their wrists and ankles.

Raskova walked over to the opening. "We have a problem."

Savitskaya joined her. They were hundreds of feet up a cliff face. The only way they could escape was on the horse. The pilot looked down at Tina who appeared self-satisfied. The creature jumped up and down, then ran to the chamber's entrance to keep watch. Savitskaya then approached the horse with care, remembering when she'd tried to push it with her telekinetic ability.

The horse didn't seem to react to a physical presence the same way it reacted to a psychic one. Massoud had explained the horse manipulated fields of all kinds. Telekinesis was a little like projecting a field around an object you wanted to move. Maybe her abilities and the horse's propulsion systems operated on a similar frequency.

She clambered into the horse's saddle and examined the controls between its shoulder blades. They proved much simpler than she feared, but she shouldn't have been surprised. If the story from the Thousand and One Nights was accurate, the horse had been a gift for a king, and his son learned to fly it by trial and error. Savitskaya had little Dari, but even she could make out a few of the related Persian words. A recessed panel between the knobs suggested more controls within. She tried to find a way to open it.

Tina squealed and yipped. Someone approached.

The pilot abandoned her exploration and called out to the

bombardier. "Let's go." Tina ran from the doorway, jumped onto the enchanted horse, and took her place on Savitskaya's belt.

"I'm not going." Raskova shook her head. "Baba Yaga ordered you to let me die. I'm done with the Night Witches."

Ahmed Shah Massoud ran into the chamber and took in the scene. He looked from Savitskaya to Raskova. "What's going on here?"

Without answering, Savitskaya turned the knob that caused the horse to levitate.

Massoud sprang toward her, but Raskova grabbed him around the waist and tackled him.

Savitskaya reached toward her sidearm but grabbed Tina instead. She plucked the creature from her belt. "Stay here. Help Nika."

Tina growled a protest.

"Go. Now." She flung her hand upwards and the little creature jumped and landed on the ground.

"You can't do this!" Massoud threw Raskova off, then drew his own sidearm and aimed. Tina leapt on his face and dug her claws into his beard, yanking hard. He dropped the pistol and Raskova kicked it away.

"Please, Katya," called Raskova. "Don't take the horse to Baba Yaga. She only wants it for the powers she'll gain. She doesn't care about you or the Night Witches or anyone else."

Savitskaya turned so Raskova wouldn't see her tears.

Baba Yaga didn't scare Yekaterina Borisova Savitskaya, but the pilot had a duty. She had promised to return the horse to Baba Yaga and she would see the mission through. It broke her heart to leave Tina behind, but she also had a duty to her sister Night Witch. If Tina returned with her, she had no doubt the creature would report what Raskova had done to Baba Yaga. If losing Tina saved Veronika Raskova and gave her a fighting chance to stay alive in the mujahideen stronghold, so be it. If Raskova could find a way to help keep extremists from taking hold in Afghanistan, even better.

She reached down, and patted her newfound steed's neck, and gave a bitter smile as she remembered an old American idiom. "Horsefeathers" captured her feelings about duty as she steered the flying machine toward Tajikistan so she could deliver it to Baba Yaga.

Message received: Remember The Office of the Aberrant and the President must have full deniability in this matter.

Dangerous Waters

Lee O'Connell

The overhead sky was a deep gray. Lightning flashed across it with booming thunder heralding each strike. A waterspout formed just to the south of the island and made its way east, sucking up fish as it passed. The young woman dove deeper and angled away, awaiting its inevitable dissipation.

Bahia hated this cold land and could not wait to return south to more reasonable weather; reasonable being blue skies and warm sun. Her name in Portuguese meant Bay, the place where she was born. Her hair was long and blond, her sky-blue eyes large and luminous. Her perfect button nose flared when she was angry, which was often. Her mouth was a tight slash across her face, except for the rare occasions it opened into a full-lipped generous smile. That was when those around her should be scared. It was never good when Bahia smiled.

Born off the coast of Portugal, her mother had struggled to tame Bahia. She was temperamental, independent, and strong-willed, which made for a challenging childhood and an amazing adult. When she thought she was right, there was no swaying her; she was exactly like her mother. This was both good and bad. Bad, because it meant they clashed constantly from the time Bahia was born. Good, because she would follow in her mother's footsteps, assisting the OTA with secret operations and be really, really good at it.

The Office of the Aberrant, using the US military as cover, had expressly requested her particular assets for this mission. She had everything necessary to complete it successfully: strength of character, independent thinking, and those specific attributes that ran in her family.

Bahia had instantly recognized the opportunity when she was recruited for the OTA and was one of their best assets in any ocean. Not willing to work for a salary, the bargaining had been difficult for the men assigned to work out her agreement. They found it particularly aggravating to be dealing with a woman who thought she knew better than they did on how things worked on the high seas. It was a blow to their egos, which were accustomed to holding all the power of the secret US intelligence agency and receiving unquestioned respect. Bahia didn't think much of their tactics and definitely wasn't putting her life on the line unless each operation was run her way. Period.

For this mission, her handler was named Johnson. It was always a challenge when her handler was a man. Growing up, her mother had limited her contact with the opposite sex. Johnson was charismatic and handsome, tall with chiseled features, dark hair and, she thought, dark eyes, though he refused to look at her directly, so she wasn't sure. She hated that. It went against her nature to not look a man in the eye. Johnson patently refused. On top of that, he wore earplugs, the kind you can still hear through, just muted. Now that really aggravated her. They managed to hammer out the details of the mission and she was off.

Bahia leapt up onto the rocks, landing on a particularly hard and abrasive outcropping with a groan. She hoped she wouldn't have to wait too long. Her long hair whipped around her face as she looked left and right, waiting impatiently for a particular Russian research vessel in the dismal, cold, gray sea. Having done her research, she knew the USSR research vessel *Akademik Tryoshnikov* would be passing close to where she was perched. Not too close, as the coast here was riddled with rocks, too shallow for the large vessel to get near, but not too far away to miss seeing her. The scientists on board had spent the spring studying the effects of ice on the vessel. Collected data would be important for the ongoing planning of Russia's projected new Arctic research platform, unimaginatively named *Severnyy Polyus*, Russian for North Pole. The installation would be able to drift through the Arctic for years at a time. She scanned the horizon again, watching the waterspout dissipate in the distance.

Aleksandr Ivanovs set his binoculars down and sipped his coffee. He thought about his wife at home, *his* Tatiana. And the baby. He couldn't forget that unfortunate accident. He hoped she would have her shape back by the time he returned. He had not bargained on a baby complicating his life. And ruining his wife's perfect hourglass shape. He harrumphed to himself at the thought.

"Ivanovs!"

"Sir." Aleksandr turned around quickly putting his coffee down and sloshing it slightly over his hand. He ignored the burn and saluted smartly as he smoothly stood up.

"Anything?"

"No, sir. Nothing moving but a polar bear and her cub."

"Beautiful. I love polar bears, don't you? So powerful and deadly, but with a certain grace."

"Yes, sir." He didn't like this particular captain, showing up at odd times, like he didn't trust his subordinates to do their job. The captain would pop in unexpectedly and pretend to be friendly. But Aleksandr knew better. He never let his guard down with this one.

"Get on with it then." The captain turned and left.

Aleksandr sucked in a big breath and let it out, his body relaxing again. He thought about his remaining time in the military and what he would do afterward. He had only a month left in his military obligation. They were trying to convince him to stay, to reenlist and serve his country for another term.

Ha. Not a chance. The bureaucrats were such bumbling idiots. Just because he was a scientist, did not mean he would do just *any* research. His true work had nothing to do with stupid ice floes or the effect subzero temperatures had on different microbes. It was so much more important. But they thought, *oh, he's a scientist, we'll assign him to the research vessel, all research is the same, obviously.* They were such imbeciles. The only redeeming value of his stupid assignment was that it was less taxing than whatever else they might have had him doing for the last three years.

With his photographic memory and the few supplies he had brought with him, he continued with his own research in his spare time, what little of it there was. It was challenging on a constantly bobbing ship, but nonetheless, he managed some small successes. He was getting so close. When he got back to his impeccably clean and unmoving lab, he would be able to finish up his doctoral thesis, turn in his research, and bask in the glory that would be his. He would go down in history for this one discovery. The perfect germ warfare weapon. And he, Aleksandr Ivanovs, would be rich, would be respected, would have anything he wanted handed to him by the Kremlin. He sighed, contented, and took another sip of his coffee.

He thought of Dimitri, his previous research partner. It had been unlucky that he had poured the warfare sample into his own vodka glass. Well, that is what happens when you drink in a lab. So unfortunate. Aleksandr chuckled to himself, thinking of how inconsolable Dimitri's wife had been. But that had been all right. He had enjoyed consoling Tatiana. Why she had ever chosen that fool he could never figure out. Well, brains were not what he admired in her, no not her brains at all. And now Tatiana was his, at least until he tired of her.

Aleksandr picked up his binoculars, took a last sip of the now cold coffee, and got back to work. Everyone had to do double duty on the research vessel. The scientist was filling in for the navigational watchman, who had come down with a stomach flu, or so the medic thought. The watchman was not long for this world though, Aleksandr knew. He wasn't a medic, but he *was* a germ warfare researcher and he had needed to develop and test something he was actually interested in. The watchman who had reprimanded him and insulted him seemed a perfect specimen—besides, there were no mice handy. So, Aleksandr had brought him a coffee as reparation, just as he had given Dimitri his final vodka. Ha. He had laughed all the way back to his bunk.

Now he, a respected researcher, had to fill in for the dolt. That was okay though, he could think up here while he did the idiot's mindless job. Aleksandr looked for whatever didn't show up on radar, moving his binoculars left to right marking off each section of the grid in his mind as he completed it.

Bahia sat on the rocks jutting out into the sea watching polar bears ambling by, a mother and her cub. The mother bear walked languidly, fearing nothing, queen of the arctic. The cub was bounding and nipping at her muzzle. She opened her mouth in a wide yawn and the sun, which had just peeked out from the gray sky, glinted off her razor-sharp teeth. The storm was moving off and Bahia relished the momentary sun warming her arms.

When she had met with Johnson, they had devised a way of communicating while he was undercover on the Soviet ship and she was on the shore. He had a powerful, yet tiny laser that he would signal her with if the target was on the ship and coming toward her. It was Johnson's job to make that happen.

She never knew why a particular target was selected, only that it was. She waited for the bears to move on, keeping her gaze firmly on the approaching ship. When the bears had gone far enough for the mother to not be a bother to her, she relaxed her vigilance. The ship was just close enough now. She kept watch, waiting for the speck of light that would tell her it was a go. She rubbed her arms to get a little more blood running through them. This weather was ghastly and she couldn't imagine living here.

There was the signal, the brief red flash.

It was showtime. Bahia started waving, sure they would see her, as she was sure they wouldn't have missed the majestic bear and her cub. She waved franticly, trying to look as scared and desperate as a woman alone out on these deadly waters should look.

Aleksandr continued his rhythmic checking of the area surrounding the ship, marking off each quadrant as he scanned the horizon. He turned back to where he had seen the bear, hoping to get another glimpse of it; what a story to tell. The bear had moved on, as he had supposed it would, but he saw something moving on that little spit of land sticking out into the water. Refocusing his binoculars, he gaped. A woman? Was that a woman? The scientist in him wanted to confirm his findings before sounding the alarm. His eyes hurt he was concentrating so intently, trying to confirm what his brain said he was seeing. She seemed to be alone out there. Quickly he scanned the rest of the horizon for another boat. He radioed the radar operator if he had anything on his screen. He didn't. Where had she come from? She wasn't there when the bear went by, he was sure of that. She seemed to be half in and half out of the water. What happened? Had there been a boating accident? With no answers, finally, he sounded the alarm.

The ship's captain answered. "What is it?"

"Sir." His voice quivered slightly. He had never had anything of significance to report before. "There's a woman, starboard side."

"Dead or alive?"

"Oh, alive sir, very much alive."

"I'll be right up. Meet me on the bridge."

Once he arrived, the helmsman came over and asked where. Aleksandr pointed and handed over his binoculars.

The helmsman chuckled "She looks cold and half dead, I'd say we better send out a lifeboat. She'll need warming up and I'll volunteer. Skin to skin's the best way you know."

"This is serious!" Aleksandr sputtered, "How can you joke?" but he knew, this guy could always joke.

Aleksandr kept scanning the horizon, there *must* be a boat out there. She couldn't survive in this weather for very long, even with it being summer here. She was lucky on that count.

The captain burst onto the bridge. "Where?"

Aleksandr handed him the binoculars and pointed. The captain stared for a full minute before barking, "Send a lifeboat. Now. Goncharov, who's up?"

Johnson, code name Goncharov, immediately stepped forward. "Ivanovs and Petrov, Sir."

"Good." Growled the captain. He turned to Aleksandr, "Get to it and see what happened. Keep your eyes open." He put the binoculars back to his eyes with a worried look on his face, scanning the seas to the left and right of the woman. His ship was a research vessel and held nothing of strategic importance, but the captain didn't trust this. There was no reason for anyone to be out there.

Bahia kept up her frantic waving, pretending to cry, wiping at her eyes every once in a while. She made sure her face looked as scared and exhausted as she should be. Intermittently, she let herself slip precariously down towards the water, grabbing onto the rocks and pulling herself back up, chest heaving with exertion. She yelled help, knowing that even though they couldn't hear her they could read her lips, and a truly stranded woman would not be thinking about whether they could hear or not. She would be screaming her heart out, so that's what Bahia did. It was her best performance yet, she thought and then, there, a second tiny pinpoint of red light coming from the stern of the ship. Her target was coming.

Bahia watched as they lowered a lifeboat and it started toward her. She slipped into the dark water, but still held on to the rocks, she hoped it looked like for dear life. As the boat came closer, Bahia slipped under the water, wanting to lure the target into the water. She swam around in the shadowy depths, counting off ninety seconds. When no one jumped in to save her, she resurfaced, grabbing onto the rocks again. Coughing up water, weakly she cried out, "Help me."

Ivanovs shouted in Russian, "Are you okay?"

"Oh, thank goodness!" she replied in Russian. Though, she wasn't worried about him understanding her. He just needed to hear her voice.

"How did you get here?" Aleksandr asked. He reached into the bottom of the boat and came up with a life preserver—a ring buoy. He threw it and it landed not too far from her.

Bahia looked scared, "I can't reach it," she yelled, her one arm that was not hanging on to the rocks, splashing out for it. She let herself get banged against the rocks by the constant push and pull of the waves, not too much, but enough to look realistic. Bahia didn't want to let go of the rocks yet and so she stretched out her arm as far as she could, panic suffusing her face.

The buoy was slowly bobbing its way in her general direction, the waves and the current pushing it along. If it didn't bypass that little jut of land, she should be able to reach it soon without letting go of the rocks.

They were quite some distance apart because of the rocky shoreline. The boat couldn't approach too closely or the current would slam it against the rocks and then her mission would be done with no effort on her part.

Bahia decided she better get the preserver which was starting to veer around the rocks. It would allow her to get a bit closer to the boat so they could hear her better. She let go of the rocks, allowing herself to slip under the water, but quickly resurfacing, sputtering and crying. She paddled weakly toward the buoy, holding herself back from using her true strength. Bahia was lucky to have such strong arms in this current but still did her best to look as if she were in imminent danger of drowning any minute. Though in point of fact, she could have been in their boat, sitting on their laps with little effort. Finally, she nabbed the preserver, just as it was about to bypass her.

Bahia was glad of the preserver, it allowed her to get her voice in range. It was important that he could hear her clearly. She started swimming weakly as she asked, "Who are you?"

Aleksandr stated with authority, "Aleksandr Ivanovs, research scientist with the vessel, *Akademik Tryoshnikov.*" Bahia was excited to hear confirmation that it was indeed her target. Johnson had come through. "And who are you? And how did you come to be here?" His curiosity was overwhelming him, even as he felt some little niggling in his gut that all was not as it should be.

Ivanovs noted the proximity of the rocky shore and the slight drift of the boat in the direction of the woman. "Petrov! Watch out!" He yelled at the sailor manning the boat. "Hold back, she's coming toward us, you don't want to run her over for god's sake."

Aleksandr was leaning over the gunnel. "What's your name?" he shouted, cupping his hands around his mouth.

Johnson had insisted he choose Bahia's code name. It was the only point she relented on. "It should be the most beautiful seductress of all time. Perfect."

She hesitated only a second, before answering, "Helen. My name's Helen."

When she said her name, he reacted viscerally, as if Cupid had shot an arrow into his cold, dark heart. Confused, he shouted, "But where is your ship?" He had been trying to keep an eye out for a boat. He knew occasionally there were pirates, even here in these frigid waters, who would lure you away from your ship then suddenly there would be a swarm of able-bodied men who would overtake you. They would get a ransom from the captain to give you back alive.

Bahia, her eyes filled with sadness, said, "It sunk so fast, there was an engine problem. I think we hit the rocks and it just started going down. It all happened so quickly. I don't know how I made it out alive." Her voice caught, she was breathing hard, "I… I haven't seen anyone else." She sobbed, knowing the salt water on her face would disguise the lack of real tears.

"Can you kick your feet?" The woman's long hair was tangling across her face from the waves and the current, and as she swiped it off her face, she nodded. "You need to get closer so I can get you in the boat. You must be freezing." Aleksandr wasn't sure how she was still alive. It was a balmy fifteen degrees Celsius but he knew the water temperature must be near four degrees Celsius. Hypothermia was a real concern. "How long since your vessel went down?"

"I don't know, not very long. After we hit the rocks it was so quick, I don't think anybody else escaped. I had just gone on deck for some air and when we hit, it threw me off into the water." Bahia pushed her hair out of her face again and shuttered, her eyes seeking his, though he was too far away for it to have any impact.

She made sure she didn't get too close to the boat yet. He wasn't quite ready, so she kept herself moving slowly away from the dingy, while at the same time, using one arm, the one not holding on to the preserver, to weakly paddle toward him. In effect, she was not moving at all, but she counted on the waves and movement of the boat to hide that fact.

Thinking he might be ready to commit to truly saving her, she sobbed and sunk below the surface, her hand sliding down the preserver, grabbing at it feebly. Underwater, she smiled, a brutal, enchanting smile and then, composing her face into a half-drowned, slack-jawed look. She pulled herself back up when it appeared her target wasn't yet ready to dive in and save her.

Petrov was yelling at Aleksandr as she resurfaced, "You idiot, you're going to capsize us and we'll all die out here!" The man was fighting to keep the boat stable while Aleksandr was leaning far over the side, his head wildly looking left and right as he scanned the water for her.

"Helen! Helen!" Aleksandr screamed as the dingy tilted precariously in the waves.

"There!" he yelled when he saw her. He slumped back into the center of the boat. It righted itself as his weight settled over the keel line. "I thought I lost you."

Good, Bahia thought. *It's getting more personal. He wants to save me. I can work with that.* She smiled inwardly. Time to up her game.

"I'm so c-c-cold." She stuttered as she inched closer to the boat. Her voice, soft and melodious, took on a dreamy quality. She looked wildly around, "Where is my boat? Where is my Bobby?" She knew that one of the signs of hypothermia was disorientation and it had been long enough for her to start losing it. "What happened?" She slurred this last but projected her voice to be sure it arrived in his ear, undeterred.

The Russian scientist felt a warm tingle all over his body. His heart rate accelerated and he started to sweat under his jacket. "Bobby? Who is Bobby?" Aleksandr yelled. "Did he survive with you? Did you see him after your boat went down?"

"My love, my sweet love. Where's my Bobby?" she gasped, a forlorn look on her face as she kept looking around, shivering violently as she slowly made her way closer to the pitching lifeboat.

Bahia checked the research vessel as she looked for her lost "Bobby." It was still keeping a safe distance away and hadn't sent out a second boat yet. Still, she needed to work faster before the captain decided to send more men to save her. These two were helpful, but still had guns with them. One wrong move on her part and she could be shot.

Bahia was trying to balance staying just far enough away that they couldn't reach her while being close enough to be heard. Even better if she could look into his eyes, but it wasn't quite time for that yet. She let her arms pretend to slip farther off the preserver, as if she were losing her strength. the agent screamed as Bahia gulped in saltwater and forcefully coughed it up. She glanced at the sky, ascertaining the changing weather. To the men, it looked like she was praying.

Petrov was having a hard time with the lifeboat. The currents here were strong and wanted to fling his small boat onto the rocks and be done with him. Petrov backed the boat away from the rocks to make sure they didn't land in the drink as well. It would be just like this captain to feel they deserved the consequences of their incompetence and leave them here, drowning woman or not. He fought for control of the vessel, complicated by Ivanov yelling at him. "Petrov, watch the rocks!"

"I am, you idiot! What do you think I'm doing?" Petrov did not take kindly to being accused of incompetence, especially by the likes of this scientist, as if *he* were a real sailor.

"Well, don't hit the woman either, asshole!" Ivanovs yelled back. The waves were getting higher and storm clouds had come in while they had their attention on saving the woman. Whitecaps splashed her face, causing her to cough and cry out. Aleksandr wasn't sure how much strength she had left in her.

Aleksandr knew that protocol said he needed to keep himself safe first and then try to help her. But he was wondering if she could make it. She seemed to be losing ground fast. The waves and the currents were pushing her back towards the rocks. He was terrified she would be bashed upon them and it would be his fault and Petrov's, for not getting to her in time.

"You want to switch places? You think you can do better at handling this boat?" Petrov's face was beet red, which indicated the degree of his anger and stress. He always got red in the face when he got mad. Aleksandr thought his blood pressure must be sky-high.

Petrov was a moron. Aleksandr had never bonded with him and had been disappointed when the duty officer had ordered Petrov to man the lifeboat. He had been hoping for Andreyev. The two of them worked like greased wheels together. They rarely had to say anything, each seemed to know what the other needed without a word. But here he was with this fool.

Bahia let one arm slip back out of the buoy she was hanging onto. While the two argued, she let herself slip precariously down, nearly letting go of the buoy with both hands. She managed to get one arm back through the ring, and then ineffectually slapped at the water, as if she didn't have the strength or know how to swim to the lifeboat.

She sobbed, "I can't make it… I'm so c-c-cold." The waves were getting higher, making it hard for the lifeboat to maintain any type of heading. Bahia stayed just close enough to the rocks that it couldn't get to her. Fog was rolling in and if she'd been able, she would have smiled at this new development. It was so very helpful to her plan.

"I'm going in." Aleksandr had made up his mind.

"What? Are you crazy?" Petrov screamed at him. "You'll both die."

"She doesn't have long. I can get to her and be back in the boat in no time. And I'll have the life jacket on-it will keep me warm enough for what I have to do." He spoke confidently, but there was a nagging thought he couldn't quite grasp, a feeling of something wrong.

"Do you know the temperature of this water? This woman's not worth your life!"

"How do you know that?" Aleksandr asked, not shouting now, but speaking with determination. Now that he'd made up his mind, he felt preternaturally calm, even as the boat was being tossed about, the wind was picking up, and the woman, Helen, was going down fast. When he decided on a course, there was no stopping him. And he had to save this beautiful woman, he wasn't sure why, but he was feeling a magnetic pull toward her. He couldn't help himself, he *had* to go to her. Every time he heard her cry out, it uncharacteristically pulled on a heart he didn't know could feel so strongly for another person.

"That is someone's lover. Someone's daughter. Someone's sister. She's a person. I have to get to her."

"You can't, you idiot!" Petrov's face looked ready to explode. His eyes wide, all of the blood in his body seeming to congregate in his face, while his mouth, usually laughing slyly, was in a rictus of fear. "I'm calling the ship. Let's see what they say."

As usual, Petrov was afraid to act on his own. *He couldn't take a shit without orders to do so,* thought Aleksandr.

Petrov picked up the radio and started shouting into it, trying to hold onto the rudder and keep his tiny dingy off the rocks while he explained the situation to the captain.

Aleksandr tightened his life jacket. He grabbed a second one, hoping he could get it onto Helen while in the water. The weather was turning and he could see he didn't have much time left, another storm was coming in. The jacket would preserve some of her body heat until he could get her out of the water and her wet clothes. He heard her call out again, louder. It was almost melodious, that call for help, and it bewildered him.

His mind felt muddled, almost as if he'd been smoking pot, or taking a depressant. He shook his head trying to clear it. He couldn't eradicate the picture of Helen from his brain. "Damn!" He slumped over the gunnel, feeling a slow heavy lethargy come over him. Visions of Helen flipped through his mind like a slide show, compelling him, against his better sense, to go to her.

"I'm going over, don't run me over," he said to Petrov. He needed to be in the water before Petrov could tell him the captain had denied the request he never made to go in the water to save Helen. He wasn't waiting.

As he turned to sit on the gunnel ready to fall backward into the water, Petrov grabbed his jacket front.

"Don't be an idiot. You cannot. Go. In. The. Water." Petrov shouted into his face, shaking him as he enunciated each word.

A large wave crashed over the bow of the lifeboat, striking the scientist in the face. Aleksandr shook himself and seemed to come out of a dream state. Or a nightmare, he wasn't sure which. He felt himself again though and searched the water, looking for Helen, half afraid and half hoping she had lost the battle for her life.

Petrov had stepped back to the rudder when it seemed Ivanovs was thinking clearly again. He picked up the dropped radio and resumed yelling into it. Aleksandr looked over his shoulder at him and said, "Thanks. You're right." He almost meant it.

He turned back to the water and found Helen. She looked terrible. He had to find a way to get her to come to him. Aleksandr needed her to come to him. He needed her.

"Petrov, can you bring the boat a little closer to her?"

"I'll try. The captain says do not, under any circumstances, go into the water."

"Got it." His mind was racing. They had to get close enough for him to scoop her up. If Petrov could only take the boat closer, he knew he could get her before they crashed on the rocks then Petrov could get them out of there. It would be close, but he thought it could be done. They would have to time it perfectly. He really needed his friend Andreyev—they could do this for sure. But could he and Petrov?

Aleksandr saw her, finally, closer to the boat and farther away from the rocks. It just might work. He had to get her.

Quietly, almost a whisper in his mind, he heard her sob, "Help me. Please."

The scientist felt her plea in his gut and that strange feeling had returned. She was so much closer, if he went in now, he could have her out in moments. Then he heard her again, "Here, I'm here." He turned around a full turn before he finally spied her, just fifty feet or so away. He could hear Petrov cursing in the boat. He fought the waves to reach her. They were getting higher and he knew their little dingy couldn't stay out in this if it got much worse.

As the boat got nearly within touching distance, her hands slipped off the buoy again, and as she slowly sunk below the surface, her hands clawed ineffectually at the water. Aleksandr screamed, "No!" He looked wildly around for her but couldn't find her anywhere. Minutes went by. He continued scanning the water, looking for any indication she might still be alive. The analytical part of his brain knew she couldn't survive submerged for this long. He's lost her and he can feel his heart breaking. The longing in his soul is going to kill him he thinks as he leans out over the gunnel, still looking for any sign of her. He knows, if he sees her now, he will have to go in and damn the rules.

Aleksandr feels a tug on his arm and turns his head to see Petrov pulling his arm to get him back into the center of the boat. "She's gone. Let's go back."

Suddenly, Petrov's arm was nearly ripped out of its socket and Ivanovs was gone. Just gone. Petrov frantically looked around thinking, *What the hell just happened? Where is Ivanovs?* Holding his arm close to his body, he groaned with the pain as he looked for any trace of his mate in the water.

Bahia had gotten a swimming start, much like a dolphin at an aquarium show, and shot out of the water right in front of Aleksandr. He had been looking back at Petrov, who was looking at him, so neither of them saw exactly what happened. Aleksandr would soon know though, and Petrov would forever wonder.

She took Aleksandr down deep enough that she could let go of the scientist's body, she wanted to, at last, look into those eyes. Bahia watched as his descent slowed when she stopped pulling him. Aleksandr started flailing his arms and kicking his feet in an attempt to get back to the surface. He didn't understand and was still trying to grab Bahia and save her. She laughed exultantly at his stupidity.

Aleksander looked desperately around in the murky water trying to figure out what just occurred. As he tried to get hold of Helen and get back up to the surface, he caught sight of a huge tail, at least four feet long. His heart pounding, his mind in turmoil, scale by slippery scale, the whole of Helen came into view. The repulsion he felt overcame his inertia. He slapped at her, ineffectually, the water slowing each blow down to a slow-motion dance.

Bahia grabbed his head in a vise-like grip as he came even with her. Aleksandr was a scientist. He sat in a lab all day whereas she lived deep in the water, moving, always moving. She was so much stronger than he was. He swatted at her, like a toddler, trying in vain to get away; his horror sapping what little strength he might have had. No more the weak and drowning woman, Bahia pulled his head close to hers, forehead to forehead, eye to eye. Aleksandr gazed into those astonishingly blue eyes and felt a liquid warmth filling his body, a weakness of spirit overcoming him as if his innards had just dissolved into mush.

And then he was sinking. Into her eyes, into her soul, down to her home under the sea.

As his last breath left him, he was content. *Helen…*

And Bahia smiled.

MI-7 mission briefing:

Griffin's serum has been one of the closely most closely guarded assets of MI-7, despite the shallowness of the candidate pool on which it will work on and not drive mad or kill.

Unfortunately, several samples have been lost to us over the decades.

Your mission is to monitor the beneficiary of one of the missing serums in Hong Kong, with the hope that one day she can be turned into an asset.

Observe but do not interfere. This will maintain plausible deniability with both Hong Kong and the Chinese government. And provide us with an early warning should she decide to retaliate against Great Britain.

Unseen Secrets

A Tale of The Invisible Madame

Rowan Dillon

With practiced precision, Grayce Li brushed the white cake makeup on her face. The sponge applicator felt smooth against her cheek, soothing her jangled nerves. Her meeting may be crucial, and she must remain calm throughout. Stylized geisha-style paint hid many sins, and wouldn't attract too much attention on the multicultural streets of Hong Kong, even in 1997. Even when she wore a form-fitting jumpsuit under her silk kimono.

The disguise helped maintain her mystique, as well as her reputation. It also helped hide her emotions. It kept her safe.

Women wear makeup for many reasons. Some wear it to feel beautiful. Others to hide blemishes or enhance features. Some wear it to attract attention from potential lovers. A few use extreme makeup to shock or surprise.

Grayce wore it to be visible.

In her youth, her dearest wish had been to be invisible. She'd been born an albino, and most who saw her curled their lip in disgust. A few men, of course, desired her as an exotic, and her madam had made good use of that appeal. Eventually, she escaped that life and killed her former owners. But in general, she wanted to hide her bizarre face from the world.

A few years ago, she got her wish. Like most people who are granted their dearest wish, she quickly regretted it. Being invisible wears on the mind and spirit.

After applying her lip color and fixing her elaborate wig in place, she took a deep sigh. Today's meeting might be incredibly important, but she'd have to tread carefully.

She detested the necessity of meeting with Wěi Qí. His crime syndicate rivaled her own and grew stronger every day. Soon, he would be much more powerful than her. In addition, his practices were less savory than the typical syndicate. While she primarily traded in secrets, with only a few subsidiaries in gambling and prostitution, he trafficked in human slaves as his primary business.

Still, her sources indicated he held important information on her son. Thus, her need to meet with him.

Grayce traveled with only two guards, men chosen for their bulk and their taciturn natures. Her assistant and second-in-command, Chen Zhang, walked one step behind her. Tall with red hair, a legacy of her Irish father, Chen remained the only person she trusted with her secret, the only one who knew what existed behind the geisha makeup. Her skills at running her various businesses were matched only by her ability to calm Grayce's madness. Without Chen, she would have died from the insanity years ago.

Her traditional geisha garb, her signature look, appeared bulky. However, despite limited seamstress skills, she had designed the cut of the fabric to move with her should speed or agility be required. It would rip off easily enough if she needed full mobility from the jumpsuit. She rarely allowed herself to get into such situations now.

Wěi Qí's nondescript two-story office building lay nestled between two taller buildings, a bank and a trade office. His guards barred her entrance until she showed them her ring, the symbol inscribed on it the Chinese symbol for 'whisper.' The guard squinted at the ring, perhaps trying to remember how to read. She held her impatience in check.

The guard's expression cleared and he nodded to his companion. They parted to let her entourage pass.

The dim hallway had no decoration and stank of stale cigar smoke and liquor. A muffled scream filtered through the red plush carpeting below us. While she was long past shuddering at such evidence of human suffering, the child living deep inside her psyche cried. She silenced the whiny brat and marshaled forward.

As Grayce waited to be presented to the crime boss, his assistant frisked her and Chen. She still had a hidden weapon he missed, and she schooled her expression into perfect neutrality. She'd learned the trick to controlling her face years ago, when Madam Ziqi trained her as a prostitute. Faked emotion after a blatantly neutral face stood out like black ink on a blank page.

Wěi Qí's assistant, a short Chinese national of indeterminate age, beckoned her inside. Chen and her guards remained outside with him. The office screamed old school wealth, with mahogany and black lacquer furniture, and more deep red plush carpeting. A sideboard with two leather chairs sat to one side of his massive desk. Her counterpart appeared to be a fit shorter man, perhaps in his mid-fifties, with silver at his temples.

He stood and saluted her in the traditional manner, cupping his hands on his chest and raising them slightly. She returned the gesture at exactly the same height, granting him neither greater nor lesser status. With a wave of his hand, he dismissed his assistant, though he left the door open a crack.

Her host strode to a black lacquer sideboard, where an ornate cinnabar tea tray stood. A Gaiwan bowl steamed with fresh tea, which he poured into two cups. He gestured for her to choose one. She chose the one furthest from her.

Once they both had our teacups and settled into the leather chairs, they took the obligatory first sips. She tapped the cup to show her thanks for the tea. As the elder, Wěi Qí greeted her first. "Nín hǎo. How may I help you, Miss Li?"

She had to unclench her jaw before she spoke. "Nín hǎo, Mister Zhang. I'm given to understand you possess information I seek."

He sat back, steepling his fingers as his eyes narrowed. "Indeed? The Queen of Whispers comes to *me* for information? How ironic. Intriguing, even. And what information would this be?"

"I seek knowledge of an agent from MI-7. He was killed some years ago. I desire the identity of his killer."

He took a sip of his tea. "On the surface, this is not a matter which warrants a personal visit from you, Miss Li. What else?"

Grayce choked down a swallow from her own teacup. "This is the information I seek."

"Your own informants are quite skilled. I would even venture to say superior to my own. Why do you require my assistance?"

She kept her answer calm. "My own skilled informants' reports lead to your network."

His shoulders tensed and her own hands clenched in readiness. He didn't enjoy being accused and if he should take the accusation poorly, she would need to retrieve her hidden weapon from its sheath. Luckily, however, his muscles relaxed after a moment.

"What will you offer to pay for such information, should I possess it?"

She already stood at a severe disadvantage, as she'd come begging for a favor. If she overvalued her offer, he would understand how essential the information was. If she undervalued the price, he would dismiss her request out of hand. He may suspect an ulterior motive. Worse, he may consider her weak enough to prey upon. The best solution, though not without peril, would be to offer a nebulous price. "An exchange of favors."

He sipped his tea again, considering his options. She glanced to the door, and glimpsed his assistant, listening at the crack in the door. Wěi Qí cleared his throat. "There is something you have which I desire."

Grayce blinked once, waiting for him to elaborate.

"The woman who accompanied you. I will borrow her for one week."

The bottom of her stomach dropped away and her vision swirled. The edge of madness pummeled against her mind, but she shoved it away. It screamed as she slammed the door shut. Once again in control of her emotions, she spoke precisely. "She is not for rent."

"For sale, then. She will buy you several pieces of information."

"I have another girl, also with red hair. I can send her to you for three weeks."

He stood in an abrupt motion. "Our negotiations are complete. N☒ gāi z☒ule."

While she didn't wish to leave, she had no choice. He, as the host, had commanded her to go. She would just have to find her information a more dangerous way.

Grayce stood, careful not to upset the teacup, and gave him a parting salute. He barely returned the gesture. His assistant opened the door as she approached. She collected Chen and two guards. His assistant accompanied them to the entrance.

She didn't breathe freely until they had exited the building and rounded the corner. Even then, she hid her distress, as they remained in public. She needed to gain the sanctuary of her own office before she would give in to her frustration and panic. And the madness which clamored against its walls.

Through busy alleys lit by rainbow neon, the misty rain making the light reflect on the streets, she led her small entourage as quickly as she dared. Her geisha sandals kept her feet dry, but hadn't been designed for long strides. The moisture formed rivulets of damp on her face, threatening to streak her careful makeup. Three more blocks, then two, then one.

When she entered her sanctum, a severe, white office block decorated with glass and chrome, she slammed the door and collapsed into her desk chair. After regaining her breath, she rushed to the small bathroom. With violent frenzy, she scrubbed the white makeup from her face, needing to be naked, invisible, and free. Soon, not a trace of clothing remained on her body and her body had disappeared from mortal sight.

Grayce gave into the invisible madness.

Chen knew the routine. Her assistant allowed her boss ten minutes to shake the panic and anxiety from her soul, and then entered with her acupuncture needles. She groped for the invisible body and dragged her to the wall, where Chen pulled the padded massage table from the wall. With cold efficiency, she strapped Grayce to the table, using soft restraints. This not only kept her in place but told Chen where her body parts should be.

Once she immobilized Grayce, still in the throes of her madness, Chen caressed her skin. Her gentle touch along Grayce's arm was like fine silk, until the pain of the acupuncture needle pierced her wrist. Chen moved her attention to her shoulder, her knee, her head. With the tiny sting of each one, Grayce regained a modicum of control. By the time her assistant had finished, Grayce was breathing more easily as her sanity reluctantly returned.

Grayce glared at the stack of intervention requests on her desk. It seemed higher this week, though Chen assured her the requests remained at an average level. With a sigh, knowing they wouldn't go away if she procrastinated any further, she yanked the top one, written on the inside of a food label.

To the Invisible Madame:

I write to you in sincere imploration. I have been abandoned by my husband of twenty years, and have four children to feed. His mother refuses to take me in, and I have no place to go. Please, grant me the blessing of your regard and luck.

Yin Yun of Tai Po Kao

She placed the letter in the 'possible' pile and moved to the next. This one had been hand-written on expensive stationery with flowery calligraphy and she almost didn't bother reading, but she forced herself to at least consider it.

Honored Invisible Madame:

My request is an unusual one. I crave your blessings and ask for your assistance. My brother is our only method of support, and he is gravely ill with pancreatic cancer. We have no resources when he dies.

With regards,
Lor Qiao

She snorted and tossed it into the 'no' pile. Anyone who can afford that paper lied about what resources she had.

Six letters later, she leaned back and cracked her back. Two letters had made her eyes itch with tears. However, she hadn't placed any in the "yes" pile yet. One letter remained, and with a sigh, she pulled it closer.

Please, Invisible Madame:
My husband is brutal, and I fear for my son's safety, as well as my own. I must lie to explain the bruises and my son's broken arm. Please, help us to escape.
Desperate for help,
Meilinn Wu

Damn. She couldn't say no to this one. A woman trying to save her son from harm stabbed her directly into her heart. Grayce ached to embrace her own son, but he had been stolen from her directly after his birth.

She pressed the intercom button on her phone. "Chen? Come in, please. We have a new project."

The night would be warm and dry, so Grayce prepared for an excursion. Colder nights grew uncomfortable, as she couldn't wear clothing and remain undetectable, and rain betrayed her presence with both sound and displacement.

Tonight, she had two missions, if she had time for both. First, she would venture into Wěi Qí's lair and try to extract her information using stealth. Second, she would scope out Meilinn Wu's house and assess her true situation. The woman seemed to be ensconced in a condominium with strict security, and even Chen's considerable talents had been unable to crack the system the day before. She might wait until Chen obtained more specialized equipment, but didn't want to leave the woman's life in fate's uncertain hands.

Even though Grayce would be safer walking along the edge of the highway, she preferred traveling on surface streets. She gathered much information in that manner, witnessing arguments, transactions, and whispered conversations. She'd compiled a great store of such information over the years, enabling her to amass considerable power in the world of the underground syndicate of Hong Kong.

She had truly earned the title Queen of Whispers.

Thus her need to beg Wěi Qí for information intensely frustrated her.

Grayce walked through the alley behind a restaurant, piles of trash barely hiding the teenager freebasing against the wall. A child of indeterminate gender, aged perhaps ten, approached him, flashing a small baggie. The junkie placed his glass pipe on a box with exaggerated care and dug into the pocket of his ripped jeans. He extracted a grimy note for twenty Hong Kong dollars. The child held out the baggie, but instead of handing over his money, the junkie lunged. The child, much quicker than their adversary, wriggled from his bumbling grasp.

After grabbing the money, the child tossed the baggie into the junkie's lap. Once they completed the exchange, the child ran down the alley, almost colliding with her. She sidestepped them and wrinkled her nose. The junkie screamed curses at the child and fell into a pile, cradling his baggie. A junkie in an alleyway provided no bankable information. She walked on.

Wěi Qí's office loomed ominously in the dark of the night. The guards outside looked different from those she'd seen earlier. Neither exhibited a trace of fatigue or boredom, but she didn't need distracted guards. She only needed someone else to enter. She must wait for such an opportunity.

A young woman walked by, barely more than a girl, her face covered in gaudy makeup. Her miniskirt looked soiled and her cropped top sleeve hung low on one shoulder. She eyed the two guards, and cocked her head in an obvious query, but they ignored her. She stalked off with a huff and a clack of cheap heels.

Creatures such as that girl both disgusted Grayce and drew her pity. Her girls were all willing sex workers, eager to earn top fees as sophisticated entertainment. She even had two fully trained geisha, conversant in culture, conversation, and the delicate arts of companionship. Thus, her public persona as a geisha didn't seem too out of place.

Footsteps behind her made her turn to watch a middle-aged businessman in an expensive, tailored suit approach the house. He nodded to the guards and they exchanged a brief, whispered conversation. As he reached into his jacket pocket for his identification, Grayce walked up to stand at his back. When the guards opened the door to grant him access, she shadowed him into the doorway.

Once inside, she gave him more room, but followed him down the hall. The soft pile carpet caressed her bare calloused feet, luxurious after the hard streets. He turned into Wěi Qí's office. However, Wěi Qí didn't seem to be inside.

The visitor sat in Wěi Qí's desk chair as if he belonged there. With quick movements, he opened each drawer of the desk, searching for something. She tapped the wooden wall with her knuckle to gauge his reaction. He froze like a deer in the headlights, staring at the door. When nothing happened, he returned to his search.

This man should not be here, not if he seemed so nervous about being discovered. Yet he'd passed the guards with ease. Therefore, he must be part of Wěi Qí's crew, perhaps a trusted underboss. Which meant she now had a very important piece of information to trade. However, Grayce needed to know the man's identity before she could leverage that knowledge into a tangible property.

He discovered a bottle of aged Maotai and grinned. He found a glass tumbler and poured himself a hefty tot. When he replaced the bottle into the desk drawer, however, it slipped and cracked, showering glass and strong-smelling liquor into the deep pile carpeting.

He cursed up a storm and, glancing nervously at the door, did his best to clean up the mess. He shoveled the glass bits into a lacquer trash receptacle and shoved it back under the desk. The room stunk.

Grayce didn't like broken glass, having been attacked with a broken bottle during her courtesan days. Her breathing quickened and her heart beat faster. She tamped down hard on the madness. Now would be a horrific time to lose control. The madness fought against her willpower, screaming to be released, but she held tight upon it with both hands of her will. Eventually, she wrestled it into somnolence once again.

After wiping his sticky hands on his slacks and downing the rest of his shot, the man pushed back from the desk and glanced around the room. His gaze lit upon the floor-to-ceiling bookshelf, covered in ponderous leather-bound volumes. He closed the last desk drawer and smiled.

Stepping to the books, he ran his hand in an almost loving caress across the book spines. He examined the dust they left on his finger with a curl of his lip. Then he pressed his hands against a group of red books. Nothing happened.

He tried again in a different spot, then a third. Soon, he'd tried at least a dozen possibilities, and she had to steel herself against laughing. Did this man think Wĕi Qí would have such an easily discovered secret panel? Surely, anything the syndicate boss had would be much more heavily guarded than by the trite movie cliché of a chamber hidden in the bookshelves.

Voices in the hall halted the intruder's efforts. He strode to the door and waited until the voices passed. Then he slipped out of the office and back down the hall toward the entrance.

Grayce followed him. She needed to discover this man's identity, and if possible, why he was snooping in Wĕi Qí's inner sanctum. Had this search been his only purpose? Or had breaking the liquor bottle cut short his mission?

Once outside the building, the man got into a white delivery van. She cursed and grabbed onto the passenger side door handle, balancing on the running board. She hoped he wouldn't take the highway.

Luck was with her, as he remained on surface streets. Even so, the whipping wind chaffed her skin and her knuckles cramped as she held tightly to the door handle.

Three miles later, he parked at a posh, flat building. As Grayce followed him through the secured entrance, she narrowed her eyes at the address, which seemed familiar. The same address she had planned on visiting later that evening. Meilinn Wu's flat.

Grayce held her breath during the elevator ride to the penthouse suite, for silence's sake. When the man walked to Meilinn's flat, she snuck in before he closed the door.

The impeccable flat had been decorated in blond wood, white leather, and frosted glass. A woman, presumably Meilinn, came in from the kitchen, a stained apron over her blue silk dress. Her petite frame and bob haircut matched the photograph Chen had shown her. She bowed her head at the man.

"Welcome home, my husband. Dinner will be on the table in five minutes."

Meilinn hurried back into the kitchen. She had set the dining table, though only for two people. Grayce glanced at the digital clock on the stove. How had it gotten to be nine already? Their son must already be asleep.

The husband grunted and took off his jacket, tie, and shoes. He placed them in their designated spots and sat at the table. Meilinn rushed in, carrying a glass filled with ice and brown liquor. He lit a cigarette and blew smoke in his wife's face.

Grayce covered her mouth to avoid a cough. Meilinn hurried in and out of the kitchen several times, bringing rice, peppers, and beef arranged on serving platters. When she served her husband, sweat beaded on her delicate facial features. Once she prepared his plate, the wife prepared her own and sat, her gaze fixed upon the food.

As they ate, Grayce drifted toward the hallway. Perhaps he had an office where she might glean more information. She already knew his identity, thanks to the bizarre coincidence that made him Meilinn's husband.

According to Chen's report, Jue Tung Wu ran three successful noodle restaurants in the tourist section. He spent most of his time there. Why he had spent the evening rifling through a powerful crime boss's private papers hadn't been part of that intelligence. The restaurants must be part of Wĕi Qí's domain, which would at least explain his ability to enter the crime lord's offices.

Four doors opened off the hallway. Only two stood open, revealing a dim master bedroom and an immaculate bathroom in white and black tiles. Another might be the boy's room. She wished the fourth stood open so she might explore. She touched one door handle, then another, but both were closed. Either might make a noise if she pushed it open.

A cry startled her. She flattened against the wall as Meilinn rushed by. The wife entered her son's room, making soothing noises.

"Shut that brat up, woman! I don't want to hear all that when I come home!"

Her shushing noises held a tinge of desperation.

Jue Tung stomped down the hall, grabbing something from the bedroom before shoving the door open. Grayce gritted her teeth at the sight of the strap.

Her conscience screamed at her to stop the beating, but she must make good use of their distraction to enter the fourth room, closing the door behind her but not pulling it shut.

As an albino, she automatically shielded her eyes in bright light, so her eyes got used to the darkness quickly. A large desk stood near the window. The lights of the city filtered through the sheer curtains. One sign blinked on and off, giving the room a cheesy film noir look.

Grayce sifted through the contents of the desk. She found several bills relating to the restaurant, a tax bill, a bribery demand, and several checkbooks to different banks. A few terse notes from Wĕi Qí confirmed that Jue Tung must indeed work for him. A stack of personal and business letters she didn't have time to read beckoned to her. She listened for sounds and held the first one up to the window.

A request for a charitable donation, a final demand from a dry cleaner, a note from a brothel... she stared at this last, certain this was also one of Wĕi Qí's establishments. She memorized the address and picked up the final letter.

She stared at the name at the top, dumbfounded. Oscar Edwards. She knew the name. She knew the man. She had known him intimately.

He'd been dead for five years.

Wishing she could have brought a camera with her, Grayce read through the letter, memorizing every word, before replacing the stack.

Nothing tonight had gone quite as planned. Each incident had revealed something new and surprising, leading to the next. She didn't like things to be so chaotic. Chaos destroyed her carefully laid plans. But this new piece of information almost ruined her control.

Her heart beat even faster than earlier, and again the incipient madness hammered on the walls she'd erected around her sane mind. It wanted out, and now. She told it to wait, just a little longer.

She'd transcribe the letter when she got home and puzzle out what it might mean later. Now she must escape this flat.

Grayce listened at the office door. Meilinn's sobbing and her son's wailing covered many sounds. She inched the door open to peek out, but no one appeared in the hallway. With silent steps, she let herself out of the office and padded down toward the front door. Jue Tung wasn't in the living room. She didn't care if he remained in the child's bedroom or elsewhere. She just thanked the luck goddess Gong De Tian for her lucky break and slipped out of the flat.

Rather than bothering with the elevator, Grayce ran down the stairs and into the warm night.

When she regained the sanctuary of her home, she wrote down the words from the letter. Then she sat and stared at it for a good ten minutes before her mind would form any questions. The letters turned to abstract designs in her mind, swirling and dancing, writhing into nonsense and reforming into artistic scrawls.

Could Oscar still live? Impossible. Oscar couldn't still be alive. That meant someone was using the former MI-7 agent's name to conduct business. He'd known his days were numbered and had given her the invisibility serum for safe-keeping.

They had brutally murdered him within the next twelve hours.

She took the potion and used the powers it granted her to avenge his death. She relived this vengeance many times in her nightmares, but she'd do it all again, given the chance. However, that oh-so-satisfying vengeance had stripped her of one vital piece of information.

Who had taken their son.

Finding her son had become her obsession. Those who had orchestrated Oscar's murder later stole her son at birth. Over the last five years, lead after lead had turned into dead ends, sometimes literally.

The most recent lead had brought her to Wěi Qí, but she wouldn't pay his price. Even that lead paled in the light of this new revelation.

Now it seems his underling, Jue Tung, had information she needed.

She would have to arrange a meeting with the man. The fact that she knew he wasn't loyal to Wěi Qí would be a distinct advantage. Still, she had little proof of his perfidy.

Still, Jue Tung wouldn't know she had no proof. She'd still lean on him and see what squeezed out. Perhaps his guilty conscience would be tickled enough to provide proof for her.

Grayce returned then to the body of the letter, puzzling out what the words meant. She spoke English well enough, but it wasn't her native language. She felt certain some hidden meaning or nuance lay beneath the simple missive.

Respectable Mr. Wu:

The favor you granted me after my last visit was indeed an invaluable help in my mission. I thank you for your time and look forward to enjoying your hospitality again on my next visit.

Respectfully yours,
Oscar Edwards

Once she had safely transcribed the letter, and she felt certain she'd remembered every word, the madness crept back, refusing to be put off any longer. With her last coherent thought, she slapped the intercom button to Chen's bedroom. Her assistant would need to work hard to bring Grayce back this night. The madness became worse when she denied it. Hopefully, she would recover in time to meet Jue Tung tomorrow.

The very darkness which shielded her now swallowed her.

The Ser Wong Fun restaurant had become a favorite among the community of spies, crime bosses, and those who fear the light. The room itself remained dim, the gloom of secrecy heavy upon each patron. Booths were curtained and sound-proofed. Many an illegal transaction had been discussed over their famous snake soup, behind heavy black velvet curtains lined with gold fringe.

Shrouded in the shadows, Grayce often used it for her clandestine meetings. She still wore her geisha makeup, but this way inconsistencies in her appearance could not be studied.

Grayce sat in the dark booth while Chen stood outside with her guard escort. Jue Tung sat down opposite her, peering through the gloom. "I am here. You said you had knowledge I needed."

She nodded once. "I do. You also have information I wish to have. I suggest a trade."

He let out a derisive snort. "I need to know what you offer before I can even think about a trade."

She clenched her jaw and folded her gloved hands. "Wěi Qí would very much like to know that one of his underbosses seeks to betray him."

Jue Tung caught his breath. "You are mistaken. I would never betray him."

"Then why did you rifle through his private papers last night?"

His jaw worked as he digested this knowledge. "What do you propose to do with such an accusation?"

Keeping her tone even, she replied, "That depends on if you have the information I seek."

"And that is?"

"You've received a letter from Oscar Edwards. I need to know who sent it and from where."

He let out a sharp laugh. "I would presume it was sent by Oscar Edwards. As far as I can tell, he lives in London. How do you know about the letter?"

"My methods are my secret, Mr. Wu. You must be aware of my specialty. When is his next visit?"

With pursed lips, he glared toward her. "He hasn't told me when he's coming again."

She leaned back about two inches. "The real Oscar Edwards did not send the letter. You will find out who did and when they are returning."

"I will, will I? What proof do you have of my supposed betrayals?"

She blinked several times before answering. "Do you deny your actions?"

His dusky skin shaded to red. "I refuse to even answer that. I don't believe you have any concrete proof of your accusations. The Queen of Whispers should be more cautious before she makes claims. Oh, yes, I know who you are. Wěi Qí made certain I could recognize you on sight, even through your geisha costume." He rose, tossing her a contemptuous look. "Goodbye, Queen of Whispers. Perhaps you will be more circumspect in your blackmail next time."

She whispered, "Wait, Mr. Wu. I have your proof."

He sat back down, raising both eyebrows, his expression skeptical.

"When you searched Wěi Qí's desk, you broke his bottle of Maotai. The proof is all over his carpet and still sticky on the wood of his desk drawer. While his staff may clean it quickly, he will have absolutely noticed it."

Her quarry paled at her words, and she knew she had hit home. However, he remained canny enough not to give himself away in words. "How is that proof the intruder was me?"

She smiled sweetly, though she knew he could barely see her face in the gloom. "Do you wish to test that theory against Wěi Qí's generous spirit and trusting nature? Or do you forget that the guards will have remembered your entrance and exit?"

Jue Tung did provide her with information, she granted him that. However, what he provided proved less than helpful. She balled up the hand-written note with frustration and threw it against the wall.

Three years? The imposter wouldn't be back in Hong Kong for three years! Her resources, though generous enough for most of her needs, did not stretch to safely traveling to London. It would break her agreement with MI-7 and the war she was fighting against them in the shadows would be dragged into the light.

Even more frustrating is that she needed to leave Jue Tung in place until then, as he had the only connection to this imposter. Which meant she dare not turn him into Wěi Qí. Eventually, he might even realize this himself.

In the meantime, she had to extract Meilinn and her child before his brutality killed them. Chen had offered several suggestions, but she had rejected each one so far.

Meilinn, though quite lovely, would never be a courtesan, so Grayce couldn't place her in one of her entertainment establishments. Not only did she have no training, but from her brief meeting with her, Grayce could tell the woman did not have the vocation and she refused to place her unwillingly into such a profession.

A home for such displaced or abused wives would be almost as bad as being homeless. Such places were poorly funded and rife with crime. Meilinn and her son would be ripe for exploitation.

If Grayce possessed greater resources, she might send her to a town in the countryside, perhaps set her up with a small farm. However, as she considered that option, a notion formed. She buzzed Chen's intercom.

"Chen, come in please."

While working, Grayce tended to wear a sari and a turban. Though neither were culturally appropriate, only her assistant would see her in the office, and the clothing remained comfortable and form-fitting enough that Chen could track her location. The silk felt good against her skin.

When her assistant entered, notebook and pen in hand, Grayce gestured for her to sit. "Find a list of recent widowers in country estates. Find several who are older, perhaps interested in a trophy wife, but not interested in carnal relations with said wife. Bring me a list of them, and how much they are willing to pay for such a wife."

Chen raised her eyebrows. "This is for Meilin? You are looking to profit from her?"

She let out a chuckle. "No, not profit. The money will go to her, but through a proxy, so her husband cannot get hold of it should things go wrong. We shall arrange a simple trust. If the fee is high enough, we can arrange it so they live on the interest while the child receives the money as a college fund."

Chen nodded and scribbled notes.

There must be some traditional older men with decent farms looking for a woman to keep his house, but willing to forgo physical pleasures.

If she couldn't keep her own son safe by her side, she might at least arrange for someone else to find that safety.

In order to ensure that Jue Tung accepted his wife's disappearance, he must believe her dead or unrecoverable. A construct of this nature would take some preparation.

Once Chen found several suitable candidates for marriage, she arranged a meeting with Meilin. When Chen showed her their photographs, she chose one. The gentleman in question was a handsome older man who ran a large rice plantation on the mainland. The fact that his wife had left him with two young children helped sell the deal. Meilinn might be a mother to them as well as her son.

Grayce then searched the alleyways for a proper fall guy. Again, the night grew warm and dry, almost too warm. The sweat on her skin shone in bright light, so she remained in the shadows.

Raised voices attracted her to the same alley she'd traveled before, on her way to Wĕi Qí's office. She found the same teenaged junkie, once again packing his glass pipe with pure cocaine.

With an invisible smile, she noted the details of his physical appearance. His hair had been shorn close to his head. His clothing, while not rags, were grimy and torn. He had surprisingly bright eyes in the gloom, and with great delight, she noted two tattoos. The words 'power' and 'faith' in Chinese adorned either side of his neck in prison-blue ink.

With such identifying marks, a frame would be simple.

When she returned to her office, she glanced at the paperwork Chen had arranged: new identity cards, birth certificates, and a death certificate for a fictional husband. These created Meilinn's new persona, Lau Dawei, with her infant son, Kuo Kuo.

They could now be extracted and taken to Macau to their new life. Once Meilinn had been removed from danger, Grayce could work on her vengeance.

The next day, once Jue Tung left for work, Chen picked Meilinn and her son up. Grayce had cautioned the woman to leave everything except perhaps a bag for grocery shopping. That bag might contain a few items, but nothing that would be missed. She wasn't going on a vacation. It must appear that she and her son had been taken while on her daily errands. Human trafficking was a very real and present danger in Hong Kong.

Sending another note to Jue Tung, they met at Ser Wong Fun. Once again ensconced in a private booth, she folded her hands.

He crossed his arms. "What do you need now? I already told you Edwards won't be back for three years."

"This is not about Mr. Edwards. This is about your wife. There was an incident at the market today. My informants have brought me details."

He dropped his arms and sat up straight. "What? What about my wife? What's she done?"

"She had been shopping. I'm afraid your wife was attacked."

His anger fell away. "My son? Is my son injured?"

At first, she had only wanted to pretend his family had been murdered. However, the absence of a body would make that problematic. She also needed to keep the police from the incident. With luck, this variation would also maintain her hold upon Jue Tung. She dropped her gaze and shook her head. "They were both taken."

"Taken? By who? Kidnappers? Is there a ransom note?"

Grayce shook her head, the beads in her geisha wig swishing back and forth. "My team is working on that. However, preliminary information indicates they were taken to be sold. My informant was almost taken as well, and as a favor to her and to you, I will take on this case. That being said, I need to know what parameters we should work within. Do you give me latitude and judgment in dealing with the attackers?"

His face had lost all expression, which she took to be shock at the news. He nodded.

She clasped her hands. "Very well. If we cannot find them, or if they have been killed, do I have your permission to enact vengeance?"

He nodded again.

The junkie slept in his alley. A niggle of conscience bugged her at setting this hapless waste of space up to be framed and murdered, but she remembered how he had lunged at the child. This sort of person had no honor left. His soul would at least find some redemption, being instrumental in saving two other lives. She hid behind a restaurant trash bin, dressed in her black jumpsuit and a cowl. She needed tools for this job, and tools required being visible. However, she didn't need to advertise her presence.

Footsteps echoed down the alleyway and she turned, half-expecting the same child she'd witnessed before. Instead, an older man approached the junkie, tall and wiry. He poked the drug-addled man with his shoe. When he got no response, the man bent to rifle through the man's ragged pockets.

The junkie moaned as the thief turned him over. The man kicked the sleeping junkie in his side, hard and vicious blows that would have woken anyone merely sleeping. The junkie, still in a drug-infused haze, just mumbled and batted at nebulous things around his head.

The thief pulled out a knife, the metal glinting in the dim light. He bent to slice the junkie's throat, but Grayce's blade came more swiftly.

She stabbed the blade up through his lower back and into his left kidney, her other hand covering his mouth to muffle any screams. Then she pulled the knife out and plunged it into the side of his neck, behind the carotid artery. She pushed it further forward, across the trachea. His screaming stopped. His hot blood spilled all over the junkie.

Skipping back before the blood splattered on her suit, she let him drop into the grimy alleyway. With a quick search, she found some distinguishing marks. While he didn't have a tattoo, he sported a rather spectacular blue Mohawk and multiple piercings along his right ear. That should be plenty for identification.

Instead of bringing on the madness, the killing brought her soul peace. When she returned to her home, she relaxed into a long, hot bath to remove the stink of vengeance and sweat.

She brought the details of the thief to Jue Tung, along with reports of his death. "I have been unable to trace your wife and son. However, I have killed the man responsible for their abduction. They may be beyond our reach by now, but I shall continue to investigate."

Of course, Meilinn and her son would never be recovered.

Information was power. Jue Tung was even more beholden to her than ever. And when the supposed Oscar Edwards returned, she would have power over him as well.

And one day she hoped she would have enough information and power to find and take back her son.

From the private journal of Director Balaoo, Directorate of Altérité Security:

It is my sworn duty as head of Directorate of Altérité Security to keep France safe. A necessary, honorable role that I would not wish upon any good man, woman, or beast.

To do my job, I'm often faced with terrible decisions. Not merely distasteful, but onerous.

I am constantly having to choose which solution is the lesser of two evils to protect France from the forces that would destroy her. I have learned to embrace the lesser evil for the greater good.

And there is no lesser evil greater than our most effective agent, a body stealing spirit known as The Phantom.

May the divine have mercy on my soul.

The Exchange Room
A tale of the Phantom of the Abyss

Aleathia Drehmer

The triangular park on the corner of Rue Paul Valliant and Rue de Villier became Aline Marchand's second home after she ran away from the first one. Paris provided her an invisibility she'd never dreamed was possible.

Her first home in Mornac-sur-Seudre, now a distant memory, was the opposite of Paris. Aline had spent a lifetime surrounded by the deep smell of salt and oysters, with seagulls circling overhead in a predatory fashion. The silence of the commune weighed heavier on the mind than one would imagine. White-washed stone buildings from centuries before, brightened by ridiculously colored shutters with neat signs affixed to the doors, became the maze for her daily trance.

The small town was popular with tourists. When they came for long weekends in the summer, the rich visitors from Paris and Toulouse looked down their noses at the town's people dressed in their shabby clothes fit only for oyster farmers, poor artisans, and harvesters of salt.

Aline was tired of their behavior, but deep in the dark center of her being, she was envious too.

Blaring sirens from an ambulance that raced down the street to save another life broke her from the memories of her first home. The park comforted Aline in the hours of sunrise to sunset. She was nothing more than a street rat to the passersby, like all the other homeless teenagers in the vast, intricate city. She did her best not to bother anyone with her state of poverty even though she placed a cup and a small sign in front of her, but never actively begged or engaged anyone.

On her corner, Aline watched the bustling agents and office workers on their way into the Directorate of Altérité Sécurité, or DAT, down the block. This group of people was peppered with nurses in scrubs and doctors in their long white coats making their way to the hospital on the other side of the government building. The morning was crisp and their legs moved past her at a quicker rate than usual, the staccato strike of various kinds of shoes each playing a different line of music in the symphony of city life.

With her sketchbook and charcoal in hand, Aline watched them intently. Some faces turned the corner at the same time every day, while others had less meticulous schedules and couldn't be counted on. The café at the edge of the DAT building was a beacon for them all. Each of them exiting with a false sense of energy and rich, buttery croissants to start their day.

Aline's stomach growled. *Be quiet, mon amie, it does not concern you.*

The runaway continued to sketch the faces of her regulars, each page of her book a different countenance. The days blended together for her, manifested only by the details she could add to each drawing. None of the people noticed her. Aline had a knack for existing without raising awareness of this. She'd been on this corner for months like clockwork and became to the others like a bench or shrubbery, some inanimate object they wouldn't miss if she happened to not show one day.

Her parents hadn't missed her. They never came looking. Aline hadn't minded that fact, had counted on it. She came to Paris to disappear in a sea of humans amongst the infinitely old buildings and streets.

She made enough money in a day to keep her fed and caffeinated. It kept her from needing to sell her body to live. Aline kept her desires low and willed herself to survive on little. The thought occurred to her that she was happier living with nothing on the streets of Paris than she had been in her warm bed at Mornac. She was equally safe between the two. At least on the streets she battled only potential abuse from strangers rather than exposed bouts from those who were supposed to love her. This made a difference to Aline.

On that day, like all the other days since she started sitting in this park, an overwhelming feeling of dread interrupted her drawing. It happened, as always, at 7:34 in the morning. Aline studied the group of people heading to their jobs, trying to find which one of them caused this feeling in her. She spotted a woman dressed impeccably in a black pantsuit, hair in a chignon so tight it pulled the features of her face taut. The dark glasses occluded her eyes, but Aline felt the power of the woman's stare, regardless. She was unsure if her gaze met the woman's eyes.

Was she looking past me? Has this woman mistaken me for someone else? Aline fixed her eyes on the face and began drawing automatically, in a trance, as if the pencil had a life of its own. The graphite scratched the paper furiously, and with a pressure she rarely used.

The woman in the dark glasses pursed her lips and turned away from Aline, who sat cross-legged in the grass. This was when Aline noticed a faint white scar on the outer left cheek, barely visible from under the sunglasses. The woman stomped off, high heels clicking a hypnotic rhythm. Aline watched as the woman presented a badge at the long fence of the DAT and disappeared around the corner into the highly secured building.

Aline spent the rest of the day at the park, her cup nearly full of coins, which would ensure at least a meal. She'd been saving the extra each day for a new sketchbook. The light faded in the small park as she gathered up her things. Aline tugged the knit skullcap from her backpack and pulled it down over her spiky blond hair. The warmth of the day was fading rapidly as she covered her Frankie Goes to Hollywood t-shirt with a hoodie and her favorite black coat. Living on the streets meant layers, mostly black layers so at night you remained invisible to the police and predators in the alleys and side streets.

"Bonjour, Aline!"

She turned to see who had called her by name. "Ah, Bonjour, Claudia. How are you?"

"Good, good my friend. Are you ready to go?" asked Claudia.

Claudia was Aline's mentor in this crazy metropolis. She was a runaway that Aline had met on her first night in Paris. The girl had lived on the streets many more months than Aline and gave her an education. Since that first night, they'd struck up a friendship and were sure to find each other at the end of each day so they could maneuver the sordid nights in the city together. There was safety in numbers. It was warmer, too, when you had someone to sleep next to. Claudia was very tall and thin with her red hair always in a braid to keep it out of her face and to not draw unwanted attention, but it did anyway.

"Yes, it's colder than usual, don't you think?" asked Aline.

"I suppose. You'd think we'd be used to the cold by now," said Claudia, "Hurry up! I'm starving."

The two girls wandered their way towards the industrial district by the river. Many of the shipping yards were dark at night and more sheltered than the usual places that harbored street people. They had a routine of getting food first and then scouring where they would sleep for the night. They tried to not stay in one place too many nights in a row to avoid an ambush by other homeless people or the cops.

"I want McDonald's," stated Claudia.

"Again? I'm tired of it. Can't we just grab something at La Ferme de Levallois today?" said Aline.

"Come on. I'm sure you've sat all day. Let's walk. It'll be nice and warm us up before we go find a place to sleep."

"Fine. I guess it's cheap enough," Aline said, followed by a deep sigh.

The girls sauntered down Rue de Villiers as they situated their backpacks for even weight distribution. Aline stared intensely at the door of the Directorate of Altérité Sécurité as they walked by, willing the woman to come out of the building again, but the lobby was dark except a faint glow from the security desk. She felt that something sinister was going on inside the secured high-rise, but she didn't know enough about it to think of what it could be.

"Aline, come on," Claudia said tugging on her arm, "This is our street. Are you okay? You look like you've seen a ghost." The two girls crossed and made a left turn onto Rue Louis Rouquier.

"I'm fine, but I saw a woman today I've never seen before. She made my skin crawl. This woman stared at me. No one ever sees me on that corner. It was weird. But, I have this strange feeling every morning as if someone is watching me."

"It's probably nothing, and you're always paranoid," Claudia said as she laughed louder than she should have.

Aline stood silent for a moment, knowing that Claudia lived on the streets like her, but had not suffered the childhood trauma of a father's late-night wandering hands.

If she had, Aline thought, *she'd be paranoid too.*

Shaking the thought from her head, she said, "Whatever. Let's eat!"

They ran across Rue de President Wilson, dodging traffic, eliciting dirty looks and loud horns from the drivers running late on their commute home. Aline didn't care.

At least they have homes, she thought.

She'd lived in a house all her life, but it had never been what anyone would have recognized as a home. There were no warm fuzzy feelings of being loved, only drunken screaming and the reality of balled fists.

The McDonald's was bustling with hungry teenagers and tired blue-collar workers looking only to have their bellies filled. The food's quality was of no consequence. Aline carefully counted out the coins in her pocket for her standard meal of a double cheeseburger and small fry.

"Can I have a glass for the water fountain?" Aline asked the cashier as the girl handed her bag across the counter. The girl frowned and looked at Aline suspiciously before handing her a small clear plastic cup.

With bags in hand, the two friends walked back up Rue de President Wilson to the spacious Parc de la Planchette.

The children's play area was the closest end of the park to them and given the time of day, no children were running about. The two girls climbed the metal dinosaur and sat cross-legged with their backs against the cool metal on either side of the opening to the slide. Their bags made loud crinkles as they reached in to enjoy the warm, salty selection they had purchased.

"So this lady, do you think she's a spy?" asked Claudia around a mouthful of food.

"I don't know. I see tons of people walk behind the gates of that building every day and they could all be spies, but none of them have ever given me a side glance," Aline said. She wiped her fingers on a napkin and rifled through her backpack to find her drawing pad. The light was fading rapidly.

She flipped through the pages quickly, all those faces collected without them knowing, until she landed on the mysterious lady. "Here. Look at her."

"She looks like a bitch. Maybe she just hates homeless people?" Claudia offered.

"It felt like more than that. I'll look for her tomorrow," said Aline, disappointed her friend wasn't as leery of the woman as she was. She stuffed her drawing pad back into her pack. They finished the rest of their meal in silence.

The girls wadded up their empty bags and rolled them down the slide before they shot themselves out of the dinosaur's mouth, both of them laughing. Aline struggled to get out of the bottom in the dark and bumped her head. Claudia snickered as she picked up the garbage beneath her friend's feet.

"We better hurry if we want to get a good spot down by the docks," Claudia whined.

Aline said nothing in return as she adjusted her pack. They walked the length of Rue de President Wilson until it ended at the Seine River. There were still a few people in the riverside parks that separated the roads from the water. Most of them were other homeless, staking claim to benches and areas under the trees. The two girls found one of their favorite rotating spots to sleep near a warehouse that had a stairway and deck leading to an office upstairs. The ground was soft and somewhat sheltered there. Claudia rolled out her blanket on the ground and laid closest to the wall, using her pack as a pillow. Aline shook out her blanket and placed it over top of them. They slept spooned together for warmth and safety until the morning light would wake them again.

The next morning, Aline set up in her usual place in the park. Her senses were acute and keenly looking for the mysterious woman from the day before. She'd come a little early to be sure not to miss her opportunity to sketch more of the woman, and to see if the interaction the day before was merely happenstance. She continued her drawing routine, adding more details of the usual suspects as they filed by.

Her stomach tightened, and the hairs on her arms stood up. She looked at the old leather-banded watch she'd stolen from her father: 7:34 am, just like yesterday. Aline shot her gaze upward to find the woman, but her face wasn't in the moving crowd. Instead, there stood a very handsome man, sharply dressed in an old hat and dark glasses in the same style as the woman's. It gave the man a slightly effeminate appearance.

The hat doesn't match the suit, Aline thought.

But this man stared at her the way the woman had the day before. Perplexed, the automatic drawing began again over the mystery lady's portrait. When she snapped out of the trance, the man had gone. Aline sat looking at the morphed drawing of the woman and the man. Their essence was the same.

I don't like that mean man, a voice in Aline's head said.

"Shhh. It's fine. Don't worry, mon amie," said Aline under her breath, looking around her periphery to see if anyone was watching her.

He will hurt us like Daddy did.

"No, he won't, ma chere. We don't even know him. Go to sleep."

I'm afraid.

"Shhh, shhh, shhh. Go to sleep." She reached into the bag beneath her knee and pulled out a worn, faded pink rabbit with only one eye.

It's okay, they won't hurt us.

Aline closed her eyes and tried to control her breathing, her heartbeat hammering in her chest. She couldn't afford to let her secret out. It was too dangerous.

Erik marched past the girl in the park, his mind churning over the possibility that this young woman held for his plans. His current mission to take down Pascal Leblond, the infamous human trafficker of Montmartre, was being thwarted by someone inside the DAT. He'd been vigilant, as always, about keeping his missions to himself. It was a matter of personal preservation. His mode of functioning was the DAT's best kept secret, of the utmost security clearance. He was their premier intelligence agent. He rarely got his hands dirty, which was for lesser agents. His work supplied the rest of them with something to do.

His anger at the whole situation caused his fists to ball and a storm to swirl across his face. Whoever had interfered with his mission would pay. He wasn't used to being thwarted. Usually, he got what he wanted when he wanted it.

As he walked through security he flashed his badge which read Erik Mantoph. That wasn't his name. He was only Erik, but in his business, they frowned upon people running around with a singular name, as if they were pretending to be Madonna or Prince.

He waited in a small pool of other agents and office workers gathered by the elevator. Unlike most people, Erik loved elevators. These were times he could study people closely without suspicion. He could place bugging devices, GPS locators, and learn personal details that would come in handy in various ways in subsequent encounters. Erik touched as many people as he could in those short travels.

The elevator emptied by the time Erik reached his floor. He again had to swipe his badge for the doors to open. After hesitating, the heavy doors opened into the spacious and breathtaking office of the Assistant Director of the DAT, Henri Legrand. Erik stepped through the doors and removed his sunglasses.

"Erik. Hello. What brings you to the top of the world?" said Henri.

"Deceit and annoyance, what else?" Erik said flippantly. Henri raised his eyebrows at the comment and waited for the explanation that was sure to follow.

"Who else knows about my current mission?" Erik said.

"No one but you and I, Erik. Why?"

"I have spent the last two weeks surveying my target in various disguises until I got into his secured building, only to overhear him acknowledge to an associate of his that someone was trying to kill him," Erik said nearly breathless with anger.

"Certainly you don't think I had anything to do with it? You must have slipped up somewhere," said Henri as he stood behind his grand mahogany desk. Despite his short stature, he commanded a certain amount of respect, even from Erik.

Erik's face, usually expressionless, filled with comical disgust at the suggestion that he was to blame.

"Listen here, Henri, don't be insane, no one finds out anything from me. You must have a mole."

"Highly unlikely, but do what you must. Figure it out. The mission needs completion," said Henri with finality and sat back in his black leather chair. His fingers steepled in front of him with index fingers resting on the tip of his nose.

Erik had walked away from Henri's desk during their heated discussion and stood in front of a large window overlooking the Seine River. He contemplated his next move when the girl in the park abruptly floated back into his mind.

"Henri, there is a woman, a girl really, who sits in the park every day. Two days in a row she has noticed me out of the throngs of people rushing past in the morning. She has a book she writes things down in, and sketches passersby daily. I want to know who she is," Erik stated matter-of-factly.

"Do you have her name? Just look her up."

"I don't, and it's too risky to get that close to find out just yet. But I took her picture this morning with the camera in my glasses while my stare held her. The girl locked eyes with me, though she couldn't see beneath the glasses. Do you have facial recognition software on your computer?"

"I believe so. Send me the photo," said Henri. Erik pulled out his phone and transferred the photo of the girl to Henri. He sat in front of the computer, and Erik stood behind him, leaning in close. The two men waited for a hit. It wasn't long before the program spit out a match.

"Aline Marchand," said Henri, "reported missing by a friend several months ago from Mornac. Seems like no one has followed up. Parents never reported either. Looks like you have yourself a runaway, Erik."

Erik's face cracked slightly into what might have been considered his version of a smile. *This will work perfectly*, he thought, strolling over to the window with his hands behind his back, *perfect indeed.*

Erik left Henri's office and descended to the basement. This was a refuge for maintenance workers, and he looked out of place in the dark, sterile hallways. He turned to the left, his footfalls echoing through the silence that existed before he arrived. At the end of the hall, he turned again. Halfway down there was another elevator, a small one, only large enough for two people, if they were not too big in size. This lift differed from the rest in the building as it required a special code entered into a keypad and a swipe of the badge. Access to the code for this elevator was restricted.

Erik stepped into the cold, coffin-like space and waited as it slid down several floors. It had only one destination, and the inside buttons were directional. The car halted with a soft bouncing that never ceased to make Erik's insides roil with nausea. Although his mind expected it, his different bodies never got used to it. Slowly, the doors opened onto an observation deck that served as his office. It was a steel box with a desk overlooking the floor below. His mission equipment stored in the lockers to one side and his files stored in neat cabinets to the other. Erik stood at the glassless window and looked down. A knowing smile peeled his face.

Below, hundreds of bodies lay still on cots, each with their individual state-of-the-art life support system. Ventilated, they lay atop pressure relief mattresses designed to prevent bedsores. Feeding tubes kept their bodies alive and other tubes carried away their waste. The out of sync groan of the machines reverberated like an ocean of undulating flesh and escaped air.

Erik's hands gripped around the steel window frame as he leaned forward, looking for Norbert.

"Where the hell is that idiot?" he said under his breath, but the nature of the room carried his voice.

"You..... rang?" said Norbert as he popped up from a bedside. Norbert's attempt to imitate Lurch didn't go over well.

Erik's lips pursed in annoyance.

"Get up here. We have work to do," Erik barked.

Erik watched as the balding, middle-aged man lumbered toward the stairs that lead up in a spiral. He didn't much care for Norbert, but the sensitive and secret nature of his lair required a person whose morals had done a fair bit of backsliding. The "body farm," as they called it, stored all the spy's "disguises." Death had made him a ghost but one with the power to possess other humans and subvert their minds.

He could control them, but when he did this, their bodies died unless put on life support when he transferred to another human. Erik didn't care about these people and would've rather just left them for dead.

There are too many people in the world as is, I'm doing the planet a favor.

This power gave him a god-like complex, but also made him an excellent spy who could take on the form of anyone he needed. Over time, he found keeping the bodies worked to his advantage, thus the creation of the body farm.

This gift of taking life came with a cost to himself.

Erik had to inhabit another body within seconds of leaving his current one. It took ingenuity and precise planning. His movements had parameters, having to be within a mile of someone previously on life support or someone he'd touched. This detail limited his freedom as much as it expanded it. The possibilities were infinite if he worked it out right.

Consequently, Erik touched many people without them knowing. He became a master at it. In his pocket, he always kept a tiny cage containing a cockroach. Sometimes he had to leave bodies to perish if they jeopardized his identity or if he'd used them to their limit, which left a telltale scarring that covered the skin like a roadmap. In these cases, he used the roach as his escape. This was never pleasing, but it worked in critical times with no other way to survive.

Norbert, he thought, *what have you been up to?*

The man still hadn't finished his way to the office through the maze of bodies. Erik watched him make minor adjustments to dials and turn off alarms as he weaved his way toward the stairs. Knowing the darkness within himself, Erik easily recognized it in Norbert. He had found Norbert at a hospital on the day they fired the man for "inappropriate touching of patients" and diverting narcotics. Norbert's career as a nurse was over, and in the wake of looming prosecution, Erik found it easy to convince Norbert to do his dirty work. In addition to the dropping of charges, he would have access to whatever drugs he desired and free rein to carry out his other predilection on the unconscious bodies.

Heavy footfalls echoed against the high ceiling as Norbert's boots contacted the metal stairs. Erik turned to wait for his hulking body to appear in the doorway.

"What do you need, boss?"

"You know I hate it when you call me that. It's Erik."

"Sure thing, boss," Norbert said with a grin.

"Whatever. I will need to check out the old beggar man's body for the day, the one that feeds the birds. I've got to watch a girl in the park for a bit. Do you remember where he is?"

"A girl?" said Norbert, licking his lips as a dreamy expression oozed across his face, "Should be number 250, over in the vagrants and street people section. Let me get the ledger and check."

There was only one drawer in the office to which both men had a key, and this was so Norbert could access the ledgers. Two large green books sat in the drawer like twin orphans. One book held the assigned number for each body, their abduction site, any obtained personal information, and the mission or missions assigned to them.

Erik had to be meticulous about his use of each live disguise as to not raise suspicion. The psychological curse the Frankensteins had placed on him required Erik to watch the bodies closely. Using a single body too much or too often caused it to scar and become deformed. The second green ledger tracked the use of these unfortunate souls by their number, date, and times on and off of life support.

"Yes, here it is. Do you want me to get an exchange ready, boss?"

"For the millionth time, you idiot, stop calling me boss! And yes, get an exchange ready. I'm not sure if the girl will still be there when I make my way up. Call Bernard and let him know I'll need a ride to the surface," said Erik, stomping off down to the exchange room.

Down the winding stairway and off to the right was a small room they had dubbed "the exchange room" in which one body was taken off life support. Erik hated this room with its drab paint and clinical coldness. He wasn't a man of flourishes, but he didn't mind the finer things in life, when he had life. At the back of that room was a sink, and a mirror lit with buzzing fluorescents.

I look terrible in this light, he thought, staring at his reflection.

Erik didn't much care for his appearance. He could be in the most exquisite body, male or female, and still feel hideous. The human suit he wore now was his favorite, clearly noted by the scars forming across the chest and arms. It was the one he felt most alive in, the only one in which he felt distanced from the disfigurement of his youth. The man to whom this skin had belonged was tall with a head of chestnut hair, silver eyes that glinted, and chiseled features. Erik would've been jealous of such a being when he was alive, and the fact that he got to portray him didn't save the mental lashings he flagellated himself with daily. Plainly, he was a miserable ghost of a man.

The wheels on the bed of Body 250 squeaked every dozen revolutions, sending out a shock wave of sound that reverberated in the sparse environment. It was as if a doom was inching forward to envelop him. Erik shook this thought from his mind. He didn't have time for mental wanderings and daydreams. Norbert arrived with the body and pushed it up the ramp into its proper place.

"You ready, boss, for the old swapperoo?" said Norbert, with his crooked teeth on display like a recurrent nightmare.

"You're an impossible man."

Norbert mumbled something under his breath. It was barely audible, but Erik's hearing was masterful.

"At least I *am* a man."

Erik lay down on the bed directly next to Body 250. He had to be close enough to touch it. Norbert removed the machines from the lifeless shell as Erik reached across and touched its arm with the intention to possess it immediately. He watched with the eyes of the old beggar man as Norbert effortlessly attached the man he had just been to a different machine at the head of his own bed that would keep it alive. Erik imagined all the cracks in people's lives he'd created over these lifetimes, stealing their bodies and breaking their families. He smiled at all the fractures he'd continue to make for a government he cared nothing about.

On the other side of the vast room, a garage door slowly rolled up. It clicked into place when it reached the top and an ambulance pulled in. The smell of diesel exhaust permeated the air. The vehicle sat idling.

"Why does that fool never shut the engine off? That carbon monoxide lasts forever in here," Erik said to Norbert.

"Don't know, boss, why don't you ask Bernie yourself?" said Norbert, laughing. It was a cackle really, but that'd been splitting hairs.

"You're infuriating! You know the damn kid is mute, and he hates being called that," Erik said through the mouth of the old beggar, his voice raspy with a lifetime of unfiltered cigarettes and harsh living. It took Erik a moment to get settled in the new body with its physical limitations of old age and depravity. He limped toward the ambulance.

Bernard stood outside the ambulance near the back, waiting for Erik. He was mute, had always been. The poor boy had spent his quiet life wanting to be a paramedic, to save people. He'd trained and passed the tests, but safety regulations prevented his being hired. The ability to communicate vocally was a must in the real world, but it mattered little to Erik. The less talking, the better.

The ambulance acted as transport and a mobile unit for exchanges. Bernard was his getaway driver and could accompany him on long trips around the continent. Bernard had pulled him out of many bad moments before Erik was exposed or killed. He liked the kid, as much as he was naturally able, but mostly endured him because he was quiet. They communicated via text and if Erik was in a jam and couldn't text he had an emergency button that would signal Bernard his location.

The hospital across the street from the Directorate of Altérité Sécurité provided a perfect cover. Bernard would go into the hospital's underground parking lot and at the far corner which appeared to be a wall, would activate a device that opened a hidden door to the secret body farm. They dared not do this too much during the day, but Erik couldn't very well go traipsing through the DAT hallways looking like a filthy beggar.

Once to the surface, away from the hospital, Erik exited the back of the ambulance and hobbled his way over to the park. He had to do what each body would allow. He had power, but not superpowers that allowed him to change the mechanical function, or lack thereof, inherent in the body's cells and muscles. He felt useless and old in this body and hoped he wouldn't have to wear it long. It did nothing for his self-image.

Erik checked a few garbage cans along the way to the edge of the park to make it look good. There was a bench near the grocery and café which gave him a direct line of sight to Aline. He pulled a bag of seed from the dirty jacket pocket to feed the pigeons and wait.

At the cusp of the evening, with purple hues infiltrating the sky, Erik saw another girl step toward Aline. The two girls chatted like they were familiar with one another as Aline stuffed items into the backpack she carried everywhere.

I need that book.

Aline's friend was gangly and awkward next to her. Erik thought the two looked an odd pair—one red-haired and tall, the other spiky blond and short.

Neither is beautiful, he thought, *homely even.* Erik shifted his gaze as the two girls advanced toward him. He listened intently to their conversation.

"Did you see that crazy lady today?" asked Claudia.

"No, it was a man today. I had the same feeling, though—the creeps. After he left, I had drawn his face over part of the woman's face. I don't know what to think," Aline said, shivering and looking around.

"Again, you're totally paranoid," said Claudia, lightly jabbing her friend's arm.

"Maybe…," whispered Aline.

"Do you want to share a real sandwich today? I made some okay money," Claudia stated.

"Sure, if we can agree on meat!" said Aline. The girls entered the grocery that stood between the DAT and the park. Erik maintained his spot on the bench. He'd waited all day to know where Aline would go. He hadn't counted on the friend, but he would deal with it when the time came.

Aline and Claudia emerged from the grocery with their dinner, cut through the triangular park, and headed further down the block until they hit Rue de President Wilson. Despite being in the old man's body, Erik quietly followed them until they reached the river. Neither girl had turned to look behind them. It astonished him how invisible the girls thought they were. He envied the idea, as he'd had to work hard to achieve the same thing.

Maybe they don't feel important enough to stand out? Erik thought as he watched them sit in a small play area in front of the river promenade to eat their dinner. He'd wait again as they settled in their resting spot and for them both to fall asleep. When the girls emitted light snoring noises, he made his move.

Erik crept up in the dark. Aline slept on the inside with Claudia curled around her. The old beggar man's hand reached out and touched Aline. Erik possessed the body, leaving the old man to die in the grass, the breath escaping him in a gurgle. The moment he entered Aline's body, his mind replaced hers and he was about to get settled into this new territory when something strange happened.

There was a gasp. "What are you doing, bad man?" a small voice yelled and tried to push him from Aline. It startled Erik.

"Help me, Claudia! Help," a child called out, the tiny voice of Fayette shouted into the stillness of the damp river air.

Claudia awoke, "Aline… what is going on?"

"The man, the bad man is here!"

At once, Claudia saw the old man gasping and dying on the ground next to them with his hand on Aline. Inside Aline's body, Fayette was trying with all her might to push Erik out. She wasn't strong enough to overcome him.

The chaos of the situation was something Erik had encountered only once before.

She has another personality; he thought, looking around to see if anyone heard the screaming rattling off the walls of his brain.

Gathering his wits, he touched Claudia with Aline's cool, slim hand and subdued her quickly. The small child's mind, inside Aline, wailed and clutched her throat as the breath left her. Erik, now inside Claudia, clutched his ears at the noise. He felt blind in the darkness and reached out a hand to touch Aline's body again. This time when he possessed her, he'd killed Fayette.

He waited a moment, nervous, but no one else emerged. Erik sat up and looked at the two bodies dying right before him. He normally didn't stick around to watch this part of the game. He had always left the dirty work of body collecting and death to Bernard. When the old beggar and Claudia had drawn their last breaths, he pressed his emergency button for pick up. He stood, grabbed the backpack, and headed toward the park where the two girls had eaten before.

Bernard pulled up alongside the small park where a young girl sat, his lights off and waiting for another word from Erik. The girl walked confidently over to the driver's window, and Bernard rolled it down half-way. He, of course, said nothing.

"It's me, Bernard. It's Erik."

Erik saw the mute pull out his phone to text him something. "I don't have my burner phone. I must have left it in the pants of the old beggar." Erik, moving strangely in the new body, ran back to the lifeless heaps under the deck. He fished the phone out of the beggar's pocket. Erik, climbing into the back of the ambulance, texted Bernard. "Get me back to the farm. I've been out too long."

The paramedic nodded his head as he looked in the rearview mirror. Erik didn't mention the fresh corpses to Bernard, which were fifty feet beyond them. Dead street people never caused much suspicion, most of their deaths fell under exposure or natural causes. They rarely made the papers with no one to claim them, so he left their existence out of Bernard's head.

Bernard pulled the ambulance through the secret entrance, shut the vehicle off, and waited for instruction. Erik climbed out of the back of the vehicle, jumping down to the floor in this new, spry body. When he slammed the heavy door, it rang through the vast basement like a shock wave. He half expected all the bodies to wake from their eternal slumber. He needed rest and revitalization. Erik had stepped over the boundaries of his ability to function properly.

"You can go to bed, Bernard. I won't need you anymore tonight, but be ready in the morning. Early."

The man nodded in his usual silence and walked off toward his bunk room in the far corner of the basement, away from the bodies.

"Norbert! God damn it, Norbert, where are you?" Erik screamed. Norbert emerged from his own bunk room looking several shades of high.

"Yeah, boss?" said Norbert, stumbling toward Erik, but working hard to maintain a straight line.

"Are you wasted? Whatever. Are you sober enough to do an exchange?" Erik asked.

"I can do them in my sleep. I like the new body, boss, she's… ripe," said Norbert with a look on his face that disgusted Erik.

He knew the man's past and did not imagine that Norbert's vile traits had left him when he took this job. He thought it would have only gotten worse without oversight. Erik had been desperate for someone to run the body farm, someone without high standards and even fewer morals. He questioned himself in times like these and half wondered if saving Norbert from a life in prison had been the right thing to do. Erik wasn't one to talk about morals, but having Norbert disappear from the general population may have been the one good deed he'd ever done.

"Stop looking at me like that Norbert, before I knock you out."

"Ooooo, she's young and feisty too! Just the way I like them."

"Just hook me up, you imbecile!"

They walked to the exchange room in silence. Erik fidgeted in the new body. Its center of gravity was lower with soft flesh in unusual places. The sound of her quiet voice shocked him compared to the way he delivered the words in his head. He didn't inhabit women as often as men because of these reasons. Something complicated them with so many behaviors and nuances to remember.

"Got a hitch in your giddy-up, boss?" Norbert snickered. Erik didn't respond, only glared at the attendant with annoyance.

Erik had other things to worry about besides Norbert's snide remarks. He knew he shouldn't have left the old beggar's body out there, but he'd been startled by the girl's second personality. Erik was glad it was a scared child trapped inside her mind and that she was easy to kill. He hadn't meant to jump into Claudia, but those things happen.

Erik sat on the cot in the exchange room, waiting for Norbert to retrieve his machine from his quarters. He knew the scoundrel had reached his room when the haunting opening of *Rien! En vain j'interroge* from *Faust* rang out, filling the room. He had instructed Norbert to start it whenever Erik went into his final exchange of the night.

"I'm so sick of this damned opera," mumbled Norbert.

"What was that?" asked Erik.

"Nothing, boss."

The music carried Erik back through the centuries to his death and afterlife when he'd haunted the stage of Palais Garnier. He grew up as a stagehand who moved from shadow to shadow. He listened to everyone's conversations, knew their weaknesses and their secrets. Erik had longed for a life in front of the lights, but his facial disfigurements never allowed him such pleasure. After the misstep with Christine, he'd fallen in love with Olympia, a strikingly beautiful soprano with a voice that made his body writhe with pleasure. When he'd finally built up enough courage to tell her so, she shunned him publicly. The embarrassment mortified him. Erik could still feel the bite of the rope around his neck as he jumped from the catwalk at the end of her final performance of *Faust*.

And he jumped into the body of the person who took his hanging body down.

Now, he moved about the world in any body he wanted. This power coursed through his consciousness, but he often missed the opera house and his lair near the edge of the underground lake. He missed Olympia and had stalked the mechanical woman across the decades trying to convince her of his love. No matter what lengths he went to, she never reciprocated. All he had left were the memories of the opera house and his obsession with Olympia. He looked for her in all corners of the world when he was on missions. When the pull of nostalgia became too strong, he had Bernard drive him by the Palais Garnier to soothe his wisp of a heart.

"Boss? Erik? Helllooo?" said Norbert, waving his dirty, musty hand in front of Erik's.

"Get that disgusting thing away from my face. Are you ready?"

"Just waiting on you," said Norbert.

Erik laid down on the cot, his essence encased in Aline's body. Norbert wheeled in the husk of a body to the cot beside him. It was the only body in which Erik felt marginally handsome and therefore had become his favorite costume. It was the only one he could stand to look at in the mirror. He transferred into the empty man now disconnected from the various machines that sustained meaningless life. There was a tingle under his fingertips, nothing extravagant as a real feeling. He'd not had those in so long.

He was a ghost. He had no life, and was forced to exist in another body after finishing his work. Erik could not survive any other way, but often chose a lesser needed body as the repeated use made them degrade over time. If something happened in the night, he needed to be in a face that blended into a crowd. Erik constantly prepared for whatever disaster lay in wait.

After Norbert finished transitioning the exhausted Erik into his resting body, Erik rose from the cot and walked to his private quarters to lay down on his bed. He watched over his shoulder as Norbert started hooking up Aline's body with the basics. Erik never slept long so he didn't bother having Norbert attach him to the usual machines. He didn't trust the imbecile to keep his perverse fingers to himself.

"Don't bother me if you can help it," Erik said to Norbert without looking at him.

"Sure thing, boss. I'm going to… have my hands full."

Breathing was all that mattered in the initial stage, and Norbert would do the work of undressing her, hooking her to the monitor, and putting in her catheter later. Besides, he wanted to take his time with this one. It'd been a long time since he'd been given a nubile body to take care of. He noted that her skin was smooth like marble and was looking forward to washing the dirt off it. Norbert planned on taking his sweet time with her.

He weaved through the long lines of inanimate humans that made up the body farm and peeked into Erik's apartment. He was already asleep.

"I can't stand this god damned opera," said Norbert under his breath as he quietly entered the open door and turned down the volume.

Norbert closed the door behind him and depressed a button on the outside of the room that closed the rolling garage door and locked it. He made his way back up to the office to find a number for the new girl, "Aline" Erik had called her, and checked the piece of paper in his hand to see if he had the girl's name correctly.

He took a key from his pocket and opened the small drawer in the desk containing the ledgers. Norbert entered Aline's personal information, which Erik had given him earlier, into the ledger and closed the book. He pulled the second one out to find a number for the girl. His finger ran down the list of bodies in their numbered slots until he came to an empty one in the female section. The previous body had either worn out or had been left for dead. 49. That was where Aline was going. With her name in that book, he put it away without locking the drawer. He'd have notes to add later once they finished the exchange.

Norbert looked out of the window of the office, trying to recount how many bodies he had handled in his time with Erik. They only had 250 beds and with the numbers recycled again and again, the specifics had moved past him in a blur. He supposed it didn't help that he was high most of the time. His duties had been ingrained in his mind and he performed by muscle memory. The details of who, what, where, and when were up to Erik.

In the exchange room, Norbert stood over her with his hands in his pockets, fiddling. He hadn't even removed her clothes, and he was excited. Erik rarely brought home such young girls as he didn't find them especially useful. When Erik had returned in this body, he'd explained to Norbert that this girl seemed particularly invisible to the world, yet she was smart and observant. She might come in handy when Erik needed to skirt the dark streets of Paris and obtain information he might not otherwise get in the older, more sophisticated human husks that populated the body farm.

He leaned in close. *I better get to work.*

Excited, Norbert removed the girl's clothes piece by piece, making a mental note of their order so he could redress her when the time came. It was his duty, but he also looked at it as a striptease just for him. It didn't matter that she was on a ventilator and unresponsive. In fact, Norbert preferred it. No talking, less chance of hearing, "No."

Concentrate, you fool.

Erik was particular about the bodies appearing precisely as he had found them. Norbert thought this was ludicrous. Would a person look exactly the same every time you saw them? It made little sense to him, but he wasn't the premier spy around this joint. He was just the body man.

When Aline was fully naked, he stood over her and stared. His excitement grew. She looked fragile without the black, punk-rock exterior, child-like even. Norbert inserted the IV and placed the electrodes of the monitor on her chest. He caressed the naked flesh in a way this girl wouldn't have permitted when she was awake. He turned his back on the girl for a few seconds to grab his other supplies.

Just as Norbert attempted to place the catheter, taking his time with her delicate parts, the girl's legs clamped together.

Norbert looked up to see her eyes open wide with horror. Her nostrils flared, and her lips moved around the breathing tube, which kept her from speaking.

Oh shit, oh shit, oh shit. Did he just jump into this body while I had my back to him?

"Boss… I'm really sorry. I didn't mean to touch her, it's just that she looked so delicious. Lay back down, I'll get the tube out for you. Crap."

The girl's body stayed rigid and wild-eyed but lay back down until the breathing apparatus was removed. Once extubated, she sat up on the cot in her nakedness and looked around for her clothes without saying a word.

"Sorry, boss. Here, let me get the clothes," Norbert said, fumbling around in a panic. He gathered the neatly folded pile of clothes he'd placed in the order he removed them, from outside layer to inside layer. He set them on the cot next to the naked body and the boots on the floor in front of the clothes.

I can't believe I just felt up Erik. Norbert, though attracted to the woman, could not bear to look at her nakedness knowing it was actually his boss.

She dressed quickly, placing her boots on last, but still said nothing. Norbert waited for the litany of derogatory remarks from Erik. It seemed very unlike him to hold back. In fact, he'd never held back before. Without hesitation, the woman landed a right cross to his jaw.

"Erik, what the hell?" Norbert said, holding his face. A small trickle of blood ran from the corner of his mouth.

"Erik. Who the fuck is Erik?"

Norbert stood there looking perplexed.

"Who the hell are you then?" he asked the woman. Her voice sounded different from when Erik had possessed her before. Now it was raspier with more edge. The way she held her body and her facial expressions seemed to contort the fragile angel he touched a moment ago.

"Sinclair."

This time she struck him with a roundhouse that dropped him to the ground. Before Norbert could audibly protest, she grabbed him by the scruff of his shirt and punched him repeatedly. Norbert grappled at her legs, at anything that would give him traction, but came up empty. She let go of his shirt, shoving him so hard that when his head hit the cold cement floor, it sounded like a cracking melon.

The pent-up rage from all the years of protecting Aline from their father's abuse channeled into this man who had just done the same. Sinclair kicked him in the ribs with her boots, making him sputter and cough up blood. She delivered one more well-centered punch to his face and Norbert appeared lifeless on the floor, blood spilling from his eyes, mouth, and nose.

From where his body fell, the pitched angle of the exchange room caused the pooled blood to run down the ramp. It snaked its way onto the body farm floor to a drain at the center of the large room.

Sinclair's arm felt damp, and blood pulsed from where her IV had ripped out, staining her favorite shirt. She looked on the back wall near the sink, found bandages to cover the wound, and carelessly wiped the blood on her black pants.

She stared at Norbert's body lying lifeless on the cold metal floor.

Disgusting pig. She bent over and rummaged through his pockets. *I need a damn cigarette.*

She patted him down and in the right side leg pocket of his scrubs, she found a familiar sky blue pack of Gauloises, nearly full. She located the lighter beneath the pack and stood tall, tapped out a smoke, and pulled it loose with her lips.

Once out of the exchange room, Sinclair looked around, unsure of where she was, then lit the cigarette, disregarding the danger of fire in the oxygen-laden room. With Aline gone, there wasn't anything she loved more than smoking.

It stunned her when she saw the bodies lined up in the warehouse. Tendrils of smoke escaped her open mouth and circled her head. She didn't know how to get out, or where to start. Beyond where she stood, an elevated room hung suspended in the air with a winding staircase spilling out of the bottom. The faint sound of opera wafted through the air and weaved itself in with the mechanical alarms of the machines.

She climbed the spiral stairs to find an office. To her left, an elevator caught her eye, and she immediately pushed the button. Sinclair waited, and nothing happened. She struck the button again with force repeatedly until she noticed the card reader blinking red.

Damn it, she thought, and struck the device with her bloody palm.

The office had a desk and the standard file cabinets and shelves along the walls. She tried opening them one by one without luck, her anger growing by the minute, until she got to the desk. While she expected the desk drawers to yield the same results, it surprised her when a slim, almost hidden drawer opened easily.

Inside were two green ledgers. She pulled them out on the top of the desk, the ash of her cigarette fell onto a book. She wiped it off with the side of her hand, leaving a sooty smear, and opened the cover. Sinclair turned page after page filled with lists of names and dates. She looked out the window at the neat rows of bodies lined up across the large space and then back to the names. She turned to the last page with writing on it and saw Aline's name and information. Rage welled up inside her as she slammed the book shut.

What a sick asshole. Stepping around the desk, Sinclair went to the window that overlooked the cave of human bodies with her hands balled into fists on the sill.

It was rare for her to get this vantage point in life, to be the driver of the body she lived in. Aline hadn't let her come out to play much, stating Sinclair was "too dangerous." Sinclair always laughed at this. It wasn't untrue. Her rage could tear people apart, but hadn't she—hadn't *they*—earned every ounce? Sinclair wished Aline would've let her kill their father when she had the chance that night, but Aline had run away to Paris. Aline always had them doing the right thing, when Sinclair wanted to do what would make them feel better.

She crushed her cigarette out on the desktop, and the smell of burning varnish stung her nose. She lit another smoke immediately and looked down below. There was another room, softly lit and with opera music seeping out from the cracks in the open window. In the dark, near the back wall, stood a parked ambulance.

That's my ticket out.

The butt of the smoke still smoldered in the fine wood, and she hoped it would burn the whole disgusting place down. Sinclair grabbed the ledgers, gave the body farm one last look, and headed back down to the exchange room to find her bag.

She stuffed the books firmly into her backpack and rooted around until the soft cover of Aline's drawing book brushed her fingers. Aline had collected things about people, strangers, but Sinclair wasn't sure why. Sinclair only knew that she came to the surface and sketched horrible faces for Aline. The two girls felt connected and disconnected at the same time.

The music coming from the other room intrigued her. It wasn't anything Aline or their parents had listened to, and Sinclair thought the music fractured the air with a sense of superiority.

She left the exchange room. The bottom of her heavy boots soaked up the mixture of her and Norbert's blood and tracked it down the ramp. The music drew her toward the room with the open window. The door was locked tight, but she could see inside. The bad man that had frightened and killed her sisters, Aline and Fayette, lay on an undulating mattress. He may have scared them, but he didn't scare Sinclair. Despite the different body, she knew he was the same one who had caused Sinclair to surface that day in the park to sketch his picture. She wanted to get in there and kill him for what he'd done but realized he looked like all the other bodies in the room—inhuman.

He has to pay for all of us, Sinclair thought as she looked over her shoulder at the hundreds of bodies stolen and lives erased.

In desperation, she wanted to unhook them all from their life support so they could die in peace. She didn't want them to be a part of his dirty work, then discarded when they were no longer useful like Claudia and that old beggar man. But if she couldn't kill Erik, he'd just take more innocent souls to replace the ones she destroyed.

There has been enough killing.

She turned back to look toward the hulking shell of Norbert lying in a pool of his own blood. Sinclair had taken him by surprise, and she sensed he'd not expected that she was capable of such fury. Norbert was still breathing, with a bit of a gurgle, as blood intermittently ran out of his mouth down the side of his face. She thought about killing him. He was the scum of the earth, wasn't he? But as tight as security seemed to be in this dungeon, she imagined his death would only bring more people and she might never make it out. Sinclair thought no one would mind if Norbert got roughed up. He deserved it.

She rifled through the rest of his pockets, found a keycard badge and a simple flip phone. The badge, she assumed, worked the elevator and maybe the doors to whatever was above this den of iniquity. Sinclair wasn't sure what was in the building above, but if the security was consistent with the basement, she'd never make it out alive. She'd have to stick with the ambulance.

Sinclair flipped open the phone and checked the contacts. There were only two names listed, Erik and Bernard. She dialed the first number, and a ring came from inside the locked room, making an unpleasant contrast to the opera. Sinclair ended the call. She didn't want to wake that man, Erik.

The girl walked through the maze of bodies toward the ambulance parked at the rear of the building in the shadows. Sinclair noted the garage door behind the vehicle as she got closer and knew for sure this was how she would get out.

Under her breath, "Well, since this badge says Norbert, I will have to assume that Bernard drives the rig." She lit another cigarette and sat on the bumper facing her escape route and thought about how she would pull this whole thing off.

First, I need to get out of here, then I'll deal with Erik.

With one long haul, she finished the smoke, its hot cherry lighting her fingers and the edge of her nose. She snubbed it out on the concrete floor and kicked it under the passenger's side wheel of the ambulance. She tried pulling on the rolled down garage door, but it wouldn't budge.

When she opened the back door of the ambulance, she realized instantly there weren't too many places she could hide, at least not well. The driver could see the area in the rearview mirror, and a passenger could turn to see her easily. Sinclair checked the glove box and the visors for a remote for the door but came up empty. She opened and closed cabinets, deciding she couldn't even squeeze into the biggest one without significant pain. Sinclair sat on the long bench seat, which snapped into place with her weight. Immediately, she stood and lifted the bench to find a large open space.

This must be where they hide the freakish bodies from authorities. Sinclair laughed to herself as she became a freak and climbed in to hide.

Some hours later, she awoke to a commotion of voices echoing through the massive warehouse. Despite how the conversation rang and boomed off the ceiling, she found it hard to make out the exact words being said. Hidden under the bench inside the ambulance added another muffled layer to the sounds. Sinclair figured Norbert had finally woken up from his 'nap' to find all his shit missing, face bloodied, and her gone.

The shouting, she imagined, came from Erik giving Norbert a once-over.

"What do you mean she's gone? How the hell did this happen?" Erik screamed.

"Well…I was undressing her and kinda taking my sweet liberty with her when she sat right up in the bed and I thought it was you and I about shit myself. So, I unhooked the ventilator thinking you would yell at me like you are now, but you didn't."

"And…," said Erik pacing, his fists clenched at his side and jaw set tight.

"The girl looked over at the pile of clothes so I handed them to her, she dressed and then beat the shit out of me. That's the last thing I remember. Look at my damn face!"

"Did she leave her bag?" Erik asked, "and how did she get out?"

"Uhhh… she stole my badge and my phone," Norbert said as he leaned over to tap his leg pocket, "and my smokes. Damn bitch."

"Go up to the office and alert security that the girl is running around the building somewhere. We have to find her. She couldn't have gotten far."

"But Boss, how is she alive if you took over her mind?" said Norbert.

Erik bristled. "When I took her in the field, she had another personality that came up. I didn't think to mention it, because after I subdued them both, it seemed all clear. She must've had a third personality lurking in there who woke while you terrorized her body, you pervert."

"She told me her name was Sinclair," admitted Norbert.

Erik looked at him with befuddlement but said nothing.

As Norbert climbed the stairs, he felt the weight of the beating he'd suffered both physically and mentally. At the office, he noticed the bloody palm print on the badge reader. As Norbert turned to go back down the stairs, he noticed the cigarette put out on the desk and then the top drawer wide open.

"Oh no. No, no, no, no," he whispered to himself.

Hesitantly, he walked toward the desk, praying the whole time that the ledgers would be there when he looked. Nothing. He called security to alert them about the girl, giving them her physical description.

Despite the pain in his head, Norbert raced down the stairs and into the exchange room. Blood covered the floor and walls, the backpack, gone. His shoulders slumped.

Norbert turned to look at Erik. "It's worse than we thought, boss."

"Dear God, what now?"

"I can't find her bag. And there was a bloody smudge on the badge reader by the elevator. And... the ledgers are gone, stolen," said Norbert.

"*What?* You've done it this time, Norbert, seriously," Erik said as the body he inhabited colored slightly in the cheeks! "Get the exchange room ready. I need my favorite female body immediately. I need to see Legrand."

With this, Erik stormed back to his chamber, unwilling to wade into the bloody exchange room floor. He needed to think about what he would tell the Assistant Director.

Erik could have just gone up to Legrand's office as he was, however, he was not sure if the girl was still lurking in the building. She undoubtedly saw him lying there, and he couldn't risk the possibility of being ambushed in the hall.

Why hadn't she tried to kill me?

After about fifteen minutes, Norbert knocked on the wall of Erik's quarters. "I set the exchange room up, sir."

"Very well, after you do the exchange, wake up Bernard and get him out on the streets. I have to find this girl and get those ledgers back. I will need him close by."

They made the exchange, and Erik rose in the beautiful woman's sleek body which had been fully dressed by Norbert before the body swap. The high heels struck the metal of the stairs, creating a ringing through the solemn sea of machines and shells of humans. At the elevator, he saw the bloody swipe for himself and mentally prepared for a blitz attack from this more rugged and rage-filled girl. He had a bad feeling about this, a panic he was unaccustomed to feeling.

With his task complete, Norbert walked over to Bernard's sleeping quarters to wake him, since he no longer had a phone to text him. When Bernard woke, he instinctively reached for his tablet.

"I don't have my phone. That crazy bitch we brought in last night stole it and escaped."

You look like shit. Do you want me to fix that cut? Bernard typed onto the screen of his iPad without sending the message.

"Not now. The boss wants you out there waiting. He just went up to the top. I'm no genius, but if she gets out with those ledgers, the social and political implications will come down on all of us."

With that, Norbert turned and went back to the exchange room, limping and groaning with each movement, to clean up his face and change his clothes.

The noise in the warehouse quieted down, and Sinclair felt the driver's side of the ambulance dip slightly as someone got into the front cab. The engine turned over, and an overwhelming smell of diesel exhaust filtered in from the back of the vehicle filling the compartment. Her throat burned from the fumes. She held her breath to keep from coughing.

Behind her, the garage door rumbled to life, and the ambulance's automatic notification alarm activated as the vehicle backed up.

Almost there.

The elevator ride to Henri Legrand's office was akin to a journey to the bowels of hell. Erik had no interest in telling his superior that an enemy with incriminating evidence was loose somewhere in the DAT, or worse, escaped into the free world. The elevator door opened into the bright expansive office full of windows.

"What is wrong?" asked Legrand, "The look on your face is hideous, and you *never* come up this early."

Erik stood stock still for a moment. How could he tactfully relay this mess and still leave himself in a good light? Almost automatically, he paced around the office. He glanced out the window, took a deep breath, and started in.

"Henri, we have a problem. Possibly a very serious one."

"Hmm, we always solve the little messes you get yourself into."

"This one is different. I was asleep when it happened, so it's not my fault. I will relay it to you the best I can from what little I got according to that worthless Norbert," Erik paused for a breath, "That runaway we took yesterday… she escaped."

Legrand looked puzzled. "I don't understand how that can happen. Don't they all die when you take them?"

"They do, but when I took her initially, she had a different personality inside her, which I killed. She showed no signs of having another. It's rare for me to find this. This only happened one other time in all my subversions," Erik explained.

"What happened that time? Did anything come of it?" Legrand asked.

"No, I killed that second personality, and it was over."

"What threat does this runaway pose? It's your word against hers and we know which side the law will fall on. We are well connected."

"She stole the ledgers in which I recorded all the personal information of every individual I've taken for the last few years. Thank God Norbert doesn't have a key to open the cabinet with all the archives," said Erik.

Henri's face drained of all color, and he slumped into his high-backed chair. His silver hair, always perfectly in place, fell onto his forehead. Silence fell over the room, and they could hear only a faint muffled sound of the city outside the windows. The assistant director looked grim. "This could destroy your cover and put the Directorate of Altérité Sécurité in serious jeopardy. Where *is* the girl?"

"We think she might be in the building. She stole Norbert's badge, and there was a bloody handprint on the elevator in the basement. I alerted security already. We did that as soon as we knew she'd left the body farm."

The ringing of Erik's phone cut the conversation short. He pulled it from his pocket. It was Norbert. Erik cocked his head in confusion as he remembered that the girl, Sinclair, had stolen the attendant's phone. He cleared his throat and answered the call.

"Hello."

"Is this…Erik?" asked a somewhat familiar voice.

"Speaking," he said, resolving to keep it short and let the woman drive the conversation.

"Listen freak, I have your books on all the zombies down there in the basement which seems like something Interpol or Amnesty International would love to hear about," Sinclair said.

"What do you want for the ledgers?" he asked, trying to get a better understanding of her personality and intentions.

"Money, but not a lump sum. You'll give me 3,000 Euro a month for as long as I want, and your precious zombie farm stays secret. It's the least you can do for killing my sisters."

Erik placed his hand over the receiver and looked to Henri Legrand, who waited, tapping his fingers on the desk.

"She wants 3,000 Euro a month for as long as she wants to keep silent, but we don't get the ledgers back."

Henri frowned. "That isn't ideal, but we spend more than that a month keeping your damn flesh puppets alive. Pay her and hope for the best. Maybe we can track her. Is she still in the building?"

Erik placed the phone back to his ear and distinctly heard the city in the background. He shook his head at Legrand. "Okay, we'll play."

"I want the first installment today. Have your tongue-tied friend drop it off tonight at the western side of the Arc de Triomphe at 7:30 pm. No funny business. If anyone tries to touch me or follow me, your secret is out. I'm sure by now you've seen your creepy nurse's face and you know I'm not joking," said Sinclair, slightly breathless and knowing that she would have copies of the ledgers made in case they reneged their deal, "I'll call you tomorrow with a number for a post office box."

With his jaw clenched, Erik snapped the flip phone closed. He stood by the window, rigid and shaking. She had beaten him at his own game. He could taste the blood in his mouth from where he'd bitten his cheek hard.

I'll get this little bitch. She will pay for this tenfold.

Over a year had passed since Sinclair had her run-in with Erik and his gruesome body farm in that sub-basement. She'd kept her word about not releasing that information to anyone and still received her monthly payments via the post office box. She set the box up across the city from where she was living. She hired someone to remove the check from the box, wait a few days, and deliver it to her work.

Sinclair settled in the Saint-Ouen district of Paris, mostly because it was close to her work and she could walk. There were parks close by, and she would often sit in one of them and observe the motions of people and cars. She did this on days when she missed Aline, when she missed her sketches and quiet calm. She herself could still draw, but there had been a lightness and beauty to Aline's work that contrasted with Sinclair's harsher dark images.

With the money, she'd rented a one-bedroom house that faced Impasse Mousseau. It had an enclosed terrace with a table shaded by an umbrella. There were plants and flowers around. Sinclair never imagined she would live a life like this.

Shortly after renting the house, she landed a job as a hostess at Ma Cocotte Café and had been there for almost a year. Now, in the café bathroom, Sinclair looked at herself in the mirror and smiled at her reflection. The hard edge to her face had softened with good living and for the first time in her life, she was happy. She'd even fallen in love.

A knock at the door distracted her from her reverie.

"Just a minute," Sinclair said.

"Sinclair? It's Julie. Christophe is waiting outside for you."

"Merci!"

Sinclair tidied her hair a bit and removed her hostess vest. Tonight was their six-month anniversary, and he'd purchased tickets to the opera. She stepped out of the bathroom and peered across the café. She saw his silhouette outside the door. He was tall and handsome with a rugged jaw. His strength and intelligence made her fall in love with him all over again.

This had been Sinclair's last shift as she had the next week off as they'd planned a string of fun activities around the city. She opened the door, stepping into the fresh evening air, and he smiled at her with his steel-gray eyes glinting in the setting sun. Sinclair kissed him as they embraced.

"Bonjour, mon amie! Are you ready?" Sinclair said.

"Yes, my love, but we should take a cab to give you more time to get ready so we won't miss the start of *Faust*. If we don't get there before it starts, we will have to wait until intermission."

The walk was only five city blocks, and it normally did not take too long, but Sinclair agreed. She still had to shower, change, and do her hair. Christophe arrived already dressed in his fine, black suit with his charcoal wool overcoat completing the ensemble. In the cab, Sinclair thought dreamily about her night out. She'd never been to the opera before, and it was thoughtful of Christophe to plan something so fancy and special for their anniversary. When the cab pulled up in front of the house, her boyfriend paid the driver and then opened the door for her as if she were a princess.

Christophe unlocked the terrace gate with the key she'd given him last week, in anticipation of their anniversary. He wasn't moving in, not yet, but she wanted him to see her when he wanted to.

"I'm having a cigarette first. You go ahead. I'll be only a minute. Just a few quick puffs," Sinclair said.

Christophe nodded and walked to the door, "Don't be too long, we have a tight schedule tonight. The rest of the week will be free and easy. I promise."

She smiled at him then sat at the table watching the sun set over the park across the street while she inhaled deeply on the cigarette. Christophe didn't like that she smoked, and she'd cut back to please him. Life changed so much this year it felt like a dream. Sinclair pinched herself.

Still awake. After one more long drag on the smoke, she crushed it out in the small ashtray on the table and went inside.

When Sinclair opened the door, Christophe stood smiling by the dining table next to a bouquet of gorgeous flowers. He held a red box with a white satin ribbon. She brought her hand to her mouth in shock, and tears welled in her eyes, but she didn't let them fall. Sinclair was never the crying kind, but the sentiment touched her heart.

"Do you like them?" Christophe asked.

"They're beautiful," said Sinclair as she walked over to the flowers, caressed their velvet petals and let herself get lost in their aroma, "What did I ever do to find such a wonderful man like you? I love you."

"I love you too, my dear, now get ready. You can open your gift after."

Sinclair kissed Christophe on the mouth and headed into the bathroom. He watched her close the door and waited for the water to come on. The sound of the shower door clicked into place. He stood in front of the gilt-framed mirror. A devilish smile crossed his face, and his eyes darkened.

She thought she could get the best of me, thought Erik inside the deadly handsome man's body, *that bitch won't see it coming.*

Gently, Erik lifted the mirror off its hook to reveal a small keycode safe. It'd taken him months to find her and then have her fall in love with the man she called Christophe. Sinclair had been hesitant at first, still cautious and leery of men after the incident at the DAT, but eventually, she softened under his well-practiced charm.

Erik had endured this sappy relationship to get the ledgers and pay her back for blackmailing him. It had taken a year of patience, which he found was always in short supply. Part of him relished the chance to have a budding romance like this, and to make it believable, he'd pretended that Sinclair was Olympia. It was the only way he could pull it off. His disdain for this woman almost made him human. As Christophe, she welcomed him into her personal space, which gave him time to learn her weaknesses.

Last week, like a fool, she'd given him a key to her house as part of their anniversary. He'd spent every moment she was away at work searching the house for the ledgers. When he finally located the safe, he spent the last few days running through every imaginable combination of numbers to find the code. This afternoon, while Sinclair was at Ma Cocotte, he punched in the corresponding numbers on the alpha-numeric keypad spelling Aline's name as a last-ditch effort.

The door to the safe popped open and there they were in all their green glory. The code was so simple, Erik was ashamed that he hadn't thought of it sooner. He thumbed through the ledgers to be sure they were the originals and smiled when he saw pages upon pages of Norbert's elegant script.

He'd left the ledgers in the safe. He had unfinished business with Sinclair, and he wanted to see the look in her eyes when he destroyed her, once and for all. So tonight, as she showered, he opened the safe and removed the ledgers, placed them in a briefcase he'd hidden behind the bookcase by the door. He hung the mirror and waited.

The water had just turned off, and he could hear Sinclair humming in the bathroom. Erik heard the buzzing of a hairdryer and then the rustle of a gown. All the while, the woman hummed a tune he couldn't recognize. The thirty minutes it took for her to get ready felt like an eternity as he was desperate for his end game.

Sinclair emerged from the bedroom in a sapphire gown with her blond hair, now long, resting in curls about her shoulders. Her makeup was delicate, and she smelled of rosewater. He pulled the shiny red present from the table and handed it to Sinclair as he bowed at the waist.

"For you, madame."

"You are too sweet to me," said Sinclair, undoing the ribbon from the box. She opened it slowly to find a diamond bracelet. "It's perfect."

Erik placed the shining bracelet on her wrist. "Are you ready?"

"I've never been more ready in my life."

He gripped her wrists tightly, jumping into her body and subverting her mind. Then, just as quickly, he went back into Christophe's body before it hit the floor. Sinclair fell onto the carpet, choking and gasping with a look of terror in her eyes.

"Me too," he said.

When she stopped breathing, he pulled a cell phone from his pocket and texted Bernard to pick him up at the corner of Rue Carnot and Avenue Gabriel Peri. Erik texted Henri Legrand next, *It's done.*

Erik smiled at his handiwork. He pulled the briefcase with the ledgers from behind the bookcase, locked the door, then the terrace as he left. The gate creaked in an eerily ancient way that ended in a clang, reverberating in his ear.

Down the block, he threw the keys in a trash can. It would be a week before anyone even thought of Sinclair as missing, and it would appear she'd died of natural causes as his subversions never left a trace of malice.

There was a gasp, a terrible, guttural choking sound, and the gowned woman sat upright clutching her throat. She screamed into the empty room.

"I'm going to kill you for what you did to Sinclair, you bastard," said Vivienne.

The look in her seething eyes spoke of nothing but revenge.

The Authors of the Abyss

Mattea Orr's most recent work appears in the anthology, *Transcendent*, from Transmundane Press. She has a Master's in English Literature from SUNY Binghamton and lives in New York with her husband, three children, and any number of cats.

John L. French is a retired crime scene supervisor with forty years' experience. His first story, "Past Sins," was published in Hardboiled Magazine and was cited as one of the best Hardboiled stories of 1993. John's first book was *The Devil of Harbor City. Past Sins* and *Here There Be Monsters followed.* His other books include *Souls on Fire, The Nightmare Strikes, Monsters Among Us, The Last Redhead, The Magic of Simon Tombs, The Santa Heist* (written with Patrick Thomas), *When the Moon Shines,* and *Mortal Sins.*

There's been a debate among certain obscure and drunken literary scholars about whether **Patrick Thomas** was raised by Cthulhu or a leprechaun in a Manhattan bar. What there is no arguing about is that Patrick is the award-winning author of 50+ books including the beloved fantasy humor *Murphy's Lore* series and universe of books, the darkly hilarious *Dear Cthulhu* advice empire, the *Bikini Jones* series, the *Mystic Investigators* paranormal mystery series, the Jack Gardner Mysteries (with John L. French) and is the creator of the *Agents of the Abyss.* Patrick's book *Nightcaps* was thrown at a suspect on the show *CSI. Dear Cthulhu* is a part of *Destinies: The Voice of Science Fiction* radio show on WUSB. His *Soul For Hire* story *Act of Contrition* was made into a short film.

As Patrick T. Fibbs, he writes middle readers including the *Babe B. Bear Mysteries, The Undead Kid Diaries, Joy Reaper Checks Out,* as well as the *Ughabooz* kids' picture and chapter books, and the YA *Emotional Support Nightmare.*

Please visit him at www.PatThomas.net and www.PatrickTFibbs. com.

In 1994, **Robert E. Waters** joined the board and computer gaming industry by becoming the Managing Editor of The Avalon Hill Gaming

Company's quarterly magazine *The General*. Since then, he has continued in the field as a writer, editor, designer, and voice-actor for other studios, including TalonSoft and BreakAway Games. In 1999, he became an assistant editor for the fantasy magazine *Weird Tales* and remained so until 2006. His first professional fiction sale came in 2003 with "The Assassin's Retirement Party." Since then, he has sold over 70 stories to on-line and print magazines and anthologies, including *The Grantville Gazette*, Eric Flint's on-line magazine dedicated to his award-winning Alternate History series, *1632/Ring of Fire*.

Robert has also published nine novels, including media tie-ins for several gaming studios, his most recent for Mantic Games and titled THE LAST HURRAH, which showcases their brutal tabletop sports game *DreadBall*. With Charles E Gannon, Robert co-authored the *Ring of Fire* novel 1636: CALABAR'S WAR (Baen Books, April 2021). Robert is also the co-author with Eric Flint on 1637: THE TRANSLYVANIAN DECISION (Baen Books, November 2022).

Robert currently lives in Baltimore, Maryland with his wife Beth, their son Jason, and two rambunctious cats named Snow and Ash.

David Lee Summers is the author of a dozen novels and numerous short stories and poems. His most recent book is the novella *Breaking the Code* about Marines recruiting code talkers in Navajo country during World War II while a Skinwalker is on the loose. His short stories have appeared in such magazines and anthologies as *Cemetery Dance*, *Realms of Fantasy*, and *Straight Outta Tombstone*. When he's not writing, David operates telescopes at Kitt Peak National Observatory. Find David on the web at www.davidleesummers.com.

Lee O'Connell is a writer and an artist. Writing and painting have been her refuge, allowing her to escape the chaos of daily life, since she can remember.

Although her formal education is in the sciences, she has taken myriad writing courses and workshops. That said, the most intense learning has been as a member of her local writers group.

Lee has published two poems, has written a plethora of stories, and looks forward to her first published short story.

Rowan Dillon is Christy Nicholas who writes under several pen names, including Emeline Rhys, CN Jackson, and Rowan Dillon. She is an author, artist, and accountant. After she failed to become an airline pilot, she quit her ceaseless pursuit of careers that begin with the letter 'A' and decided to concentrate on her writing. Since she has Project Completion Compulsion, she is one of the few authors with no unfinished novels. Learn more at www.greendragon.com/2022/03/rowandillon.

Aleathia Drehmer is the creator and editor of *Durable Goods: The Missouri Collective* which features poetry from high school students affected by trauma. She was once the editor of *In Between Altered States*, co-editor of *Full of Crow* and *Zygote in My Coffee*, and art editor of *Regardless of Authority*. Aleathia currently has two collections available, *Running Red Lights* (Gutter Snob Books) and *Looking for Wild Things* (Impspired) with a forthcoming collection of poems on grief, *Layers of Half-Sung Hymns* (Cajun Mutt Press) coming out later this year. You can follow Aleathia's adventures in the world at www.aleathiadrehmer.com

Sometimes it takes a monster to keep the Abyss at bay.

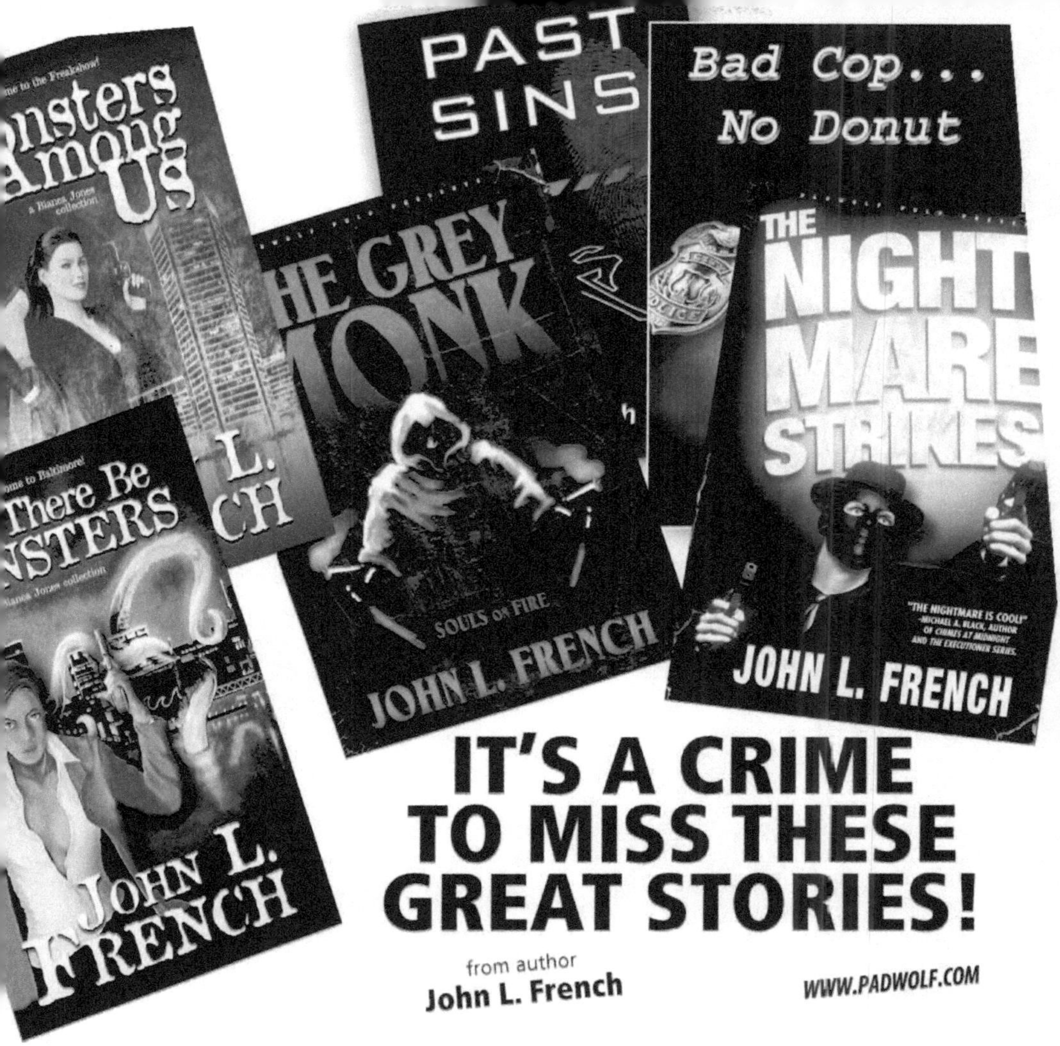

Monsters Among Us
a Bianca Jones collection
JOHN L. FRENCH

Welcome to Baltimore!
There Be Monsters
a Bianca Jones collection
JOHN L. FRENCH

PAST SINS
THE GREY MONK
SOULS ON FIRE
JOHN L. FRENCH

Bad Cop... No Donut
THE NIGHTMARE STRIKES
"THE NIGHTMARE IS COOL!"
-MICHAEL A. BLACK, AUTHOR
OF CRIMES AT MIDNIGHT
AND THE EXECUTIONER SERIES.
JOHN L. FRENCH

IT'S A CRIME
TO MISS THESE
GREAT STORIES!
from author
John L. French
WWW.PADWOLF.COM

APOCALYPSE 13
DEFCON 1

MERMAIDS 13
TALES FROM THE SEA

Camelot 13
Edited by
John L. French and Patrick Thomas

LUCKY 13
EDITED BY EDWARD J. MCFADDEN
Thirteen Tales of
Crime & Mayhem

You can't get better than 13!

DOWN THESE
MEANS STREETS
of Magic & Monsters walk the

MYSTIC INVESTIGATORS

THE STARSCAPE PROJECT
As his quest begins, an artificial intelligence life form enters the galaxy and launches a series of covert attacks against the Empire. The Teconeans assume that the Federation is responsible, and galactic peace is about to unravel. As Stryker chases his nemesis into Teconean space, he finds himself thrown into the middle of the battle. Knowing that Earth will be the aliens' next target, Stryker must decide whether to let them destroy the Empire, or to join forces with his Teconean enemies against the invaders. The key to the mysterious aliens lies buried on the moon of Kennedy Prime, and it's up to Stryker to solve the puzzle before war begins. The fate of the galaxy is at stake.

ZONE OF THE TENTH DGREE
In 1912, an alien ship crash lands in the Atlantic Ocean, setting up a secret colony that remains undetected for centuries, allowing them to manipulate some of the most important events in human history -- from the sinking of the Titanic to the Bermuda triangle to global warming. Now, the technology of the 26th century has uncovered the aliens' distress beacon, and it's a race against time as the Navy tries to stop a terrorist armed with a nuclear weapon from destroying the colony and triggering an all-out war as the mother-ship approaches

Now available from
PADWOLF PUBLISHING

DEAR CTHULHU
The advice column to END
all advice columns

The Collected Advice Columns Of Dear Cthulhu
GOOD
ADVICE
for
BAD
PEOPLE
PATRICK THOMAS

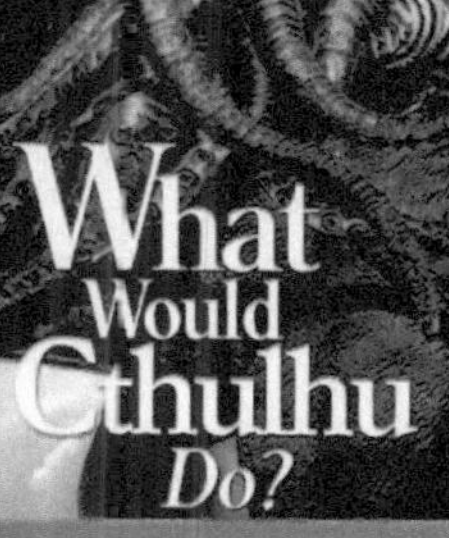

CTHULHU
KNOWS BEST
The Collected Advice Columns Of Dear Cthulhu
PATRICK THOMAS

AVE
Dark
DAY
RICK THOMAS

The Collected Advice Columns Of Dear Cthulhu
What
Would
Cthulhu
Do?
PATRICK THOMAS

The Collected Advice Columns of Dear Cthulhu
CTHULHU
HAPPENS
PATRICK THOMAS

The Collected Advice Columns of Dear Cthulhu
CTHULHU
Explains It All
1. Humans are pathetic
2. Cthulhu Knows Best
3. Ask What
   Would
   Cthulhu
   Do?
4. Obey Cthulhu
5. Buy This book!
PATRICK THOMAS

WWW.DEARCTHULHU.COM
WWW.PADWOLF.COM